Russian
Comic Fiction

Russian
Comic Fiction

Edited, Translated,
and with an Introduction
by
GUY DANIELS

SCHOCKEN BOOKS • NEW YORK

First published by Schocken Books 1986
10 9 8 7 6 5 4 3 2 1   86 87 88 89

Library of Congress Cataloging-in-Publication Data
Main entry under title:
Russian comic fiction.
1. Short stories, Russian—Translations into English.
2. Short stories, English—Translations from English.
3. Russian wit and humor.   I. Daniels, Guy.
PG3286.R89   1986   891.73'01'08   85–26208

Manufactured in the United States of America
ISBN 0–8052–0815–1

To Vladimir Solovyov and Elena Klepikova

Contents

Russian
Comic Fiction

INTRODUCTION

*The true homeland of comedy is a
despotism without too many gallows.*

—Stendhal, *Racine and Shakespeare*

I

For our *Auslander*'s stereotype of Russian literature
as unrelievedly gloomy, we can blame other things besides
our own ignorance: above all, the vagaries of the Russian
comic spirit. The brilliance and vigor of that spirit cannot
be called into question. Throughout the history of "classical"[1] Russian literature, it enjoyed undisputed supremacy
on the stage. Without exception, the few eighteenth-century
Russian plays that remain worthy of mention are comedies;
e.g., Fonvizin's *The Hobbledehoy* and *The Brigadier
General*, Kapnist's *Chicane*, and Krylov's *Trumf*. And
so are the two greatest plays of the nineteenth century:[2]
Griboyedov's *Woe from Wit* and Gogol's *The Inspector
General*. Again, most of the major poets, from Derzhavin
through Krylov, Pushkin, and Lermontov to Nekrasov,
were masters of comic verse; as were numerous minor
poets, like A. K. Tolstoy. But in the realm of Russia's
greatest literary achievement, the novel, the behavior of
that comic spirit has been decidedly skittish. Except for
a few brief visits to the dark abodes of Dostoyevsky's

---

[1]Loosely, in the sense of "prerevolutionary"—the literature we
are dealing with in this anthology.
[2]I.e., right up to *The Sea Gull* (1896), which incidentally Chekhov
called a "comedy"—though one should probably not plump too
hard for the modern meaning of the word in this case.

novel-tragedies, it has pretty much avoided the domain of the "Great Prose Realists"; and for all the splendor of that one isolated edifice, *Dead Souls,* the "Russian comic novel" as a genre unto itself can hardly be said to exist.

The same is true of short fiction. There are plenty of humorous sketches (Chekhov alone wrote hundreds of them) but only a few first-rate comic stories. Hence the limited scope of this collection.

Of the six authors represented here, only one—Gogol—was primarily a creator of comic fiction.[3] Indeed, in a sense Gogol was *the* creator of the comic short story. "How the Two Ivans Quarreled" (1834) is perhaps the best, and certainly the first, masterpiece of its kind. It had, however, at least three worthy predecessors: Pushkin's "History of the Village of Goryukhino" (written in 1830 but not published until 1837), and Krylov's "Panegyric in Memory of My Grandfather" and "Caib" (both 1792). All three of these stories easily qualify, artistically, for inclusion in an anthology like the present one. But "A History of the Village of Goryukhino" was left unfinished, and breaks off so suddenly as to leave the reader dangling in midair. As for "Caib," it is available in a fine English version by Bernard Guilbert Guerney in his *Treasury of Russian Literature.* So that the logical place for us to begin is with "A Panegyric in Memory of My Grandfather"—of which the present English version is, to the best of my knowledge, the first to appear in print.[4]

II

There were two brief periods during the reign of Catherine the Great (1762–96) when satirical journalism flourished—when there were not "too many gallows." The

---

[3] Saltykov, it is true, largely specialized in satirical stories and sketches; but most of them are either too journalistic to qualify as fiction, or too bitter to be comic.

[4] Perhaps unduly conspicuous by its absence from this collection is Nikolai Leskov's best comic story, "The Steel Flea." But its length would have set it squarely (and unfairly) in competition with Gogol's masterpiece, "The Two Ivans." "The Steel Flea" is best read in another context—preferably in William Edgerton's scrupulously edited and translated *The Satirical Stories of Nikolai Leskov.*

earlier period (roughly, 1769–74) began with the found-
ing by Nikolai Novikov of the first of his two satirical
magazines. It ended rather abruptly when Novikov became too outspoken on such subjects as serfdom and
corruption in high places.

The second period began about 1789, when a young
man of twenty named Ivan Krylov, who had already
written a number of keen-edged comedies, founded a
satirical publication of his own. By all rights that period
should have ended almost as soon as it began, in 1790,
when Catherine, thrown into a panic by the French
Revolution, imprisoned such "troublemakers" as Novikov
and Alexander Radishchev.[5] And it might well have, but
for the courage of the young Krylov. Even though his
first publication closed down amid the wave of arrests,
the undaunted Krylov promptly founded another, in the
pages of which he was too outspoken on almost everything. This second period ended, in effect, in 1792, when
the police descended on the printing establishment of
"Krylov and Associates," and put the young trouble-
maker under surveillance. It is characteristic of Krylov
that, even after this, he launched a third journal (in 1793).
But things were getting much too hot, and he had to
leave St. Petersburg in a hurry. He didn't return to the
capital until some 13 years later, in the reign of Alexander
I—about the time he began to write the fables that would
bring him world fame.

One of the many astounding things about Krylov is
that before he was twenty-five he was writing satirical
prose pieces that place him among the most outstanding
"sons of the French Enlightenment" in Russian letters.
(Although one of his favorite targets was Russian imita-
tion of French foppery, he was an early admirer of
Molière and Beaumarchais, and was deeply committed
to the views of Voltaire, Montesquieu, and the French
philosophes generally.)[6] Of course most of the other

---

[5] For the "illegal" publication of his famous *Journey from Petersburg to Moscow*, an impassioned attack on serfdom. Radishchev,
a highly educated nobleman who attended the University of Leipzig
in the days of its Goethian glory, was the common ancestor of all
Russian revolutionaries.

[6] He came by these authors via self-education. When he sold his
first original work for sixty rubles (he was fifteen years old, and
supporting his widowed mother and younger brother largely by
means of translations), he took out the payment in copies of
Racine, Molière, and Boileau.

significant writers of Catherine's reign were also nourished on the ideas of the French Enlightenment; but in their satire they did not venture beyond the persiflage of courtiers' (or merchants') manners and morals. Krylov, though hardly so radical as Radishchev, did not hesitate to ridicule arrogance and injustice wherever he found them: if on the throne, why then so much the worse.

He did this, moreover, with surpassing lucidity (like Voltaire's, his prose is far more readable today than that of most nineteenth-century authors) and a sharpness of bite peculiarly his own. Witness, for instance, the following from "Caib," an oriental tale in the manner of Montesquieu. The Caliph Caib (actually Catherine) is the most splendid of all sovereigns, and a great patron of the arts. True, all the poets in his realm are starving, and he would never, never let one of them so much as put one foot inside his palace. But on the other hand:

> Caib commanded that they sit for portraits in sumptuous dress, and that those paintings be hung in the finest rooms of his palace, for he sought in every way to encourage learning. And, as a matter of fact, in all his realm there was not a single poet who did not envy his own portrait.

On the subject of "poetry and power," the twenty-three-year-old Krylov seems to have been a good deal more sophisticated, in the year 1792, than was Robert Frost in his old age a century and a half later. Accordingly, he was hardly one to rhapsodize about "westering"— or "eastering," as I suppose we would have to call the kind of national expansion practiced by Catherine at the expense of indigenous tribes:

> Alexander the Great cut his way through many kingdoms with the sword, conquering and destroying thousands of tribes, apparently so that he could wet his boots in the ocean surf and then brag about it back home. (From "Panegyric.")

These two portraits of autocrats obviously belong in the same gallery with those produced earlier by Voltaire and Montesquieu. But in his "farcical tragedy," *Trumf* (1800), Krylov went far beyond his French masters in ridiculing "temporal power." Vakula, the idiotic tsar of the play, is a worthy forerunner of Jarry's King Ubu—a slob beyond belief. As such, he delighted the young Pushkin, who celebrated him and his creator in an early poem. *Trumf*, although only privately performed and never published in Krylov's day, was in fact one of the most popular comedies in early nineteenth-century Russia —especially among the Decembrists.[7]

For all his gifts as a writer of prose, Krylov's favorite medium since earliest youth had been poetry; and about 1806 he returned to a genre he had dabbled in earlier, the verse fable. In no more than a few years he emerged as the greatest fabulist of modern times, *and* the most popular —at any rate in nineteenth-century Russia, where his *Fables* ranked second only to the Bible in sales.

His astounding success in this genre has tempted critics and literary historians to offer a variety of explanations. That it was substantially due to his consummate art in putting colloquial Russian into fluent verse, plus an originality not to be found in any other modern fabulist, most of them agree. But there is also a rather widespread notion that his popularity is equally due to a latter-day, passive "peasant wisdom." The implication here is that in his fables he renounced his earlier intransigence and came to terms with temporal power.

The best answer to such calumny is given by Krylov himself, in a little fable called "The Cat and the Starling" (1825). The starling, a "philosopher," lives in the same household as the cat. One day when the cat has missed a meal and is meowing about it, the starling begins

> . . . to teach him,
> Saying, "You're a fool. It's quite unnecessary
> To suffer hunger pangs while that canary
> Is right there in that cage where you can reach him."
>
> "My conscience, though—" "Why listen to your
>   conscience?
> Believe me, it's a lot of nonsense—
> An old wives' tale for simple-minded folk.
> To those who think big, it's a joke.
>
> "In life's great struggle, might
> Makes right.

---

[7]As was the custom with such dangerous writings, *Trumf* circulated (widely) in manuscript. It was not published until the Eighties—some forty years after Krylov's death in 1844.

I'll prove my point to you by demonstration."
Then, citing one by one each concrete situation,
He set forth in detail his whole philosophy.

It suited hungry Tom right to a tee:
He dragged the poor canary to the floor
And ate him up. He tasted good—tasted, in fact, like
                                                more.

"Thank you for teaching me," he said, "that it's not
                                                wrong,
When one is strong,
To prey upon a smaller creature.
Thank you again for making me a sage."
Then, pouncing on the starling's cage,
He ate his teacher.[7a]

No doubt about it: this is the same Krylov who wrote
"Caib" and "Panegyric."

III

It is a sobering thought that one of the gloomiest
periods in Russia's history—the reign of the "pewtery-
eyed" Nicholas I (1825–55)—produced its greatest comic
genius, Nikolai Gogol. And it is not only sobering but
dismaying to reflect that Nicholas, who was the sworn
enemy of Lermontov and contrived to make the last
years of Pushkin's life miserable,[8] sometimes just couldn't
seem to do enough for Gogol. He personally intervened,
for instance, to permit the first production of *The Inspector General;* and during the writing of *Dead Souls*
he responded to Gogol's appeals for financial help with
two handsome grants. Now the "Prussian tsar" was
occasionally obtuse; and this trait of his is nowhere more
evident than in these magnanimous gestures—considering
the ultimately devastating social effect of the two works in
question. On the other hand, we can be sure that when

[7a]*Fifteen Fables of Krylov,* ed. and trans. Guy Daniels (New
York: The Macmillan Company), pp. 13–15.
    [8]Nothing could be farther from the truth than Vladimir Nabokov's
characterization of Pushkin as a "serene" conservative in his later
years—the very period when he was writing poems like the one
that begins: *"Please God, don't let me go mad!"*

the already-demented Gogol—some five years before his death by self-imposed starvation—published his infamous *Selected Passages from Correspondence with Friends* (1847), its abject eulogy of autocracy came as no surprise to Nicholas. The book's shock effect was reserved for the author's radical friends—like Belinsky, whose outrage and dismay were vented in his celebrated letter to Gogol.

The foregoing represents only one aspect of that great enigma of Gogol which is such a fertile field for scholarly exploitation: not only fertile but fragrant with hints of homosexuality, masturbation fantasies, impotence, etc. These delightful fringe benefits of scholarship are of course denied the Soviet investigators, what with the persistence of Russian puritanism from the tsarist era on into the present (and the foreseeable future). On the other hand, they are abundantly supplied—as foreign scholars are not —with something equally dear to the heart of the literary historian: Gogol's laundry slips. Armed with these and other memorabilia, they bravely enter the lists to joust with their Cold War enemies, who are armed with copies of Freud. And in the ensuing mêlée, more often than not, Gogol gets completely forgotten as both sides begin shouting—the Russians with hurrays and the Americans with boos—"Belinsky! Belinsky!"

Poor Vissarion Belinsky! Such is his reward for being the first (along with Pushkin) to recognize Gogol's genius, and to proclaim it in no uncertain terms.

All this hullabaloo is really quite unnecessary. What Belinsky did was to hail Gogol as, first of all, an *artist* of unprecedented originality, one of whose gifts was realistic portrayal. Just what Belinsky meant by his own phrase ("naked reality," or some such) is perhaps best left to him to explain. In any case, his concept is certainly less narrow than one might gather from either the Soviet critics or the more dogmatic of the American Slavicists.

According to the Soviet gloss of the Gospel of Saint Belinsky, Gogol was first and foremost a "critical realist," and hence an impassioned exposer of social evils. Nay! the American specialists cry out (if not in unison, then almost). Belinsky was dead wrong! Gogol was a "pure artist" who cared not a fig for social justice; and his characters do not accurately represent "real life."

Hm—as Ivan Ivanovich might mutter. Who can say for sure whether Gogol "really cared" about social justice?

Or whether his characters were "true to life"? Literary criticism, one would have thought, had outgrown such puerile questions long, long ago. Perhaps the moral here is that criticism would do well to steer clear of Cold War politics and the like.

In any case, we are not likely ever to know more about Gogol's *motivations* than he himself did—which was precious little, apparently. But we do know two things of far greater importance: that his art was astonishingly original; and that it had a tremendous social effect—perhaps even more than if it had been impeccably "realistic."

It was Belinsky, as we have said, who first recognized Gogol's stature as an artist and called public attention to it—in an article centered upon *Mirgorod,* Gogol's second collection of Ukrainian stories, which included "The Two Ivans." [9] For this alone he deserves something better than the downgrading of him that has become fashionable among us. I was therefore much gratified, upon looking again at Vladimir Nabokov's marvelous (and often misleading) book on Gogol, to rediscover in it a spirited defense of Belinsky against the "little conceptions" of "some modern American critics." Elated by this unexpected moral support, I turned for further enlightenment to Vladimir Vladimirovich's comments on Gogol's Ukrainian stories.

Those comments led off with an abrupt dismissal of Gogol's first collection, *Evenings on a Farm near Dikanka,*[10] whose "charm and fun have singularly faded." True enough. So I settled back in pleasurable anticipation of some deep and delightful insights into *Mirgorod*—and particularly into those two masterful tales that established Gogol's fame as a maker of comic fictions: "The Two Ivans" and "Old-World Landowners."

And what did I learn? I learned: 1) that Gogol is *not* a humorist; 2) that his misconceived fame as such is based solely on those faded *Evenings*—except that: 3) it is also based on *Mirgorod;* 4) that both *Evenings* and *Mirgorod* leave Nabokov "totally indifferent"—except that: 5) when he reread the former it *didn't* leave him totally indifferent.

Well. If made by a lesser author, such muddle-headed

---

[9]"The Two Ivans" had first been published in a magazine in 1834. *Mirgorod* appeared (in two volumes) in 1835.
[10]Published (also in two volumes) in 1831–32.

pronouncements would of course be beneath one's notice. But when they occur in an otherwise brilliant book by perhaps the most "prestigious" author of our times, duty demands that we hoist the red flag signaling "Danger!" [11]

Nabokov's *Nikolai Gogol* is in some ways the most important—and by all odds the best-written—book on its subject. That it should be read goes without saying. What doesn't go without saying is that it is also the worst possible introduction to the Gogol of "The Two Ivans" and "Old-World Landowners."

The best introduction is still the one penned by Belinsky.[12] Struck by Gogol's tremendous originality, Belinsky came up with a phrase which still serves, perhaps better than any other, to mark the watershed between the literature of the old school and modern fiction—of which Gogol and Sterne are the greatest forerunners. In "Old-World Landowners," "The Two Ivans," and "The Nose" (said Belinsky) Gogol "made everything out of nothing."

Exactly. In "Old-World Landowners," as in a play by Beckett or Ionesco, *nothing happens*.[13] The old couple just "drink and eat, and eat and drink and then, as people have done since time immemorial, die." This is what Belinsky calls "spareness of plot" (*prostota vymysla*). The real matter of the story lies elsewhere: in that marvelous alchemy by which the "nothing" of everyday trivia somehow becomes "everything"; and in Gogol's uneasy, ambivalent vision of the world, with a backdrop of gloom behind every comic bit.

In "Old-World Landowners" these elements are fused into a perfect work of art, appropriately low-keyed. In "The Two Ivans" they are jumbled together—in an unbridled exuberance precluding perfection but making for greater comedy—with whatever else comes to hand. One of these odd items is a wild parody of a Flemish painting

---

[11]This is the same red flag (by now somewhat tattered) that I was compelled to hoist on the publication of Nabokov's version of *Eugene Onegin*. (See my review in *The New Republic*, April 3, 1965.)

[12]In his aforementioned article ("On the Russian Short Story and the Short Stories of Mr. Gogol"), which appeared in *The Telescope* in 1835.

[13]Krylov, in his fables "The Titmouse" (1811) and "The Knight" (1816), brought off the same feat brilliantly. Gogol is indebted to him, as well as to Sterne, for his schooling in the art of "the absurd."

in which the action has "only one spectator: the boy in the enormous frock coat, who stood rather quietly picking his nose."[14] Another is a bit of authentic, Marx-Brothers madness: "Ivan Ivanovich is of a rather timid character. Ivan Nikiforovich, on the other hand, wears big, baggy pants. . . ." And while he's at it, Gogol stands E.T.A. Hoffman on his head and makes even the fantastic trivial and vulgar (not to say unlovely). He has done this before; but never so well as when Ivan Nikiforovich's petition is spirited away from the courtroom by Ivan Ivanovich's brown sow, who thereby breaks a deadlock and wins fame as literature's first *suinus ex machina.*

How now, brown sow? Are you no more than a fat adjunct to a skinny plot? Far from it! Close inspection reveals that it was the sow who set the whole thing in motion, when she (or the offer of her by Ivan Ivanovich in exchange for a gun) aroused the ire of Ivan Nikiforovich. For Ivan N. (like Gogol) was hypersensitive to hogs, the care and feeding of which, in the rural Russia of those days, was the *exclusive province of women*—toward whom Ivan N. (like Gogol, again) was even more hypersensitive. Not only that, but in textbook terms she "symbolizes the theme" of the whole story: swinishness, or, in contemporary parlance, slobism.

Gogol is the world's greatest virtuoso in the depiction of slobism (*poshlost*). The "height of this degradation" (to quote Lermontov) is of course reached in *The Inspector General* and *Dead Souls;* but the phenomenon had fascinated Gogol since early in his career. Witness the old couple in "Old-World Landowners" and the two Ivans— both of them consummate slobs, yet rivaled by all the minor characters in the story, and even excelled by the incomparable Agafya Fedoseyevna, who "ate boiled beets in the morning, talked scandal, and swore wonderfully well."

But if Gogol ranks first, he is still merely *primus inter pares,* since slobism was the favorite theme of Russian satirists generally, and his mentors were many. Chief among them were Fonvizin (one of whose characters preferred pigs to people) and Krylov. In particular, Gogol employs in "The Two Ivans" the same basic device used by Krylov in his satire of *poshlost:* the "false panegyric,"

---

[14]Cf. Auden's poem, "Musée des Beaux Arts."

whereby a naïf narrator,[15] in the course of praising his hero, "inadvertently" reveals all the latter's slobism (Mark Antony coming to praise Caesar, and then burying him).

But this was just one of many techniques employed in a story that was much more complex in its authorial attitudes than Krylov's "Panegyric." Gogol was decidedly not a clear-eyed son of the Enlightenment; nor was he an "exposer" like Saltykov or an "anti-exposer" like Dostoyevsky in "The Crocodile." More than anything else, he was an artist fascinated by the ambivalence of his own view of things, and expressing it in a subtle (not to say sly) interplay between pity and parody. In Belinsky's words:

> Indeed, to make us take the liveliest interest in the quarrel between Ivan Ivanovich and Ivan Nikiforovich —to make us laugh to the point of tears at the stupidities, worthlessness, and imbecility of these living lampoons of mankind—is amazing. But then to make us pity those idiots—pity them with all our hearts— and take leave of them with a kind of deep melancholy, exclaiming along with him, "It is dreary in this world, gentlemen!"—*that* is the divine art that is called creativity.

IV

Dostoyevsky's return to St. Petersburg in December, 1859, after ten years of penal servitude and exile, concided with the beginning of the most dynamic decade in nineteenth-century Russia. Ushered in by Turgenev's symbolically entitled *On the Eve* and Alexander II's Emancipation decree, the Sixties were (like our own Sixties in this century) a time of great ferment: of political reforms, student revolts, widespread arson, and battles of ideologies —nascent Capitalism, Socialism, Populism, Nihilism, Slavophilism, and Lord knows what else—with their attendant journalistic feuds, in which both Dostoyevsky and Saltykov got embroiled.

"The Crocodile" (1865) was the product of one such feud. This fact, together with its chronological place in the

---

[15]The narrator of Gogol's Ukrainian stories is "the bee-keeper, Rudi Panko."

Dostoyevsky canon—sandwiched in between "Notes from Underground" (1864) and *Crime and Punishment* (1866)—offers unbounded possibilities for comment on "The Crocodile" as a set of comic variations on the themes announced in "Notes from Underground," etc. Or rather, it *would* offer such possibilities if both the age and the author were not what they were. Happily, however, both are well known to the world at large: the age, because of its signal importance, not only in politics but (especially) in literature;[16] the author, because he is Dostoyevsky, whose works have been glossed and reglossed far beyond my poor power to add or detract. Since the same thing applies to Chekhov and Tolstoy, I propose to give all three of them (along with Saltykov, a marginal figure) short shrift in what follows, and discuss their stories more or less *en bloc*.

For all the great differences among the world-views of their authors, these stories have a salient common denominator: they lack that undercurrent of sympathy for the human condition by virtue of which Gogol's grotesques are so improbably alive, and his comic fictions inimitable. If there is even a hint of it to be found anywhere in these stories, it is in Chekhov's "The Culprit" and "The Exclamation Mark"—that undeservedly overlooked tour de force in "making everything out of nothing." But the young Chekhov was by no means the philanthrope he is often made out to be; and in the rest of the stories his attitude toward the greed, sycophancy, and willful ignorance of his characters in one of deadly impassivity.

He does, however, have the good grace to let his characters hang themselves, without pulling the tabouret out from under them, as Dostoyevsky and Saltykov so often do.[17] Both were practicing journalists—fiery participants in the ideological feuds of the day—and both used their gift for comedy as a weapon to destroy the enemy. In these journalistic frays, "the enemy" was likely to be both pernicious doctrine *and* the individual who preached it.

A prime instance of this is "The Crocodile." The story is of course an attack upon a whole host of enemies: the

---

[16]A few titles from the Sixties: Turgenev's *On the Eve, Fathers and Sons,* and *Smoke;* Dostoyevsky's "Notes from Underground," *Crime and Punishment,* and *The Idiot;* Tolstoy's "The Cossacks" and *War and Peace;* and Goncharov's *Oblomov.*

[17]One of Dostoyevsky's most venomous pieces of writing, by the way, is a sketch satirizing the satirist, Saltykov.

former Dostoyevsky himself (the one who was sent to
prison); his old master, Gogol;[18] his former friends, the
Liberals (who in those days, as now, were everybody's
favorite punching bag), personified by Timofey Semyonych; the "swingers" who relished the emergent Capitalism
(e.g., Elena Ivanovna); and Capitalism itself, along with
Socialism, Populism, and Culture with a capital "C." But
Dostoyevsky's Enemy Number One was Utilitarianism—it,
and its chief proponent, Nikolai Chernyshevsky, doubly
hateful because he combined the Capitalist doctrine of
enlightened self-interest with Socialist Utopian notions.

Three years before "The Crocodile" was written,
Chernyshevsky had been sent to prison, where he wrote
his tremendously popular (and tremendously bad) utopian
novel, *What Is To Be Done?* As an ex-prisoner, Dostoyevsky might have been expected to show some sympathy for
his fellow victim. And of course as a Christian he should
have hated only "the sin, not the sinner." But in this sense
he was never a very good Christian, really; and he hated
both the sin *and* the sinner—implacably.

In *House of the Dead* Dostoyevsky had remarked that
prisoners "are great daydreamers." And what is the first
thing that Ivan Matveich does after becoming a prisoner[19]
inside the crocodile? He dreams up three schemes for
the salvation of mankind, and starts working on a fourth—
because "seen from the inside of a crocodile, everything
becomes clearer, somehow."

Given the biographical facts, the cruelty of this kind
of comedy is undeniable. (It was in fact held against
Dostoyevsky for the rest of his life.) On the other hand,
the violence of the attack on utilitarianism—an attack that
had been begun in "Notes from Underground" and was
continued in *Crime and Punishment*—has been more than
justified by subsequent history: especially that of Russia
and America. "The Crocodile," in short, is a brilliant and
significant piece of polemics reflecting the "temper of the

---

[18]Dostoyevsky's original Preface to "The Crocodile"—published
in his own journal, *Epoch*, but not reproduced in later editions—
links the story's grotesquerie to that of Gogol in "The Nose."

[19]Garnett (whom I rather admire, generally) and other translators lose the point when they refer to Ivan Matveich as a "captive."
Dostoyevsky distinctly says "prisoner" in the sense of being cooped
up (*uznik*). If he had meant "captive" he would have said *plennyy,
plennik,* or whatever.

times," which now and then makes a successful reach toward comic art of the first order.

An even more partisan spirit marks (and often mars) the work of Dostoyevsky's sometime associate and sometime adversary, Saltykov[20]—so much so that his fictions often degenerate into mere journalism. Most of them, moreover, were written in "Aesopic" (allusive) language in order to circumvent the censors; and this, too, tends to detract from their survival value as literature. In fact, the only one of his longer works completely free of such blemishes is *The Golovlyov Family,* an impressively gloomy novel of the chronicle type which ranks second only to the *Fables* among Saltykov's achievements.

Although a good many of the latter are topical, they often rise (as Krylov's verse fables always do) to a level of universal application, and so endure. In "The Eagle as Patron of the Arts," for instance, the Eagle is plainly identifiable as the Tsar (at first Alexander II, then Alexander III), and the Falcon as the liberal Minister, Loris-Melikov; yet this fable still holds up as an attack on autocracy in general—and, for that matter, on such pseudo-concepts as "the Great Society." But "How One Muzhik Looked After Two Generals" is something rather different. Saltykov's chief target here is an entire social class (the high-ranking civil servants). And his secondary target is another; since his muzhik, far from being the "idealized peasant" who abounded in the more dreary "social protest" literature of the times, is clearly an "Uncle Tom," however sympathetically portrayed. Saltykov, in short, was a good deal more realistic than the kind of radical writer who specialized in grim documentaries while taking the "natural goodness" of the peasants for granted.

Tolstoy himself lapsed into this kind of naïveté on occasion. There is certainly a good dollop of it in "Ivan the Fool," for instance. (Or perhaps there only appears to be. In this marvelous realm of make-believe, you simply can't tell. Nor does it matter.)

---

[20]Mikhail Yevgrafovich Saltykov (often referred to as "Saltykov-Shchedrin," since he wrote under the latter name), was born in 1826 into a family of provincial gentry. In his early twenties he was exiled to Siberia for his radical writings. A few years later he returned to European Russia, and rose in the civil service, being appointed vice-governor of a province in his thirties. In his forties (still an unreformed radical) he retired to devote full time to writing and editing (with the poet, Nikolai Nekrasov) *Notes of the Fatherland.* He died in 1889.

"Ivan the Fool" belongs to the same period as Saltykov's "Eagle" and the Chekhov stories—the middle Eighties: a period of repression, stagnation, and "little deeds," as one Russian writer put it—and autocracy is certainly one of its chief targets, along with the State in general, militarism, *un*enlightened self-interest, and (naturally) Culture. But Tolstoy, like Chekhov, had never been one to engage in journalistic feuds; and his attitude toward the "enemy" is the farthest thing from either wrath or spitefulness. It is, rather, one of Olympian contempt—as witness his female soldiers defeating a vast army of males by heaving bombs out of as-yet-uninvented airplanes.

Needless to say, this kind of outlook is incompatible with the *lachrymae rerum* from which Gogol's comic art is distilled in the *Mirgorod* stories. (Not that Tolstoy lacked compassion: but he chose to express it in works of a different kind; e.g., in "The Death of Ivan Ilych," published the same year as "Ivan the Fool.") Still, it does serve to lift his comic anarchist tract to a high place in that "literature of satirical exposure" that put up sprouts in the reign of Catherine the Great, then withered until briefly revived in the middle and late decades of the nineteenth century, only to die in the era of Stalin, when there were "too many gallows."

A NOTE
ON THE TRANSLATIONS

Of all "classical" Russian prose, Gogol's is notoriously the most difficult to translate. To be sure, some of the other original texts used in preparing this anthology presented special problems of their own; e.g., Saltykov's rough-hewn, elliptical dialogue, or Dostoyevsky's artful use of intonations. But such obstacles are as nothing when compared to those set up for the translator by Gogol: confusing switches in tense, Ukrainianisms, and even grammatical errors. ("You try to correct it, and you spoil it," wrote the lexicographer Vladimir Dahl to the historian Mikhail Pogodin. "What would happen if he wrote Russian?")

Besides all the foregoing difficulties (too numerous to be ensampled here), "The Two Ivans" contains not a little legal gibberish, most of it archaic. In particular, the third petition—the one penned by the "scribbler" who "had three quill-pens stuck behind each ear"—is nine parts nonsense, than which nothing is harder to translate. I have done my best, though, to keep this nonsense intact—along with the awkward switches in tense elsewhere in the story.

At the same time, I have tried to respect—as some translators have not—that eloquence for which Ivan Ivanovich was famous in Mirgorod. It is nothing less than a slander upon that worthy citizen to have him say in his petition, things like "lawfully-criminal actions" (Garnett) or "legally criminal acts" (Magarshack). Ivan Ivanovich may well have been a slob, but he was a *literate* one. And what he said was that the other Ivan's acts were *zakonoprestupnyye*, which *looks* like "lawfully-criminal," etc., but

26

is actually an archaic form of "illegal"; i.e., a "stepping over" (*prestupleniye*) of the law (*zakon*).

The "sly Ukrainian," as Pushkin called Gogol, is a very tricky writer. I only hope he hasn't tricked me too often.

CIVIL SERVICE GRADES AND CORRESPONDING MILITARY RANKS

in Nineteenth-century Russia*

Civil Service Grade	Military Rank
1. Chancellor of the Empire	Commander-in-Chief
2. Actual Privy Councillor	General
3. Privy Councillor	Lieutenant General
4. Actual Councillor of State	Major General
5. Councillor of State	. . . .
6. Collegiate Councillor	Colonel
7. Court Councillor	Lieutenant Colonel
8. Collegiate Assessor	Major
9. Titular Councillor	Captain
10. Collegiate Secretary	1st Lieutenant
11. Naval Secretary	. . . .
12. Government Secretary	2nd Lieutenant
13. Provincial Secretary	Ensign of Infantry
14. Collegiate Registrar	. . . .

*Excerpted from the official Table of Ranks.

A PANEGYRIC IN MEMORY
OF MY GRANDFATHER

*Delivered by a Friend to an Audience
of His Friends, Over a Bowl of Punch*

BY IVAN KRYLOV

Dear Friends! This day marks the passing of exactly one
year since the dogs of this world lost their best friend,
and our district its wisest landowner. One year ago, to the
very day, while intrepidly pursuing a hare, he fell in a
ditch and shared the fatal cup, most fraternally, with his
bay horse. Fate, respecting their mutual affection, did not
want either of them to outlive the other. Meantime, the
world lost its finest gentleman and its handsomest horse.
Which of the two is the more deserving of our sorrow?
Of our praise? In the matter of virtues, neither was second
to the other. Both were equally useful to society; both led
the same kind of life; and, finally, both died the same
glorious death.

Still, my friendship for the departed inclines me in his
favor and obliges me to glorify his memory. For, though
many may say that his heart was (so to speak) the stable
of his bay horse, I may flatter myself that next to her, he
loved me better than anything else on earth. But even
though he had not been my friend, would not his sterling
qualities merit praise for themselves alone? And should
not his memory be exalted as one which will serve as an
example to all of our local gentry?

Please do not think, dear listeners, that I am proposing
him as an exemplar only in the matter of hunting. Not at

29

all. Hunting was among the least of his talents. Besides that, he possessed a thousand other natural gifts both suitable and necessary to us of the gentry. He showed us how a true gentleman should go about consuming, in one week's time, everything produced in a year by the two thousand common people under his authority. He provided us with notable examples of how those two thousand people could, with good advantage, be whipped two or three times a year. He had a talent for dining sumptuously and elegantly on his estate when, presumably, Lent was being observed there. And this art produced some pleasant surprises for his guests. Yes, gentlemen, all this is true! It frequently happened that when we came to dine with him at his estate, and saw all of his peasants pallid and starving, we would be afraid that we ourselves would starve at his table. Looking at them, we would conclude that for a hundred versts around, there was not a crust of bread or a consumptive chicken to be had. But what a pleasant surprise when we sat down at his table! On it was a wealth of victuals that one would have thought never existed in those parts—an abundance of which there was not the slightest hint elsewhere on his estates. Even the cleverest of us did not understand what he could still squeeze out of his peasants; and we were compelled to conclude that he had created his splendid banquets out of nothing.

But I see my enthusiasm is leading me astray from the order of thoughts I had intended to follow. Let us therefore consider the beginning of our hero's life. In this way we shall not miss one trait of those praiseworthy deeds of his—deeds that many of you, dear friends, are imitating most successfully. Let us, then, begin with his origins.

However much the philosophers may rave, claiming that in accordance with the genealogical table of the whole world we are all brothers, however often they may affirm that we are all the children of Adam, a person of gentle birth should be ashamed to own any such philosophy. And though it may be necessary and convenient that our servants should have descended from Adam, we would rather acknowledge that our original progenitor was an ass, than to have the same origins as they. Nothing exalts a person so much as noble extraction: it is his chief merit. Let the philosophers protest that a grandee and a beggar are alike in body, soul, passions, foibles, and virtues. If this be true, it is not the fault of the nobles. It is Nature's

fault that she created them in the same form as the most
vulgar commoners, so that we gentlemen have no special
features to distinguish us. It is a sign of her laziness and
negligence. I say no more than the truth, gentlemen! And
if this Nature were a living being, she would be very
ashamed of the fact that whereas she confers upon the
lowliest worm those traits proper to his condition; whereas
the smallest insect receives from her its coloring and ca-
pacities; whereas, when we consider the animal kingdom in
its entirety, it seems to us that she is inexhaustible in her
invention and variety—she, to her shame and our misfortune, has not invented anything at all by which to
distinguish us from the peasants; has not so much as given
us an extra finger as a sign of our superiority over the
muzhiks. Does she not show greater concern for the
butterflies than for the gentry? And so we must wear a
sword—a thing, so it would seem, that we should have
been born with. But in any case, thanks to our cleverness
we have found ways of correcting her defects; and we
have rid ourselves of the danger of being taken for animals of the same breed as the peasants.

Having a forefather who was wise, virtuous, and useful
to society—that is what makes a gentleman; that is what
distinguishes him from the rabble and the common people,
whose forefathers were neither wise, nor virtuous, nor
useful to society. The more ancient and farther removed
from us our ancestors are, the more illustrious our noble
strain. And it is precisely that which distinguishes our
hero, of whom I make bold to invent fitting oblation; for
it has been more than three hundred years since a wise
and virtuous man appeared in his family. And that one
man performed so many shining deeds that among his
descendants no more such things were necessary; so that
right up to the present they have been quite content to
do without wise and virtuous men, and have lost none of
their merit in the process.

Finally our hero, Jinglehead, made his appearance. He
did not yet know what he was; but already his noble soul
sensed the advantages of his birth, and in his second year
he began to scratch the eyes of his wet nurse, and bite her
ears. "That child will go far!" his father exclaimed
rapturously, on one such occasion. "He doesn't yet know
how to give orders, but he is already learning how to
administer punishment. It is easy to see that he has noble

blood in his veins." And the old man often wept for joy
when he saw with what a noble demeanor his offspring
pinched the wet nurse or the domestics. Not a single day
passed but what our little hero scratched somebody. And
as early as his fifth year he became aware that he was
surrounded with the kind of hoi polloi that he could bite
and scratch whenever he felt like it.

His all-knowing father was quick to realize that his son
now needed a companion. There were a good many im-
poverished gentry living in that part of the country; but
he was unwilling to stoop so low as to allow his son to
share his time with such people. As for providing him with
a serf's son as a companion, that struck the old gentleman
as even more intolerable. Another person would not have
known what to do. But the father of our hero immediately
relieved this distressing situation: he gave his son, as a
companion, a handsome spaniel. This, perhaps, is the
underlying reason why our hero, during all of his life,
preferred dogs to people and enjoyed himself more with
the former than the latter.

Jinglehead, being accustomed to giving orders, received
his new companion rather roughly, and started things off
by pulling her ears. But little Pepper (for such was the
dog's name) showed him that it is sometimes a mistake
to play jokes on others, relying too much on one's own
strength: she bit his arm till it bled. Our hero froze in
astonishment. It was the first time he had encountered
such a harsh response to his habitual behavior. Never
before had he been punished for pinching. His heart was
seething within him. But at the same time, he was afraid
to have a taste of combat with Pepper. And so he ran to
his father to complain of the mortal insult he had received
from his new companion. "My boy," his incomparable
father said to him, "don't you have plenty of serfs around
you to pinch? Why did you have to bother Pepper? After
all, a dog is not a servant: you have to be more careful
with a dog, unless you want to get bitten. She is stupid.
She can't be kept quiet and made to endure hardships without opening her mouth, like an intelligent being."

The precept deeply touched the heart of our young
hero, and he never forgot it. As he grew up, he often
engaged in those profound reflections for which this precept had provided the basis. He sought to discover ways
of beating his domestic animals without exposing himself
to danger, and of making them as passive as his peasants.

Or at any rate he sought to discover why the former were impertinent enough to snap back more than the latter did; and he concluded that his peasants were inferior to his domestic animals.

His doting father, having noticed that the child was beginning to think, decided that the time had come to begin his education; and he himself undertook to teach him his ABC's. In five months the pupil had surpassed his teacher and was spelling in modern Russian at least as well as his father could. Such progress frightened the old man. He was afraid that his son might learn to read fluently, and that he might take it into his head, some day, to become an academician. And so the lad's course in philology ended with the last page of the ABC book. "That's enough reading and writing for you," his father said. "You should be ashamed of learning anything more. I want you to be a distinguished gentleman. It wouldn't be fitting for you to read books."

Our hero profited from this brilliant reasoning, and learned to love all books like the plague. Not a single one found access to him, except for Rousseau's pronouncements on the harmfulness of knowledge. That was one work that earned his approbation, because of its epigraph. True, he never read it; but he always kept it on the mantelpiece. "Just read that," he would say, when anyone chanced to praise knowledge in his presence. "Read that, and you will regret being more intelligent than my bay horse. Oh, what a great man Rousseau was!" he would continue. And afterward he would undertake, slavishly, to count the pages in the book. This was his greatest concession to scholarship, and one that he made only to the author of *La Nouvelle Héloïse*.

Finally it came time for him to enter the civil service; and his rare progenitor, when bidding farewell to his son, delivered his last instructions to him. "Always remember, my darling son," he said, "that you are the owner of two thousand serfs. Remember that you are a gentleman of ancient stock, and the last of your line. Therefore, be sparing of yourself and don't follow the example of those unfortunates who, not having a crust of bread to eat, are obliged to wear out their health in the service. Behave in such a way as to avoid dismissal, and don't worry about the rest. Let the poor people seek promotions if they want to. As for us men of wealth, it is the promotions that should seek us out. Be always decorous in

your behavior; that is, don't venture outside the antechambers of important personages. Above all, avoid in-
curring the displeasure of a woman, of whatever low condition she may appear to be. The outward show of a
woman's social station is like a young sapling: however
weak and wretched it may seem, it often has roots that,
deep down in the earth, are intertwined with those of a
mighty oak which may crush you with its weight. In short,
here is my testament in a nutshell: I want you to retire
with high rank, not high honors." Whereupon he gave
him his parental blessing and two thousand rubles for the
journey. Three days after his son's departure, his illustrious
life came to an end.

For all the eagerness of our hero to profit from these
instructions, his noble soul accepted them only reluctantly.
Or to put it more precisely, he approved but half of
them. That is, in accordance with his father's advice, he did
not want to work; yet on the other hand he did not want
to grow old sitting in antechambers. These two rules of
conduct estranged him from two of his uncles, and from the
government service, and made of him a philosopher. The
frivolities of high society soon became tiresome to him.
He noticed that wherever he went, either he himself
yawned, or others yawned at him. And so he conceived
the peaceable intention of withdrawing from the world,
having everywhere seen indications that he and it were not
suited to each other.

A rare magnanimity and an incomparable modesty—
these two amiable qualities were manifest in him from
the time he first arrived in the capital. In his place, and
possessed of his illustrious family connections, a vulgarly
ambitious man would not have remained aloof from high
society. Rather, he would have sought entry into the best
homes. But not our hero: he sat all night long in the
taverns. He fled the life of elegance; and often, after
passing the evening with a gang of zealous gamblers, he
would return modestly home minus his coat. He never
held a grudge; and he would go to dine, quite undisturbed,
in the same place where, at supper the night before, he
had taken a thrashing. He was forbearing to the extreme.
I myself have witnessed, gentlemen, with what touching
meekness he would take blows from his friends, and then
drown his sorrows in drinking with them.

I repeat: an ambitious man, in his place, would have
been seduced by the worldly vanities and examples of high

society. But not he. When he heard that someone of his own age had received a decoration, that another person had been given an appointment, and another an award, he remained indifferent. None of these things touched his great soul; and he would listen to such news with a yawn. "It may very well be," he would say, "that some day I shall have to feed half of these civil servants. It's enough that I have two thousand serfs: that kind of rank will always assure me first place in my part of the country." Usually he concluded his comments with the words, "Vanity of vanities." And then, surrounding himself with a dozen bottles of port, he would sit down to a game of faro.

From this you can easily deduce, gentlemen, that the company he kept, while not elegant, was sportive. True, civil servants sometimes mingled with them; but as a rule the first two dozen bottles would establish complete equality and friendship in the gathering. However, this was not a tiresome kind of friendship, carried on for five years or so. No, it was a free and noble camaraderie, such that frequently, even before they had concluded their mutual pledges of affection, they would be pulling at each other's hair—quite without malice, of course, and often merely to pass the time.

There, gentlemen, you have a picture of his life in the city. He did not go in pursuit of happiness, but sought pleasures of another kind. He did not make the rounds, paying social calls at great houses, only to yawn with boredom. Instead, being a lover of freedom, he would often go to sleep under the table at his own friendly gatherings. He had no aspirations toward attracting, some day, the attention of the whole world upon himself: it was enough for him that his name was well known in all the taverns and coffee houses. And he had no intention of ever becoming a statesman. Not that he was lacking in intelligence; on the contrary, gentlemen, he was only too clever. It often happened that for this very reason he was given a thrashing by his companions of the card table, where he chiefly made a show of sharp wits. But since intelligence is persecuted everywhere in the world, he very soon tired of being intelligent and began to play cards with philosophical naïveté and a noble trust in the honesty of others. His friends, instead of being impressed by these amiable traits, cleaned him out of his entire fortune in two months' time and left our philosopher half naked—despite the fact that the northern climate is ill-suited to the practice of ascetic philosophy.

Anyone else, under such distressing circumstances, would have lost heart. Anyone else would have become desperate. But not he. Without the slightest vacillation he simply stayed home, waiting with great and heartfelt humility for his creditors to take him off to jail. Like Julius Caesar, he did not try to escape his fate. He did not even go beyond his front gate, although in the darkness of the night he could have walked along the street in only his sleeveless sweater and slippers without violating the decorum of the city. Nor did he seek any help in his misfortune. "What must be, must be," he said, and yawned fearlessly.

And destiny rewarded him for his faith. Just at the moment when it seemed that he had been abandoned by the whole world; when all doors were closed to him except the doors of the city jail; when in his kitchen, as in Rome, there remained not a trace of its former glory; and—most catastrophic of all—when his famished cat, looking for a stale crust of bread with all the zeal of Columbus seeking the New World, knocked over and broke his last bottle of port—when, I say, all these misfortunes had been heaped upon him, one of his uncles, renowned for his parsimony, in the practice of which he had gone without supper for twenty years, finally decided not to eat dinner either, and so left our hero an inheritance of five thousand serfs and 100,000 rubles.

Do you suppose this turned him into a proud man? Not a bit of it! That very same evening he went to see a wine merchant of his acquaintance, had a drinking bout with him, and then very modestly spent the night at his establishment, lying on a bare brick floor.

But already his passions were on the wane. And so, profiting from his past misfortunes, he no longer desired to seek good luck in any suit of cards whatsoever. He obtained a rank in the civil service and then retired, having decided to return to his country estate in order to embellish our district with his presence. Since he had a pronounced dislike for noisy farewell ceremonies, he left the city without notifying a single creditor. Then too, it may have been because of his modesty that he favored the French custom of leaving without saying good-bye, since the most reliable billiard-scorers have testified that, whenever he could, he took French leave of the taverns, however strongly they reproached him for it.

And so at last he withdrew from the bustle of the city and entered into a new field for the testing of his talents. And you, my friends, have seen for yourselves how brightly those talents shone.

No sooner had he arrived here, than he declared open war against the hares and assembled a numerous army of hounds. Having the interests of the peasants at heart, he was resolved to exterminate the entire race of hares. And he kept his word. True, many of his perverse peasants complained that they would rather feed the hares than an infinite number of hounds and a useless gang of hunters; that they would rather encounter hares in the grain fields than a half-hundred horses and twice as many hounds. But our hero, who knew just when and where to whip such tellers of idle tales, quieted their grumblings and persisted in his implacable hatred of the hares, like that of Hannibal toward the Romans.

In order to be more certain of extirpating them, he felled and sold his timber, meantime reducing the peasants to such a state that they had nothing wherewith to sow the fields. Imagine, if you will, the inner satisfaction felt by our hero as he rode out to the fields and found them clean as a tablecloth, so that he was free of all apprehension that a hare could conceal itself anyplace whatsoever. In three years he had cleared his land so completely that the intrepid beasts could find nothing there but death from starvation. "Tell me," someone once asked him, "wouldn't you rather see a thousand well-fed hares on your land, than five thousand hungry peasants? Isn't a man a fool if he burns down his house to get rid of the cockroaches?"

"Hold your tongue!" our hero replied. "I know very well that my peasants have nothing to eat. But in another five years the hares will abandon my land. They will flee from it as from a desert. And when that time comes, I will outwit that entire breed of cowardly plunderers by restoring the order and abundance of the past."

Ah, my friends, what a penetrating mind! Was there ever anyone, at any time, who conceived such a bold and majestic enterprise? Nero burned the splendid city of Rome in order to extirpate a handful of Christians. Julius Caesar killed off great numbers of his fellow citizens because he wanted to put down the power of Pompey, which was harmful to them. Alexander the Great cut his way through many kingdoms with the sword, conquering and destroying thousands of tribes, apparently so that he could wet his boots in the ocean surf and then brag about it back home. But none of these schemes or labors can compare with the feats of our hero. The others destroyed men in order to gain glory; but he destroyed them in order to stamp out hares.

And yet destiny, ever jealous of great deeds, did not allow him to consummate his scheme. In this he was like many other heroes who, having undertaken to perform a thousand feats in two years' time, have died in the first or second year of their enterprise.

Such, gentlemen, are the feats of our hero, which . . . But what's this? My amiable auditors have gently dozed off. Their venerable heads are at rest, like so many big, plump melons, around the punch bowl. O my dear departed friend, glory in thy triumph! Thy friends, who love thee, have inherited thy ways! For it was precisely thus that thou wert wont to doze off, at those jolly nocturnal revels, with thy nose half-submerged in a bowl of ale. If thou canst, absent thee from grim Pluto for a while, and look up from beneath the floor at thy friends. Then triumphantly tell the other dwellers in the infernal regions what a pleasant effect was produced by this panegyric in thy honor. And a fig for the disapproving stare of those envious authors who believe that they alone have obtained from Apollo the privilege of putting this world to sleep with their works!

THE TALE OF HOW
IVAN IVANOVICH QUARRELED
WITH IVAN NIKIFOROVICH

By Nikolai Gogol

Chapter the First

Ivan Ivanovich and Ivan Nikiforovich

What a fine fitted coat Ivan Ivanovich has! Really splendid! And what astrakhan! Hell and damnation, what astrakhan! Dove-gray, with a frost on it! I'll bet nobody else has that kind! For the love of heaven, just look at it! Especially when he stops to talk to somebody. Just look at it from the side. How delicious! Indescribable! Velvet! Silver! Fire! Great God! Nikolai the Wonder-Worker, Holy Saint! Why don't I have such a coat? He had it tailored before Agafya Fedoseyevna went to Kiev. You know Agafya Fedoseyevna—the one who bit off the assessor's ear?

Ivan Ivanovich is an excellent man. What a house he has in Mirgorod! A slanting porch roof supported by tall oak posts runs all the way around it; and everywhere under this roof are benches. When it gets too hot, Ivan Ivanovich takes off both his coat and his underclothes, leaving on nothing but his shirt, relaxes on his porch, and watches what is going on in the yard and out in the street. What apple and pear trees he has under the very windows! Just open the window, and the branches push their way into the room. All this is in front of the house; but you should see what he has in the garden! What *doesn't* he have? Plums, red cherries, sweet cherries, all

39

kinds of vegetables, sunflowers, cucumbers, muskmelons, sugar peas—even a granary and a forge.

Ivan Ivanovich is an excellent man. He is very fond of muskmelons. They are his favorite food. As soon as he has dined and come out on the porch in nothing but his shirt, he tells Gapka to bring him two melons. He slices them himself, collects the seeds in a special piece of paper, and begins to eat. Then he orders Gapka to bring him the inkpot, and in his own hand he writes an inscription on the paper containing the seeds: "This melon was eaten on such-and-such a date." If a guest was present, he adds: "So-and-so participated."

The late Mirgorod judge always admired Ivan Ivanovich's house when he looked at it. Yes, it's quite a nice little house. What I like is that sheds and outhouses have been added all around it, so that if you look at it from a distance you can see only roofs piled on top of one another, very much resembling a plateful of pancakes—or, better still, the funguses growing on a tree. The roofs, moreover, are all thatched with reeds; and a willow, an oak, and two apple trees lean on them with their spreading branches. Little windows with carved, whitewashed shutters can be glimpsed through the trees, and even reach out as far as the street.

Ivan Ivanovich is an excellent man. Even the commissioner from Poltava knows him. When Dorosh Tarasovich Pukhivochka comes from Khorol, he always goes to see him. And the archpriest, Father Pyotr, who lives in Koliberda, whenever he has a few people at his home, always says he doesn't know anyone who fulfills his Christian duty and knows how to live, like Ivan Ivanovich.

Lord, how time flies! Even then, more than ten years had gone by since he had become a widower. He didn't have any children. Gapka has children, and they often run about in the yard. Ivan Ivanovich always gives each of them a *bublik*,[1] or a slice of melon, or a pear. His Gapka carries the keys to the storerooms and the cellars. But Ivan Ivanovich himself keeps the key to the big trunk that stands in his bedroom, and the one to the middle storeroom; and he doesn't like to let anyone in there. Gapka, a healthy wench, goes about in a kind of slit skirt of woolen homespun. She has fine, robust calves and fresh cheeks.

---

[1] A kind of bagel (tr.).

And what a devout man is Ivan Ivanovich! Every Sunday he puts on his fitted coat and goes to church. When he has entered and bowed in all four directions, he usually takes a place in the choir loft and joins in the singing with a good bass. When the service is over, Ivan Ivanovich absolutely cannot bear to bypass the beggars. Perhaps he would have preferred not to bother himself with this tiresome business, were he not impelled to do it by his natural goodness.

"Good-day, poor woman," he usually said, when he had sought out the most crippled old woman in a tattered dress all made up of patches. "Where do you come from, poor creature?"

"From the farm, my lord. It's going on three days, now, since I've had a bite to eat or a drop to drink. My own children turned me out."

"Poor thing! But why did you come here?"

"Why, to beg, sir. To see if somebody might give me enough for a crust of bread."

"Hm! Well then I suppose you want bread?" Ivan Ivanovich usually asked.

"Oh, yes! I do! I'm hungry as a dog!"

"Hm!" Ivan Ivanovich usually answered. "And perhaps you would like some meat, too?"

"Why, I'll be glad for anything you're kind enough to give me."

"Hm! Would you be thinking that meat is better than bread?"

"It's not for a hungry person to choose. Whatever you kindly give will be good." So saying, the old woman usually held out her hand.

"Well, get along now—go with God," Ivan Ivanovich would say. "Why are you still standing there? I'm not beating you, am I?" And having addressed similar questions to one or two more, he finally goes home—or else drops in his neighbor, Ivan Nikiforovich, or the judge, or the mayor[2] to have a glass of vodka.

Ivan Ivanovich likes it very much when someone gives him a present or gift of some kind. This pleases him very much.

Ivan Nikiforovich is also a very fine fellow. His yard is next to Ivan Ivanovich's yard. They are such close

---

[2] A loose equivalent for *gorodnichy*, the appointive "police-governor" of the town.

friends as the world never produced. Anton Prokofyevich Pupopuz,[3] who to this day goes around in his brown frock coat with the light blue sleeves and dines at the judge's on Sunday, used to say that the devil himself had tied Ivan Ivanovich and Ivan Nikiforovich together with a rope. Where one went, the other would drag himself along, too.

Ivan Nikiforovich was never married. It used to be blabbed about that he had got married, but this was an absolute lie. I know Ivan Nikiforovich very well, and I can affirm that he never had any intention of getting married. Where do all these slanders come from? For instance, there was a rumor that Ivan Nikiforovich had been born with a tail in the rear. But this invention is so absurd—and at the same time so disgusting and indecent—that I don't even think it necessary to disprove it to enlightened readers, who undoubtedly know that tails in the rear are found only on witches (and on very few of them, at that)—who, moreover, belong rather to the female sex than to the male.

In spite of their great mutual affection, these two rare friends were not altogether alike. Their characters can best be gathered from a comparison. Ivan Ivanovich has the unusual gift of speaking in an extraordinarily pleasant manner. Lord, how he can talk! The sensation can only be compared with that produced when somebody is feeling your head for lice, or gently scratching your heel. You listen and listen until your head droops. Pleasant, surpassingly pleasant! Like a nap after taking a bath. Ivan Nikiforovich, on the contrary, mostly says nothing. But if he does drop a remark, just look out! It will cut better than any razor. Ivan Ivanovich is tall and skinny; Ivan Nikiforovich is somewhat shorter, but well spread out in breadth. Ivan Ivanovich's head is like a radish with the tail down; Ivan Nikiforovich's head is like a radish with the tail up. It is only after dinner that Ivan Ivanovich lolls on the porch in nothing but his shirt: in the evening he puts on his fitted coat and goes somewhere—either to the town store, which he supplies with flour, or to the countryside to catch quail. Ivan Nikiforovich lies on his porch all day (if it isn't too hot a day, he usually lies with his back to the sun) and never goes anywhere. If he happens to think of it, in the morning he will walk through the yard and look things over; then he'll go back to rest. In

---

[3]This is the same Anton Prokofyevich who shows up later with the last name of "Golopuz."

the old days he used to drop in on Ivan Ivanovich. Ivan Ivanovich is a man of most unusual refinement: in polite conversation he never utters an improper word, and he is quick to take umbrage if he hears one. Ivan Nikiforovich sometimes isn't too careful with his language. When this happens, Ivan Ivanovich usually stands up and says, "Enough, enough, Ivan Nikiforovich! Better go on out into the sun than to utter such ungodly words!" Ivan Ivanovich gets very angry if there's a fly in his borsch: he goes into a rage, shoves the soup plate away from him, and gives his host a tongue-lashing. Ivan Nikiforovich is extremely fond of bathing, and when he is sitting in water up to the neck, he orders the tea table and samovar to be set in the water, too; and he is very fond of drinking tea in such coolness. Ivan Ivanovich shaves his beard twice a week; Ivan Nikiforovich shaves his once. Ivan Ivanovich is extraordinarily inquisitive. God forbid you should start to tell him a story and not finish it! And if he is displeased with something, he lets you know right away. From Ivan Nikiforovich's countenance it is hard to tell whether he's pleased or angry; even if he is overjoyed at something, he won't show it. Ivan Ivanovich is of a rather timid character. Ivan Nikiforovich, on the contrary, wears big, baggy pants with such broad folds that if they were inflated you could put the whole yard into them, along with the granaries and outhouses. Ivan Ivanovich has big, expressive eyes the color of tobacco, and a mouth that looks something like the letter V. Ivan Nikiforovich has little, yellowish eyes, completely concealed by his thick brows and chubby cheeks, and a nose that resembles a ripe plum. When Ivan Ivanovich offers you a pinch of snuff, he always licks the lid of his snuffbox first, then taps it with his finger and, having proffered it, says, if you are an acquaintance, "May I make so bold, sir, as to ask you to do me the favor?" Or if you are not an acquaintance: "May I make so bold, sir—not having the honor of knowing your rank, your name, or your father's name—to ask you to do me the favor?" Ivan Nikiforovich, on the other hand, puts his snuff-horn right in your hands, and merely adds: "Do me the favor." Both Ivan Ivanovich and Ivan Nikiforovich detest fleas. Therefore, neither Ivan Ivanovich nor Ivan Nikiforovich ever lets a Jewish peddlar pass by without purchasing from him various little jars of a remedy against those insects—having first abused him roundly for professing the Jewish faith.

Despite certain dissimilarities, however, both Ivan Ivanovich and Ivan Nikiforovich are excellent men.

Chapter the Second

From Which One May Learn What Ivan Ivanovich Coveted, the Subject of a Conversation Between Ivan Ivanovich and Ivan Nikiforovich, and How It Ended

One morning—in July, it was—Ivan Ivanovich was lying on his porch. The day was hot, the air was dry and shimmered. Ivan Ivanovich had already been out in the countryside to see the mowers and his farm, and had already questioned the muzhiks and peasant women he met as to where they were coming from, where they were going, and why. He was terribly tired, and had lain down to rest. Lying there, he looked around at the storehouses, the yard, the sheds, the hens running about in the yard, and thought, "Good Lord! What a clever proprietor I am! Is there anything I don't have? Fowl, outbuildings, granaries, something to satisfy every whim; fruit and berry brandies; pears and plums in my orchard; poppies, cabbages, and peas in my garden. . . . Is there anything I don't have? I'd like to know if there's anything I don't have!"

Having asked himself that profound question, Ivan Ivanovich became lost in thought. Meantime, his eyes were seeking out new objects: they passed over the fence into Ivan Nikiforovich's yard, and were involuntarily attracted by a curious spectacle. A gaunt peasant woman was bringing out, one after another, garments that had been stored away, and hanging them on a clothesline to air. Soon an old uniform with frayed facings had stretched out its sleeves in the air, and was embracing a woman's brocade jacket. Sticking out from behind them was a nobleman's uniform with crested buttons and a moth-eaten collar; then a pair of stained white cashmere trousers that had once been pulled on over Ivan Nikiforovich's legs, and now

could scarcely be pulled on over his fingers. Next, another
pair of trousers were quickly hung up in the shape of an
inverted V. Then came a dark blue Cossack-style jacket
that Ivan Nikiforovich had had made for himself twenty
years before, when he was getting ready to join the militia
and had already grown a moustache. Finally, to top it all
off, a sword was displayed, looking like a spire sticking up
in the air. Then the fluttering skirts of something resembling
a grass-green caftan with copper buttons the size of a
five-kopeck coin. From behind the skirts peered a vest
trimmed in gold braid and cut low in front. The vest
was soon blocked from view by the old-style petticoat
of a deceased grandmother, with pockets big enough to
hold a watermelon apiece. All this mixed together constituted a very interesting spectacle for Ivan Ivanovich,
while the sun's rays, picking up here and there a dark-blue
or green sleeve, the red trimming on a cuff, or a bit of
gold brocade, or playing on the sword-spire, made it into
something extraordinary, like the puppet shows[4] put on in
the villages by strolling actors. Especially when the crowd
of peasants, pressing close together, watches Herod in his
golden crown, or Anton leading his goat: behind the
scenes a fiddle scrapes, a gypsy slaps his hands against his
lips in lieu of a drum, as the sun goes down and the fresh
coolness of the southern night imperceptibly snuggles up
to the fresh shoulders and breasts of the plump village
girls.

Soon the old woman came out of a storeroom, grunting
and dragging along an ancient saddle with broken stir-
rups, worn-out leather holsters, and a saddlecloth that had
once been scarlet, with gold embroidery and copper disks.

"That's a stupid woman!" thought Ivan Ivanovich.
"Next thing, she'll drag out Ivan Nikiforovich and air
him out."

As a matter of fact, Ivan Ivanovich was not entirely
wrong in his guess. Some five minutes later, Ivan Nikiforovich's baggy nankeen pants were hung up, filling almost
half of the yard. After that, she brought out a cap and a
shotgun.

"What does that mean?" Ivan Ivanovich wondered.
"I've never seen a shotgun at Ivan Nikiforovich's. What
is he up to? He never hunts, but he keeps a shotgun! What
does he need it for? But it's a fine little thing. I've been

---

[4]*Vertep*—a puppet show on the theme of the Nativity.

wanting to get one like that for a long time. I'd very much like to have that little gun. I like to amuse myself with a nice little gun."

"Hey, there, granny!" Ivan Ivanovich shouted, wiggling his forefinger.

The old woman came up to the fence.

"What's that you have there, old girl?"

"You can see for yourself—a gun."

"What kind of a gun?"

"Who knows what kind? If it was mine. I 'spose I'd know what it's made of. But it's the master's."

Ivan Ivanovich stood up and began to examine the shotgun from every angle—and forgot to reprimand the old woman for hanging it and the sword out to air.

"It's made of iron, I'd say," the old woman went on.

"Hm! Iron. Why should it be iron?" Ivan Ivanovich said to himself. "Has your master had it for a long time?"

"Could be for a long time."

"A fine little thing!" Ivan Ivanovich continued. "I'll ask him for it. What does he need it for? Or I'll trade him something for it. Tell me, granny, is your master at home?"

"Yes, he is."

"Very well. I'll come and see him."

Ivan Ivanovich got dressed, took his gnarled stick to keep off the dogs (since in Mirgorod there are many more dogs in the street than people), and went.

Although Ivan Nikiforovich's yard was next to Ivan Ivanovich's, and you could climb over the fence from one into the other, Ivan Ivanovich went by way of the street. From the street you had to go through an alley so narrow that if two one-horse carts happened to meet in it, they couldn't make way for each other but had to remain in that position until someone took hold of the back wheels of each and dragged it back into the street. As for anyone on foot, he would be adorned both by the burdocks and the flowers growing along the fence on either side. At one end of the alley stood Ivan Ivanovich's cart-shed; at the other stood Ivan Nikiforovich's granary, gate, and dovecote.

Ivan Ivanovich went up to the gate and rattled the latch. Within, dogs began barking; but when the motley-coated pack had seen the familiar face, they ran back with their tails wagging. Ivan Ivanovich walked across the yard, made colorful by the Indian pigeons fed from Ivan

Nikiforovich's own hand, the watermelon and muskmelon rinds, a patch of grass here and there, a broken wheel in this place or that, or a barrel hoop, or a lolling little boy in a dirty shirt—a picture of the kind painters love! The shade from the clothes hung out on the line covered almost the entire yard, and gave it a degree of coolness. The old woman met him with a bow, gaped, and just stood there. The front of the house was ornamented by a little porch whose roof was supported by two posts of oak—an unreliable protection against the sun, which at that time of year in Little Russia[5] shines in earnest and bathes anyone out walking in a hot sweat, from head to foot. From this it was plain to see how great was Ivan Ivanovich's desire to obtain the indispensable article, when he decided to go out in that kind of weather, even altering his set custom of strolling out only in the evening.

The room that Ivan Ivanovich entered was quite dark, since the shutters were closed. A sunbeam coming through a hole in one of the shutters took on the hues of the rainbow and, striking the opposite wall, painted on it a varicolored landscape of thatched roofs, trees, and the clothes hung out on the line—the whole thing upside down, however. All this endowed the room with a kind of marvelous twilight.

"God's blessing!" said Ivan Ivanovich.

"Ah, how do you do, Ivan Ivanovich!" answered a voice from a corner of the room. Only then did Ivan Ivanovich see Ivan Nikiforovich lying on a rug spread out on the floor. "Pardon me for being in a state of nature."

Ivan Nikiforovich was lying there with nothing on at all—not even a shirt.

"That's quite all right. Have you slept today, Ivan Nikiforovich?"

"I have. And have you slept, Ivan Ivanovich?"

"I have."

"And so you have just now got up?"

"*Just now got up?* Good heavens, Ivan Nikiforovich! How could I sleep until now? I've just come back from the farm. The grain fields along the road are splendid. Marvelous! And the hay is so tall, soft, and golden!"

"Gorpina!" Ivan Nikiforovich shouted. "Bring Ivan Ivanovich some vodka and fruit pastries with sour cream."

---

[5] I.e., the Ukraine.

"Fine weather today."

"Don't praise it, Ivan Ivanovich! The devil take it! There's just no getting away from this heat."

"So you just had to mention the devil! Ah, Ivan Nikiforovich! You'll remember what I told you, but then it will be too late! You'll pay the price in the next world for your ungodly words!"

"How did I offend you, Ivan Ivanovich? I didn't mention your father, or your mother, either. I can't understand how I offended you."

"Enough, now! Enough, Ivan Nikiforovich!"

"I swear I didn't offend you, Ivan Ivanovich!"

"It's odd that the quail still don't come at the birdcall."

"As you like. Think what you want, but I didn't offend you in any way."

"I don't know why they won't come," Ivan Ivanovich said, as though he hadn't heard Ivan Nikiforovich. "Could it be that it isn't quite the season yet? But this *should* be the time."

"You say the grain looks good?"

"Marvelous grain! Marvelous!"

After this there was a silence.

"Why is it you're hanging the clothes out, Ivan Nikiforovich?" Ivan Ivanovich finally asked.

"Well, that damned old woman let mildew get into those splendid clothes—almost new, they are. Now I'm airing them out. The material is fine, really excellent. They just have to be turned, and I can wear them again."

"I saw one thing there I liked very much, Ivan Nikiforovich."

"What was it?"

"Tell me, please. What need do you have for that shotgun that was hung out to air along with the clothes?" At this point Ivan Ivanovich proferred his snuffbox. "May I make so bold as to ask you to do me the favor?"

"No, thanks. Help yourself. I'll take a pinch of my own." So saying, Ivan Nikiforovich felt around and found his snuff-horn. "That stupid woman! So she hung the shotgun out there too, did she? Fine snuff that the Jew in Sorochintsy makes. I don't know what he puts in it, but it's so fragrant! A little like balsam. Here, take some. Put it in your mouth and chew it a little. Take some—do me the favor!"

"Tell me, please, Ivan Nikiforovich—I'm still speaking

of the shotgun—what are you going to do with it? After all, you don't need it."

"What do you mean I don't need it? I might go hunting."

"Good heavens, Ivan Nikiforovich! When will you go hunting? At the Second Coming, no doubt. So far as I know and others can recall, you haven't yet killed so much as one duck. Besides, the good Lord didn't fit you out with a constitution for hunting. You have a dignified bearing and figure. And how can you go dragging yourself through the marshes when that garment of yours which it is not proper to call by its name in just any conversation, is still being aired out? No, you require rest and relaxation." As was mentioned above, Ivan Ivanovich spoke with unusual picturesqueness when it was necessary to convince somebody of something. How he could talk! Lord, how he could talk! "Yes, dignified behavior is the thing for you. I say, give it to me!"

"The very idea! That's a valuable shotgun. You can't find guns like that anywhere today. I bought it from a Turk, way back when I was getting ready to go into the militia. And now I'm supposed to give it away all of a sudden? The very idea! It's an indispensable thing!"

"Indispensable for what?"

"What do you mean, 'for what'? Why, if robbers attack my house. . . . Not indispensable, indeed! Now, thank the Lord, my mind is at ease and I'm not afraid of anybody. Why? Because I know I have a shotgun in the storeroom."

"A fine shotgun! Why, Ivan Nikiforovich, the lock on it is ruined!"

"What do you mean? What's ruined? It can be fixed. I just have to put a little hemp oil on it to keep it from rusting."

"From what you are saying, Ivan Nikiforovich, I can see that you have no kindly disposition toward me whatsoever. You don't want to do anything for me as a token of friendship."

"How can you say, Ivan Ivanovich, that I show you no friendship? You should be ashamed! Your cattle graze on my pastureland, and I've never once laid hands on them.[6] Whenever you go to Poltava, you ask me for the use of my light carriage. Well? Have I ever refused it? Your young-

---

[6] I.e., impounded them, so as subsequently to demand payment of a fine for use of the pastureland.

sters climb over the fence into my yard and play with my dogs, and I never say anything about it. Let them play, just as long as they don't touch anything. Let them play!"

"If you don't want to make me a present of it, perhaps we could trade something."

"What will you trade me for it?" And Ivan Nikiforovich propped himself up on his elbow and looked hard at Ivan Ivanovich.

"I'll give you my brown sow—the one I fed up in the sty. A splendid sow! Just see if she doesn't give you a litter of pigs next year."

"Ivan Ivanovich, I don't know how you can say such a thing! What do I need your sow for? To give a funeral banquet for the devil?"

"There you go again! You just can't get along without the devil! It's sinful of you! By heaven, it's a sin, Ivan Nikiforovich!"

"Really, Ivan Ivanovich! How could you, in exchange for my gun, give me the devil only knows what—a sow!"

"Why is she 'the devil only knows what,' Ivan Nikiforovich?"

"Why? Just judge for yourself. This is a shotgun—a thing everybody knows. But that's the devil only knows what—a sow! If anybody else but you had said it, I might have taken it as an insult."

"But what have you noticed that's wrong with the sow?"

"Really, now! What do you think I am? To take a sow—"

"Sit down! Sit down! I'll forget it. . . . Keep your shotgun! Let it rot and rust standing in a corner of the storeroom! I don't want to talk about it any more."

After this came a silence.

"They say," Ivan Ivanovich began, "that three kings have declared war against our Tsar."

"Yes, Pyotr Fyodorovich was telling me. What kind of a war is it? And what's it about?"

"Nobody can say for sure, Ivan Nikiforovich, what it's about. My guess is that the kings want all of us to adopt the Turkish religion."

"They're fools! What a thing to want!" declared Ivan Nikiforovich, raising his head.

"So you see, our Tsar has declared war on them because of that. 'No,' he says. 'You adopt the Christian faith!'"

"What do you think, Ivan Ivanovich? Our men will beat them, won't they?"

"Oh, yes. So you won't trade the little gun, Ivan Nikiforovich?"

"You amaze me, Ivan Ivanovich. You're supposed to be well-known for your learning, yet you talk like you're still wet behind the ears. That I should be such a fool—"

"Sit down! Sit down! Forget the gun! Let it fall to pieces! I won't talk about it any more!"

At this point the refreshments were brought in.

Ivan Ivanovich drank a small glass of vodka and ate a fruit pastry with sour cream.

"See here, Ivan Nikiforovich. Along with the sow, I'll give you two sacks of oats. After all, you didn't sow any oats. One way or another, you'll have to buy oats this year."

"I swear, Ivan Ivanovich, a person shouldn't talk to you except when he's eaten a bellyful of peas." (That was nothing: Ivan Nikiforovich got off expressions much worse than that.) "Who ever heard of trading a shotgun for two sacks of oats? I'll bet you won't toss in your astrakhan coat."

"But you're forgetting, Ivan Nikiforovich, that I'm giving you the sow besides."

"What? Two sacks of oats and a hog for a shotgun?"

"What's wrong? Isn't that enough?"

"For a shotgun?"

"Of course, for a shotgun."

"Two sacks for a gun?"

"Two sacks—not empty, but full of oats. And have you forgotten the sow?"

"Go kiss your sow! Or if you don't want to, go kiss the devil!"

"Oh, you *are* touchy, aren't you? You'll see! In the next world they'll pierce your tongue with red-hot needles for saying such ungodly things! After talking with you, a person has to wash his face and hands and fumigate himself."

"Excuse me, Ivan Ivanovich, but a gun is a noble thing— the most fascinating kind of amusement. And besides, it's a very pleasing ornament to a room. . . ."

"You, Ivan Nikiforovich, have been fussing over that shotgun of yours *like an idiot child with a new toy*," said Ivan Ivanovich with vexation; because he had really begun to get angry.

"And you, Ivan Ivanovich, are a regular *gander*."

If Ivan Nikiforovich had not uttered that word, they would have quarreled and then parted friends, as always. But now something very different took place.

Ivan Ivanovich flushed all over. "What was that you said, Ivan Nikiforovich?" he asked, raising his voice.

"I said you were like a gander, Ivan Ivanovich."

"How dare you, sir, ignoring both propriety and respect for a man's rank and family, insult me with such an abusive name?"

"What's abusive about it? And, for that matter, why are you flapping your hands so much, Ivan Ivanovich?"

"I repeat. How did you dare, flouting all decency, call me a gander?"

"I spit on your head, Ivan Ivanovich! Why have you set up such a cackling?"

Ivan Ivanovich had lost all self-control: his lips were quivering; his mouth lost its usual shape of the letter *V* and became a kind of *O;* his eyes blinked so much it was frightful. This happened to Ivan Ivanovich very seldom— only when something had made him really furious.

"Then I hereby inform you," declaimed Ivan Ivanovich, "that I do not want to know you!"

"A great loss that is! By heaven, I won't weep for that!" Ivan Nikiforovich answered.

He was lying, lying! I swear he was lying! He was very upset by it.

"I will never set foot in your house again!"

"Aha, ha!" said Ivan Nikiforovich, so vexed he didn't know what to do and, against all habit, rising to his feet. "Hey, woman! Boy!"

At this, the same gaunt old woman appeared in the doorway, along with a small boy muffled up in a long, ample frock coat. "Take Ivan Ivanovich by the arm and put him outside."

"What? To a nobleman?" Ivan Ivanovich cried out with a feeling of injured dignity and wrath. "Just you dare! Come on! I'll annihilate you and your stupid master together! The crows won't be able to find where you lie!" (Ivan Ivanovich spoke with unusual force when his soul was shaken.)

The group as a whole presented a striking picture: Ivan Nikiforovich, standing in the center of the room in his full beauty without any adornment whatsoever! The old woman, gaping, with the most senseless, terrified look

on her face. Ivan Ivanovich with his arm upraised, as the
Roman tribunes are depicted. It was a rare moment! A
magnificent spectacle! And yet there was only one spectator: the boy in the enormous frock coat, who stood rather
quietly picking his nose.

Finally, Ivan Ivanovich picked up his cap. "Fine behavior on your part, Ivan Nikiforovich! Excellent! I won't
let you forget it!"

"Get along, Ivan Ivanovich! Get along! And make sure
you don't cross my path! If you do, Ivan Ivanovich, I'll
beat your mug to a pulp!"

"Just for that, take *this*, Ivan Nikiforovich!" replied
Ivan Ivanovich, making a fig at him and slamming the door
—which creaked shrilly and opened again.

Ivan Nikiforovich appeared in the doorway and tried
to add something, but Ivan Ivanovich rushed out of the
yard without looking back.

Chapter the Third

What Happened After the Quar-
rel Between Ivan Ivanovich and
Ivan Nikiforovich

And so two worthy men, the pride and ornament of
Mirgorod, had quarreled. And because of what? Because
of a mere nothing—a gander. They refused to see each
other, they broke off all relations—although formerly they
had been known as the most inseparable of friends! Every
day, Ivan Ivanovich and Ivan Nikiforovich used to send
to inquire about each other's health; and they often talked
to each other from their respective porches, and said
such pleasant things to each other that it gladdened the
heart to hear them. On Sundays, Ivan Ivanovich in his
fitted astrakhan coat and Ivan Nikiforovich in his Cossack-
style caftan of brown nankeen would set out for church
almost arm-in-arm. And if Ivan Ivanovich, who had exceedingly sharp eyes, was first to notice a mud puddle or
filth of any kind in the street (which *is* sometimes found
in Mirgorod), he would always say to Ivan Nikiforovich,
"Be careful, and don't step here, because it's not good." For

his part, Ivan Nikiforovich also manifested the most touching signs of friendship, and no matter how far away he was standing, he would always hold out his snuff-horn toward Ivan Ivanovich, saying, "Do me the favor." And what well-managed households and lands both of them had! . . . And these two friends. . . . When I heard of it, I was thunderstruck. For a long time I simply wouldn't believe it. Ivan Ivanovich has quarreled with Ivan Nikiforovich! Such worthy men! After that, is there anything solid left in this world?

After Ivan Ivanovich got home, he remained for a long time in a highly excited state. Usually, he first went to the stable to see whether the mare was eating her hay. (Ivan Ivanovich had a gray mare with a bald patch on her forehead—a very fine horse.) Next he would feed the turkeys and suckling pigs with his own hand. Then he would go into the house, where he would either make wooden dishes (he was very skillful, and could fashion various articles from wood as well as any turner) or read a book published by Liuby, Gary, and Popov[7] (Ivan Ivanovich did not remember the title of the book, because a servant girl had long since torn off the upper part of the title page by way of amusing a child), or else rest on the porch. But now he didn't busy himself with any of his usual pastimes. Instead, when he encountered Gapka, he began to scold her for dawdling about doing nothing, though in fact she was hauling buckwheat into the kitchen; he threw a stick at a rooster that had come to the porch for his usual tribute; and when a grimy urchin in a torn shirt ran up to him and cried, "Daddy, Daddy! Give me a honeycake," he stamped his foot and threatened him so fiercely that the frightened little boy ran off God knows where.

Finally, however, he thought better of it and began to busy himself with his usual activities. He sat down to dinner late, and it was almost evening when he lay down to rest on the porch. The good borsch with pigeons in it that Gapka had cooked made him completely forget what had happened that morning. Ivan Ivanovich once again began to survey with pleasure his little domain. At length his eyes came to rest on his neighbor's yard, and he said to himself, "I haven't been to Ivan Nikiforovich's yet today. I'll go over and see him." With this, Ivan Ivanovich took

---

[7]Publishers of cheap illustrated books for the semi-literate.

his stick and his cap and went out to the street. But he had scarcely got through the gate when he remembered the quarrel, spat, and came back.

Almost the same kind of action took place in Ivan Nikiforovich's yard. The old woman, as Ivan Ivanovich noticed, had already put one foot on the wattle fence with the intention of crawling over into his yard, when Ivan Nikiforovich's voice was suddenly heard: "Come back! Come back! You mustn't!"

Ivan Ivanovich became very bored, however; and it is quite likely that these worthy men would have made peace the very next day, if a special occurrence at Ivan Nikiforovich's house had not destroyed all hope and poured oil on the fire of enmity just when it was dying out.

On the evening of that same day, Agafya Fedoseyevna came to visit Ivan Nikiforovich. Agafya Fedoseyevna was neither a relative of Ivan Nikiforovich, nor his sister-in-law, nor even his gossip. Apparently, she had no reason at all for visiting him; and he himself was not too happy to have her there. Nonetheless, she used to come and visit him for weeks on end, and sometimes even longer. When she did, she took possession of the keys and took over the running of the whole house. This was very unpleasant to Ivan Nikiforovich, but surprisingly enough he obeyed her like a child; and although he sometimes tried to argue with her, Agafya Fedoseyevna always won.

I must admit that I don't understand why things are so arranged that women can take us by the nose as deftly as they do the handle of a teapot. Either their hands are just made that way, or our noses aren't better suited for anything else. And despite the fact that Ivan Nikiforovich's nose was quite a bit like a plum, she took him by that nose and led him around like a dog. When she was there, he even altered, unwillingly, his usual mode of life. He didn't lie so long in the sun; and when he did lie there it was not in a state of nature: he always had on his shirt and big, baggy pants, although Agafya Fedoseyevna by no means insisted on this. She was not one to stand on ceremony, and when Ivan Nikiforovich had a fever she would, with her own hands, rub him down from head to foot with turpentine and vinegar. Agafya Fedoseyevna wore a mobcap on her head, three warts on her nose, and a coffee-colored housecoat with yellow flowers on it. Her whole figure resembled a tub, so that it was as difficult to locate her waist as to see your own nose without a mirror.

Her legs were very short and shaped like two pillows. She talked scandal, ate boiled beets in the morning, and swore wonderfully well; and throughout all these varied activities her face did not for a moment change its expression —something which, as a rule, only women can manage.

As soon as she arrived, everything was turned topsy-turvy. "Ivan Nikiforovich, don't you make up with him, and don't apologize. He wants to ruin you—that's the kind of man he is. You don't know him yet."

That damned woman talked slander and more slander, and fixed things so that Ivan Nikiforovich didn't want to hear so much as a mention of Ivan Ivanovich.

Everything took on a different aspect. If a dog from next door ran into the yard, it was drubbed with whatever was handy; those youngsters who crawled across the fence came back howling, with their shabby little shirts pulled up and the marks of a switch on their backs. Even the gaunt old woman, when Ivan Ivanovich tried to ask her about something, made such an indecent gesture that Ivan Ivanovich, as a man of refinement, could only spit and mutter, "What a nasty woman! Worse than her master!"

Finally, to top off all his insults, his hateful neighbor put up—directly opposite his property, at the usual place for climbing over the fence—a goose-shed, as though with special intent to aggravate the insult. This shed—so odious to Ivan Ivanovich—was built with diabolical swiftness: in a single day.

This stirred up wrath and a longing for vengeance in Ivan Ivanovich. He did not, however, show any sign of chagrin, although the shed even extended over some of his own land. But his heart beat so hard that it was difficult for him to preserve this outward composure.

Thus did he pass the day. Night came. . . . Oh, if I were a painter, how marvelously I would portray all the loveliness of that night! I would depict all Mirgorod sleeping; the myriad stars looking down on it in stillness; the palpable silence broken by the barking of dogs from nearby and far away; the lovesick sexton hurrying past them and climbing over a fence with knightly intrepidity; the white walls of the houses, bathed in moonlight, becoming still whiter as the trees sheltering them grew darker, the shadows of the trees blacker, the flowers and the silent grass more fragrant, as from every corner the crickets, those indefatigable troubadours of the night, strike

up in unison their rasping song. I would depict how, in one
of those low-roofed clay cottages, a black-browed village
maiden, twisting and turning on her lonely bed, dreams
with heaving young breasts of a hussar's moustache and
spurs, as the moonlight smiles on her cheeks. I would
depict how the black shadow of a bat flits across the
white road, as he comes to settle on a white chimney-top.
. . . But I would scarcely be able to depict Ivan Ivanovich
as he went out that night with a saw in his hand. So many
different emotions were written on his face! Quietly, very
quietly, he crept up and crawled under the goose-shed.
Ivan Nikiforovich's dogs didn't yet know anything of the
quarrel between the two, and they therefore allowed him,
as an old acquaintance, to approach the shed, which was
supported entirely by four oak posts.

When he had crawled up to the nearest post, he put
the saw to it and began sawing. The noise of the sawing
made him look around every moment, but the thought of
the insult restored his courage.

The first part was sawed through; Ivan Ivanovich began on the second. His eyes were flashing, and he was
so terrified he could see nothing. Suddenly, he cried out
and went cold all over: a ghost appeared before him. But
he soon recovered himself when he saw it was a goose,
craning its neck toward him. Ivan Ivanovich spat with
indignation and resumed his work.

The second post was likewise sawed through: the
goose-shed tottered. When he began on the third post
his heart was beating so violently that he had to stop
his work several times. It was sawed through more than
halfway, when the tottering structure gave a sudden,
violent lurch. . . . Ivan Ivanovich barely had time to jump
out of the way, when it collapsed with a crash. Snatching
up his saw, he ran home in a terrible panic and threw
himself on his bed, lacking even the courage to look out
the window at the results of his awful deed. It seemed
to him that Ivan Nikiforovich's entire household—the
old woman, Ivan Nikiforovich, and the small boy in the
immense frock coat—had assembled, all of them with
clubs and, led by Agafya Fedoseyevna, were coming to
tear down his house and smash it to bits.

Ivan Ivanovich passed the whole of the next day as
though in a fever. He kept imagining that his fateful
neighbor, in revenge for his deed, would at the very least
set fire to his house. So he gave orders to Gapka to keep

a sharp lookout, everywhere and at every moment, to see whether dry straw hadn't been planted somewhere. At length, in order to forestall Ivan Nikiforovich, he decided to lodge a complaint against him with the Mirgorod District Court. Its contents may be learned from the following chapter.

Chapter the Fourth

Concerning What Took Place in the Mirgorod District Court

Mirgorod is a marvelous town! It has all sorts of buildings: some are thatched with straw, some with reeds, and some even have wooden roofs. To the right a street, to the left a street, and everywhere a fine fence. Hops twine over it, pots hang on it, and from behind it the sunflower displays its sunlike head, the poppy blushes, and fat pumpkins can be glimpsed. . . . Splendor! The fence is always adorned with objects that render it still more picturesque: either a checked woolen petticoat spread out wide, or an undershirt, or else a pair of big, baggy pants. In Mirgorod there is no stealing or misappropriation, so everyone hangs out whatever he wants to.

If you come to the square you will no doubt pause to admire the view. There is a puddle in it—an amazing puddle! The only one like it you ever saw! It covers almost the entire square. A beautiful puddle! The houses and cottages, which from a distance might be taken for haystacks, stand around it admiring its beauty.

But in my opinion there is no finer building than the district courthouse. Whether it is constructed of oak or birchwood is quite unimportant to me; but, my dear sirs, it has eight windows! Eight windows all in a row, looking directly out on the square and upon that body of water I have already mentioned, which the mayor calls a lake! It alone is painted the color of granite; all the other houses in Mirgorod are merely whitewashed. Its roof is all wood, and it would even have been painted if the oil intended for that purpose, after having been seasoned with onions, had not been eaten by the office clerks (which happened,

as luck would have it, during Lent) and the roof left un-
painted. On the front steps, which project out onto the
square, hens often run about, since the steps are almost
always littered with grain or some other edibles—which
is not done on purpose, however, but only through the
carelessness of the petitioners. The courthouse is divided
into two parts: in one is the court proper, and in the other
is the jail. In the court half there are two clean, whitewashed rooms: one is the waiting room for petitioners; the
other contains a table adorned with ink stains, and on it
stands the *zertsalo*.[8] Four oak chairs with high backs; along
the walls, iron-bound chests in which stacks of complaints
filed with the district court are kept. On one of the chests,
at the moment, a polished boot was standing. The court
had been in session since early that morning. The judge,
a rather fat man (although somewhat thinner than Ivan
Nikiforovich) with a good-natured face, wearing a greasy
dressing gown, was chatting over a pipe and a cup of tea
with his clerk. The judge's lips were located directly under
his nose, so that he could sniff his upper lip to his heart's
content. This lip served him in lieu of a snuffbox, since
the tobacco intended for his nose almost always settled
on it. And so, the judge was chatting with his clerk. Off to
one side, a barefoot girl was holding a tray of teacups.
At the end of the table, the secretary was reading a de-
cision, but in such a monotonous and mournful voice that
the defendant himself would have fallen asleep listening
to it. The judge would no doubt have done so before anyone else, if he hadn't become involved in an interesting
conversation.

"I purposely tried to find out," he was saying, as he
sipped from a cup of tea already grown cold, "what they
do to make them sing well. I had a wonderful thrush two
years ago. And do you know, he suddenly cracked up
and began to sing God only knows what. The longer it
went on, the worse it got. He started lisping and wheezing
—seemed like a hopeless case. But it was a mere nothing.
Here's why it happens. Under the throat there's a little
lump smaller than a pea. All you have to do is prick that
little lump with a needle. Zakhar Prokofyevich showed me

---

[8]The emblem of office under the Russian Empire. It had the
shape of a triangular prism, with each facet displaying (under
glass) a decree of Peter the Great, and was surmounted by the
two-headed eagle.

how to do it, and if you like I'll tell you just how it happened. I went to his place one day—"

"Shall I read the next one, Demyan Demyanovich?" interrupted the secretary, who had finished reading several minutes before.

"Ah, have you read the whole thing already? My, how fast it went! I didn't hear a bit of it. Where is it? Give it here, and I'll sign it. What else do you have there?"

"The case of the Cossack Bokitko's stolen cow."

"Very well, read it. And so, I went to his place. . . . I can even tell you in detail what he gave me to eat and drink. With the vodka they served sturgeon—unique! I'll tell you, it was nothing at all like the sturgeon that. . . ." At this point the judge clicked his tongue and smiled, and his nose sniffed from its usual snuffbox . . . "our Mirgorod store treats us to. I didn't eat any herring, because as you know they give me heartburn. But I tasted the caviar. Marvelous caviar! No two ways about it—just marvelous! Then I had some peach brandy distilled with centaury. There was saffron brandy, too; but as you know, I never drink it. It's very nice, I realize. Before a meal, they say, it whets your appetite, and afterward it adds the finishing touch. . . . Well, just look who's here!" exclaimed the judge, seeing Ivan Ivanovich come in.

"God's blessing, and I wish you good health," said Ivan Ivanovich, bowing all around with that amiability which was his and his alone. Lord, how he could charm us all with his manners! I have never seen such refinement anywhere. He was well aware of his own worthiness, and therefore looked upon our unanimous respect as his due. The judge himself offered a chair to Ivan Ivanovich, and his nose sucked up all the snuff from his upper lip—which with him was always a sign of great pleasure.

"What may I offer you, Ivan Ivanovich?" he asked. "Would you like a cup of tea?"

"No, thank you very much," answered Ivan Ivanovich; and he bowed and sat down.

"Oh, please have just one little cup," the judge repeated.

"No, thank you. Very much appreciate your hospitality," answered Ivan Ivanovich. He bowed and sat down.

"Just one cup," repeated the judge.

"No, don't trouble yourself, Demyan Demyanovich." Ivan Ivanovich bowed and sat down.

"One little cup?"

"Well, all right, perhaps one little cup," said Ivan Ivanovich, and reached for the tray.

Merciful heavens! What boundless refinement there was in that man! Words cannot express what a pleasant impression such manners produce.

"Won't you have another little cup?"

"No, thank you very much," answered Ivan Ivanovich, putting his inverted teacup back on the tray and bowing.

"Do me the favor, Ivan Ivanovich."

"I can't. Much obliged to you." With this, Ivan Ivanovich bowed and sat down.

"Ivan Ivanovich! For our friendship's sake—one little cup!"

"No, thank you. Much indebted to you for your hospitality." Having said this, Ivan Ivanovich bowed and sat down.

"One cup—just one little cup!"

Ivan Ivanovich reached over to the tray and took the cup.

Damn it all, anyway! How does he manage? How does the man keep up his dignity like that?

"Demyan Demyanovich," said Ivan Ivanovich, when he had drunk the last drop, "I have urgent business with you. I am lodging a complaint." With this, Ivan Ivanovich put down his cup and took out of his pocket a sheet of stamped paper covered with writing. "A complaint against my enemy—my sworn enemy."

"But against whom?"

"Against Ivan Nikiforovich Dovgochkhun."

At these words the judge almost fell out of his chair. "What are you saying?" he exclaimed, clasping his hands. "Ivan Ivanovich—is this you?"

"You can see for yourself it is I."

"The Lord and all the holy saints have mercy on us! *What?* You, Ivan Ivanovich, have become the enemy of Ivan Nikiforovich? Did those words come from your lips? Repeat that! Wasn't there someone hiding behind you and speaking instead of you?"

"What's so incredible about it? I can't bear the sight of him. He has offended me mortally. He has defiled my honor."

"By the Holy Trinity! How can I ever make my mother believe this? The dear old thing—every day, as soon as I start quarreling with my sister, she says, 'Children, you get along like cats and dogs! Why don't you take an example from Ivan Ivanovich and Ivan Nikiforovich? They're real, honest-to-goodness friends! Such friends! Such worthy men!" Some friends, I'll say! Tell me, what's this all about? What happened?"

"It's a delicate matter, Demyan Demyanovich. I can't tell you in so many words. You'd better have your secretary read my petition. Here, take it by this side. It's more presentable here."

"Read it, Taras Tikhonovich," the judge said, turning to his secretary.

Taras Tikhonovich took the petition and, blowing his nose as all secretaries of district courts do—that is, with two fingers—he began to read:

"From Ivan, son of Ivan, Perepenko, nobleman and landowner of the Mirgorod District, a petition, the substance of which is set forth in the following charges:

"1) The nobleman Ivan, son of Nikifor, who is known to the whole world for his ungodly, disgusting, and totally unconscionable illegal acts, did, on the seventh day of July of the present year 1810, perpetrate a mortal insult upon me, both personally as affecting my honor and likewise to the degradation and defamation of my rank and family name. The aforesaid nobleman, who is moreover of loathsome appearance, has a quarrelsome character and overflows with all manner of blasphemous and abusive expressions. . . ."

At this point, the secretary paused so as to blow his nose again, as the judge reverentially folded his arms and just said to himself: "What a lively pen! Lord, how the man can write!"

Ivan Ivanovich asked Taras Tikhonovich to read on, and the latter continued:

"The aforesaid nobleman Ivan, son of Nikifor, Dovgochkhun, when I went to him with friendly proposals, called me publicly by an insulting name which is demeaning to my honor; to wit, 'gander'; whereas it is well known to the entire Mirgorod District that I have never borne the name of that loathsome animal, and have no intention of bearing it in the future. The proof, moreover, of my noble extraction is the fact that both the day of my birth and the name I received at baptism are recorded in the parish register kept in the Church of the Three Bishops. But a gander, as is known to everyone at all versed in the sciences, cannot be listed in the parish register, since a gander is not a person but a fowl—something well known to everyone, even to a person who has not attended a seminary. But the aforesaid evil-minded nobleman, being duly aware of all this, abused me with the aforesaid loathsome word for no other purpose than to inflict a mortal insult upon my rank and station.

"2) This same lewd and indecent nobleman attempted, moreover, to encroach upon my family property, inherited by me from my father of blessed memory, Ivan, son of Onisim, Perepenko, by profession a member of the clergy, inasmuch as in violation of every law he transported to a point directly opposite my front porch, a goose-shed; which was done with no other intent than to aggravate the insult perpetrated upon me; for said goose-shed had theretofore stood in a very suitable place, and was still reasonably solid. But the abominable intent of the afore-mentioned nobleman was solely to cause me to witness unseemly incidents; for it is well known that no man goes into a shed—and *a fortiori* a goose-shed—for any proper purpose. In the course of this illegal action, the two front posts trespassed upon my own land—conveyed to me during the lifetime of my father, Ivan of blessed memory, son of Onisim, Perepenko, starting from the granary and running in a straight line to the place where the women wash their pots.

"3) The above-described nobleman, whose very names, both first and last, inspire total disgust, nurtures in his heart the evil design of setting fire to me in my own house. Unmistakable indications thereof are manifest from the following: *primo,* the aforesaid evil-minded nobleman has begun frequently to emerge from his house—something he never undertook before, owing to his laziness and the loathsome obesity of his body; *secundo,* in his servants' quarters, contiguous to the very fence which forms the boundary of my own land, inherited by me from my late father, Ivan of blessed memory, son of Onisim, Perepenko, there is a light burning every day and for an unusually long time; which is manifest proof thereof, since hitherto, by reason of his miserly stinginess, not only the tallow candle but also the oil lamp was always put out.

"And I therefore petition that the aforesaid nobleman, Ivan, son of Nikifor, Dovgochkhun, as guilty of arson, of the defamation of my rank, Christian name, and sur-name, and of rapacious misappropriation of property—but above all, of the base and reprehensible coupling of my surname with the appellation of 'gander'—be sentenced to the payment of a fine, together with all costs and damages, and that he himself, as a lawbreaker, be put into irons and, when fettered, be sent to the city jail, and that a ruling on this my petition be made promptly and without fail. Written and composed by Ivan, son of Ivan, Perepenko, nobleman and landowner of Mirgorod."

When the reading of the petition was concluded, the judge went up to Ivan Ivanovich, buttonholed him, and began to speak after this fashion: "What are you doing, Ivan Ivanovich? Fear God! Drop that complaint! Plague take it! (Let it dream of the devil!) Much better you and Ivan Nikiforovich should shake hands, kiss, and make up, and buy some Santurin or Nikopol wine—or else simply make some punch—and invite me. We'll down a bottle together, and forget the whole thing."

"No, Demyan Demyanovich, it's not that kind of thing," said Ivan Ivanovich, with the dignity that always sat so well on him. "It's not the kind of thing that can be settled by a friendly agreement. Good-bye. Good-bye to you, too, gentlemen!" he added, with the same dignity, turning to all the rest of them. "I hope that my petition will bring about appropriate action." And he went out, leaving the whole court dumbfounded.

The judge sat there without saying a word; the secretary took a pinch of snuff; the office clerks upset the shard of a bottle that they used in lieu of an inkwell; and the judge himself, in his distraught condition, spread the puddle of ink over the table with his finger.

"What do you say to that, Dorofei Trofimovich?" asked the judge, turning after a brief silence to his clerk.

"I say nothing," replied the clerk.

"What won't people do next!" the judge went on.

He had scarcely said this, when the door creaked and the front half of Ivan Nikiforovich landed in the courtroom while the other half remained in the waiting room. That Ivan Nikiforovich should appear—and in the courtroom at that—seemed a thing so extraordinary that the judge cried out, and the secretary stopped reading. One clerk, wearing a frieze facsimile of a frock coat, put his pen in his mouth; another swallowed a fly. Even the army veteran who performed the duties of messenger and porter, and who had been standing by the door scratching himself, under his dirty shirt with the stripes on the shoulder—even he gaped and stepped on somebody's foot.

"Well I never! What brought you here? How are you, Ivan Nikiforovich?"

But Ivan Nikiforovich was more dead than alive, because he was stuck fast in the doorway and couldn't take one step either forward or backward. In vain did the judge shout into the waiting room that somebody there should shove Ivan Nikiforovich from behind into the courtroom. There was nobody there but an old woman petitioner who, despite all the efforts of her bony hands, could do nothing. Then one of the clerks, who had thick lips, broad shoulders, a thick nose, drunken, crossed eyes, and tattered elbows, went up to the front half of Ivan Nikiforovich, folded his arms on his chest as if he were a baby, and winked to the old veteran, who shoved his knee into Ivan Nikiforovich's belly; and in spite of his piteous moans he was squeezed out into the waiting room. Then they slid back the bolts and opened the other half of the door. Meanwhile, the clerk and his assistant, the veteran, breathing hard from their joint efforts, diffused such a strong smell that for a long time the courtroom seemed transformed into a pothouse.

"Are you hurt, Ivan Nikiforovich? I'll tell my mother, and she'll send you a lotion. You just rub it on the small of your back and everything will be all right."

But Ivan Nikiforovich collapsed into a chair, and except for prolonged groans could say nothing. At length, in a faint voice, scarcely audible from exhaustion, he said, "Would you like some?" And taking his snuff-horn from his pocket, he added: "Take some! Do me the favor."

"Delighted to see you," answered the judge. "But I still can't imagine what made you take all this trouble and oblige us with such a pleasant surprise."

"A petition. . ." was all Ivan Nikiforovich could enunciate.

"A petition? What kind of petition?"

"A complaint. . . ." At this point there was a long pause for breath. ". . . Oof! A complaint against that scoundrel, Ivan Ivanovich Perepenko!"

"Good heavens! Are you at it too? Such rare friends! A complaint against such a virtuous man!"

"He's Satan in person!" Ivan Nikiforovich said sharply. The judge crossed himself.

"Take my petition and read it."

"There's nothing else we can do—read it, Taras Tikhonovich," said the judge, turning to the secretary with an expression of displeasure. But his nose involuntarily sniffed his upper lip, which before then it had usually done only from deep satisfaction. Such self-assertiveness on the part of his nose caused the judge even greater vexation. He took out his handkerchief and wiped all the snuff from his upper lip by way of chastising such insolence.

The secretary, after making the habitual gesture that he always went through before starting to read—without the help of a handkerchief, that is—began in his usual voice as follows:

"The petition of Ivan, son of Nikifor, Dovgochkhun, nobleman of the Mirgorod District, the substance of which is set forth in the following charges:

"1) Out of his hateful spite and evident ill will the self-styled nobleman, Ivan, son of Ivan, Perepenko, is perpetrating against me all manner of dirty tricks, injuries, and other evil and dreadful actions; and yesterday P.M., like a robber and a thief, with axes, saws, chisels, and other carpenter's tools, he broke at night into my yard and into my own shed, situated therein. With his own hand, and in a humiliating manner, he hacked it to pieces, although I on my part had given no cause for such an illegal and piratical deed.

"2) The aforesaid nobleman, Perepenko, has designs upon my very life, and before the seventh day of last month, concealing those designs, he came to me and began in a friendly and sly manner to wheedle from me a shotgun which was in my room, and with his characteristic stinginess offered me many worthless things for it, such as a brown sow and two sacks of oats. But, having by then surmised his criminal intent I tried in every way to divert him from it; but the aforesaid scoundrel and villain, Ivan, son of Ivan, Perepenko, swore at me like a muzhik, and since that time has nurtured an implacable hostility toward me. Moreover, the aforesaid, frequently mentioned ferocious nobleman and bandit, Ivan, son of Ivan, Perepenko, is of very disgraceful origins: his sister was known to all the world as a slut, and went off with the light infantry company stationed in Mirgorod five years ago, and registered her husband as a peasant. His father and mother were also exceedingly lawless people, and both were prodigious drunkards. But the aforementioned nobleman and bandit, Perepenko, has surpassed all his family with his brutish and reprehensible behavior, and under a show of piety he commits the most immoral acts. He does not keep the fasts; for on the eve of the fast of Advent, that godless man bought a ram, and the next day he ordered his common-law trollop, Gapka, to slaughter it, alleging that he urgently needed tallow for candles and oil lamps.

"Wherefore I petition that the aforesaid nobleman, as a bandit, sacrilegist, and swindler who has already been detected in theft and burglary, be put into irons and sent to jail or to a government prison, and there, as may seem best, having been stripped of his rank and nobility, be soundly flogged and sent to a penal camp in Siberia for as long as is necessary; that he be ordered to pay all costs and damages; and that a ruling be made on this my petition. To this petition Ivan, son of Nikifor, Dovgochkhun, nobleman of the Mirgorod District, has set his hand."

As soon as the secretary finished reading, Ivan Nikiforovich picked up his hat and bowed, with the intention of leaving.

"I say, where are you going, Ivan Nikiforovich?" the judge called after him. "Sit with us for a little! Have some tea! Oryshko! Why are you standing there winking at the clerks, foolish girl? Go and bring some tea!"

But Ivan Nikiforovich, terrified at having gone so far away from home and having endured such a dangerous quarantine, had already managed to squeeze through the door, saying, "Don't inconvenience yourself. I'll gladly. . . ." And he closed the door behind him, leaving the whole court dumbfounded.

There was nothing to be done about it. Both complaints were entered, and the case was in the way of assuming considerable importance, when an unforeseen circumstance made it even more interesting. When the judge had left the courtroom, accompanied by his clerk, and the secretary and the office clerks were loading into a sack the chickens, eggs, loaves, pies, cakes, and other odds and ends brought by petitioners, a brown sow ran into the room and seized, to the amazement of all present, not a pie or a crust of bread, but Ivan Nikiforovich's petition, which was lying at one end of the table with its pages hanging over the edge. When she had seized the document, the brown grunter ran off so quickly that not a one of the clerks could catch her, in spite of the rulers and inkwells that were thrown at her.

This event caused a terrible hubbub, since not so much as one copy of the document had been made. The judge—or rather, his secretary and his clerk—spent a long time discussing this unprecedented development. Finally, it was decided to write a report on it for the mayor, since the investigation of this case was more the concern of the police. The report, #389, was sent to him that same day, and out of it grew a rather curious conversation, about which the reader may learn in the following chapter.

Chapter the Fifth

In Which Is Described a Conference Between Two Eminent Personages of Mirgorod

No sooner had Ivan Ivanovich taken care of things on his property and gone out, as usual, to lie on the porch, than, to his unutterable astonishment, he noticed something red at the front gate. This was the mayor's red cuff, which like his collar had acquired a glaze, and along the edges was being transformed into polished leather. Ivan Ivanovich thought to himself: "I'm really pleased that Pyotr Fyodorovich has come for a chat." But he was very surprised to see that the mayor was walking much faster than usual and waving his hands—which as a rule he did very rarely. There were eight buttons on the mayor's uniform. The ninth had come off during a procession at the consecration of the church two years before, and so far the police force had not managed to find it, although the mayor, when hearing the daily reports made to him by the inspectors, always asked whether the button had been found. These eight buttons were sewed on the way peasant women plant beans: one to the right, and the next to the left. His left leg had taken a bullet in his last campaign, so that as he limped along, he threw it out so far to the side that he thereby nullified almost all the work of the right leg. The more rapidly the mayor maneuvered his infantry, the slower it advanced. Thus while he was approaching the porch, Ivan Ivanovich had time enough to lose himself in conjectures as to why the mayor was waving his arms so fast. He was all the more interested, because the business at hand was apparently of unusual

importance, since the mayor was even wearing his new
sword.

"Hello, Pyotr Fyodorovich!" called out Ivan Ivanovich,
who, as has already been said, was most inquisitive and
simply could not restrain his impatience at the sight of
the mayor trying to take the porch steps by storm without
raising his eyes as he quarreled with his infantry, which
was quite unable to mount one step at one fell swoop.

"A very good day to you, my dear friend and benefactor
Ivan Ivanovich!" answered the mayor.

"Pray sit down. You're tired. I can see that, because
your wounded leg hinders—"

"My leg!" cried the mayor, giving Ivan Ivanovich one
of those looks such as a giant casts at a pigmy, or a
learned pedant at a dancing master. As he said this, he
stretched out his leg and stamped on the floor. This valor,
however, cost him dear, because his whole body lurched
forward and his nose pecked at the railing. But the sage
guardian of law and order, by way of saving face, at once
righted himself and reached into his pocket as though
trying to get at his snuffbox. "Let me tell you, my very
dear friend and benefactor Ivan Ivanovich, that I've made
much worse campaigns in my day. Yes, seriously, I have.
In the campaign of 1807, for instance. . . . Oh, I could tell
you how I climbed over a fence to visit a pretty German
girl." With this, the mayor winked, and smiled a fiendish-
ly roguish smile.

"But where have you been today?" asked Ivan Ivanovich,
eager to cut the mayor short and bring him more quickly
to the reason for his visit. He would very much have liked
to ask what it was the mayor intended to inform him of.
But his refined social awareness made him realize how very
improper such a question would be; and he had to con-
trol himself and wait for the key to the riddle, although
meanwhile his heart was pounding with unusual violence.

"Very well, I'll tell you where I've been," the mayor
answered. "In the first place, I report that the weather is
fine today."

At these words, Ivan Ivanovich almost died.

"But allow me," the mayor continued. "I came to see
you today about a very important matter." With this, the
mayor's face and bearing took on the same anxious
aspect they had had when he was storming the porch.

Ivan Ivanovich came alive again, and shook as though

in a fever; but, as usual, he was not long in asking a question.

"How is it important? Is it really important?"

"Well, judge for yourself. First of all, I beg to inform you, dear friend and benefactor Ivan Ivanovich, that you . . . for my part, mind you, I don't care at all; but the policy of the government demands it . . . you have committed a breach of public order!"

"What are you saying, Pyotr Fyodorovich? I don't understand it at all."

"I swear, Ivan Ivanovich! How can you say you don't understand it at all? Your own beast has made off with a very important official document, and you still say you can't understand it at all!"

"What beast?"

"If I may say so, your own brown sow."

"But how is it my fault? Why did the court porter open the door?"

"But, Ivan Ivanovich, the beast was your own, so you are to blame."

"Thank you very much for putting me on the same level with a pig."

"I never said that, Ivan Ivanovich! As God is my judge, I never said that! Kindly judge for yourself with an open mind. You are beyond any doubt aware that, in accordance with the policy of the government, unclean beasts are prohibited from straying about in the town— especially in the principal streets. You must admit that this is prohibited."

"Good Lord, what are you talking about? What difference does it make if a hog goes out in the street?"

"Allow me to inform you—allow me, Ivan Ivanovich— that this is quite impossible. What can we do? If our superiors want something, we must obey. I don't deny that chickens and geese sometimes run out into the street, and even the square. Chickens and geese, mind you. But already last year I issued an order that hogs and goats were not to be allowed in public places. Which order I commanded to be read aloud at that time before an assembly of all the townspeople."

"Pyotr Fyodorovich, I see nothing in all this except that you are trying in every way to offend me."

"That's one thing you simply can't say, my very dear friend and benefactor—that I'm trying to offend you. Just try to remember: I didn't say a word to you last year when you put up a roof a whole yard higher than what regulations permit. On the contrary, I pretended I hadn't noticed it at all. Believe me, my very dear friend, even now I would absolutely . . . er, so to speak. . . . But my duty—in a word, my responsibility—requires me to enforce cleanliness. Judge for yourself, when suddenly, in the principal street—"

"Fine principal streets they are! Every peasant woman goes there to throw out whatever she doesn't want."

"Permit me to inform you, Ivan Ivanovich, that it's *you* who are offending *me*. True enough—that does happen sometimes, but as a rule only beside a fence, or behind sheds or storehouses. But when a sow in farrow barges into the main street and the public square, that's something—"

"Really now, Pyotr Fyodorovich! After all, a sow is one of God's creatures!"

"Agreed! Everybody knows that you're an educated man—that you know all the sciences and various other subjects. I didn't start learning to write until I was thirty. Because, as you know, I rose from the ranks."

"Hm!" said Ivan Ivanovich.

"Yes," the mayor went on, "in 1801 I was a lieutenant in the 42nd Light Infantry Regiment. Our company commander, if you would care to know, was Captain Yeremeyev." As he said this, the mayor dipped his fingers into the snuffbox that Ivan Ivanovich was proffering, and rolled some snuff between his thumb and forefinger.

Ivan Ivanovich answered, "Hm!"

"But it is my duty," continued the mayor, "to obey the orders of the government. Are you aware, Ivan Ivanovich, that anyone who steals a government document from a courtroom must be tried before a criminal court like any other criminal?"

"I'm so well aware of it that, if you like, I can teach you something. That applies to human beings—if you stole a document, for example. But a pig is an animal—one of God's creatures."

"That's all very well, but the law says 'anyone guilty of stealing. . . .' Please listen carefully: *'anyone* guilty.' Nothing is said about the species, sex, or rank. Therefore, an animal can be guilty, too. You may think what you please, but the beast, prior to being sentenced, must be turned over to the police as a violator of law and order."

"No, Pyotr Fyodorovich," Ivan Ivanovich replied coolly, "that will not be."

"As you like, but I must follow the orders of the government."

"Why are you trying to frighten me? I suppose you mean to send that one-armed soldier for the sow? I'll tell my serf girl to take a poker to him and throw him out. She'll break his other arm."

"I won't venture to argue with you. If you don't want to turn her over to the police, then do whatever you like with her. Butcher her for Christmas, if you want to, and make hams out of her. Or eat her just as she is. Only if you're going to make sausages, I wish you'd send me a couple of those that your Gapka makes so well out of hog's blood and lard. My Agrafena Trofimovna is very fond of them."

"I'll be delighted to send you a couple of sausages."

"I'll be very much obliged to you, my dear friend and benefactor. Now allow me to say just one more thing. I have been especially asked by both the judge and all of our other acquaintances, to—so to speak—reconcile you with your friend, Ivan Nikiforovich."

"What? With that boor? You want me to make peace with that coarse individual? Never! That will never be— never!"

"As you like," answered the mayor, regaling both nostrils with snuff. "I won't make so bold as to offer advice. But allow me to point out one thing. Right now you two are at odds; but when you've made up. . . ."

But Ivan Ivanovich had begun to talk about catching quails, which usually happened when he wanted to change the subject.

And so the mayor was obliged to depart without having achieved any success whatsoever.

Chapter the Sixth

*From Which the Reader Can
Easily Learn All That Is Contained in It*

Despite all the efforts made by the court to conceal the matter, the very next day all Mirgorod learned that Ivan Ivanovich's sow had made off with Ivan Nikiforovich's petition. It was the mayor himself, in a forgetful moment, who was the first to spill the beans. When Ivan Nikiforovich was told of it, he said nothing except to inquire, "Was it the brown one?"

But Agafya Fedoseyevna, who was there at the time, started needling Ivan Nikiforovich again. "What's the matter with you, Ivan Nikiforovich? If you let it pass, people will laugh at you for a fool! A fine nobleman you'll be then! You'll be worse than the woman who sells those pies you're so fond of!"

And that tireless woman talked him around! Somewhere she dug up a little man, middle-aged and swarthy, with blotches all over his face, who wore a dark blue frock coat with patched elbows—a regular bureaucratic scribbler! He smeared tar on his topboots, had three quill-pens stuck behind each ear, and for an inkpot he had a little glass bottle tied to a button by a string. He would eat nine pies at a sitting, and put the tenth in his pocket, and would fill one sheet of stamped foolscap with all manner of chicanery so that no clerk could read it aloud straight through, but would have to pause time and again to cough or sneeze. This little semblance of a man fussed and sweated and scribbled, and finally concocted the following document:

"To the Mirgorod District Court from the nobleman Ivan, son of Nikifor, Dovgochkhun.

"As a consequence of the aforesaid my petition, which was from me, the nobleman Ivan, son of Nikifor, Dovgochkhun, and so intended, jointly with the nobleman Ivan, son of Ivan, Perepenko, at which the Mirgorod District Court itself manifested its connivance. And the aforesaid insolent wilfulness of the brown sow being itself kept secret and having reached our ears from persons not parties to the case. Forasmuch as the aforesaid indulgence and connivance, as of malicious intent, falls strictly within the competence of the court; for said sow is a stupid beast, and hence all the more capable of stealing official documents. From which it is clearly evident that the frequently aforementioned sow could not but have been incited to the same by the opposing party himself, the self-styled nobleman Ivan, son of Ivan, Perepenko, who has already been detected in theft, attempted homicide, and sacrilege. But the aforesaid Mirgorod Court, with its characteristic partiality, manifested the tacit consent of its own person, without which consent said sow could never have been allowed to abscond with the document; inasmuch as the Mirgorod District Court is well provided with attendants, for which it suffices to mention a certain soldier at all times present in the waiting room who, although he has one blind eye and a somewhat damaged arm, possesses the requisite capacity to drive out a hog and strike it with a cudgel. Wherefrom is abundantly evident the connivance of the aforesaid Mirgorod Court and, incontestably, the sharing of the Jewlike profits therefrom, mutually combining. And the aforesaid, aforementioned bandit and nobleman Ivan, son of Ivan, Perepenko, who has disgraced himself, was the accomplice. Wherefore I, the nobleman Ivan, son of Nikifor, Dovgochkhun, herewith inform the aforesaid District Court in its appropriate omniscience that if the aforementioned petition is not recovered from said brown sow or from her accomplice, the nobleman Perepenko, and a just ruling in my favor is not made thereupon, then I, Ivan, son of Nikifor, Dovgochkhun, will lodge a complaint with the higher court regarding such illegal connivance of the aforesaid District Court, with due and appropriate transference of the case.—Ivan, son of Nikifor, Dovgochkhun, nobleman of the Mirgorod District."

This petition produced its effect. The judge, like all kindhearted people, was a cowardly man. He asked the secretary for his opinion. But the secretary emitted a deep "Hm" through his lips, and his face took on the indifferent and diabolically ambiguous expression that is assumed only by Satan when he sees at his feet the victim who has run to him for help. One recourse was left: to reconcile the two friends. But how go about this, when so

far all attempts had been unsuccessful? Nonetheless, they
decided to try. But Ivan Ivanovich declared flatly that he
would have none of it, and even got very angry. Ivan
Nikiforovich, instead of answering, turned his back to
the sun and didn't say a word. Then the litigation pro-
ceeded with the extraordinary rapidity for which the
mills of justice are ordinarily so famed. The document
was earmarked, registered, numbered, sewed into a paper
case, and receipted for—all in one day; and the paper case
was put on a shelf, where it lay and lay and lay—for one
year, another, and another. A great many young ladies
managed to get married; a new street was built in Mirgorod;
the judge lost one molar and two side teeth; more urchins
were running about Ivan Ivanovich's yard than before
(Lord only knows where they came from); Ivan Nikiforovich, by way of reproaching Ivan Ivanovich, had built a
new goose-shed, although somewhat farther away than
the former one, and had put up enough other outbuildings
to screen himself off completely from Ivan Ivanovich,
so that these worthy men almost never saw each other
face to face—and the case still lay, in perfect order, there
on the shelf, which had turned marblelike from the ink-
stains.

Meantime, an event of great importance to all Mirgorod
took place. The mayor was giving a party! Where shall I
find brushes and colors to paint the variety of the gathering and the magnificent regale? Take a watch, open it up,
and look at what's going on inside. A frightful hodgepodge,
is it not? Now just imagine that almost as many, if not
more, wheels were standing in the mayor's yard. What
britskas and light springless carriages were not there! One
with a broad rear end and a narrow front; another with
a narrow rear end and a broad front. One was a britska
and a light springless carriage combined; another was
neither a britska nor a springless carriage; and another was
like a huge haystack or a fat merchant's wife; another was
like a dishevelled Jew or a skeleton that has not yet shed
all its skin; another looked, in profile, exactly like a pipe
with a long stem; still another like nothing on earth—
some kind of strange being utterly hideous and most
fantastic. From the midst of this chaos of wheels and
coach-boxes loomed the semblance of a carriage with a
window like that of a room barred with a thick cross-
piece. Coachmen in long-waisted gray Cossack coats,
tunics, and gray jerkins, sheepskin caps, and forage caps

of various sizes and shapes, with pipes in their mouths,
were leading the unharnessed horses through the yard.
What a party the mayor was giving! Permit me to list all
those present: Taras Tarasovich, Yevpl Akinfovich, Yev-
tikhiy Yevtikhiyevich, Ivan Ivanovich (not our Ivan Ivanovich, but another), Savva Gavrilovich, our Ivan Ivanovich, Yelevferiy Yelevferiyevich, Makar Nazaryevich,
Foma Grigoryevich . . . I can't go on! My strength fails
me! My hand is tired from writing. And how many ladies
there were! Swarthy and fair, long and short, fat as Ivan
Nikiforovich, and so thin it seemed each one of them
could be hidden in the scabbard of the mayor's sword. So
many bonnets! So many dresses! Red, yellow, coffee-
colored, green, dark blue; new, turned, remade; fichus,
ribbons, reticules. Farewell, poor eyes! You'll be no good
for anything after this spectacle. And what a long table
was pulled out! And how everybody talked—what a
racket they raised! A mill, with all its grindstones, wheels,
pinions, and beaters, is as nothing compared to that. I
can't tell you for sure what they were talking about, but it
must have been about many pleasant and useful subjects,
such as the weather, dogs, wheat, bonnets, and stallions.
At length Ivan Ivanovich—not our Ivan Ivanovich, but
the one-eyed one—said: "It strikes me as strange that my
right eye" (the one-eyed Ivan Ivanovich always spoke of
himself ironically) "does not see Ivan Nikiforovich
Dovgochkhun."

"He wouldn't come!" said the mayor.

"How so?"

"Well, it's already been two years, thank the Lord,
since they quarreled—I mean Ivanovich and Ivan Nikiforovich; and if one of them goes somewhere, the other
won't go for the life of him."

"You don't say so!" At this, the one-eyed Ivan Ivanovich cast his eyes upward and clasped his hands. "Well,
now, if people with good eyes can't get along together,
how can I live in peace with my blind orb?"

At these words everybody laughed heartily. They
were all very fond of the one-eyed Ivan Ivanovich, because
he cracked jokes very much in the taste of the day. Even
the tall, thin man in a soft woolen frock coat with a
plaster on his nose, who up to then had been sitting in a
corner and never once changed the expression on his face
—even that gentleman rose from his seat and came nearer

to the crowd that had gathered around the one-eyed Ivan Ivanovich.

"I'll tell you what," said the one-eyed Ivan Ivanovich, when he saw he was surrounded by a rather large company. "Instead of staring at my blind eye, as you are doing now, let's reconcile our two friends. Right now Ivan Ivanovich is chatting with the women and young girls. Let's send on the sly for Ivan Nikiforovich, and then shove them together."

Everyone unanimously adopted Ivan Ivanovich's proposal and decided to send at once to Ivan Nikiforovich's house and beg him to come to the mayor's for dinner at all costs. But the important problem of who was to be entrusted with this important mission threw all of them into a quandary. For a long time they argued about who was most capable and skillful in matters of diplomacy; and finally they decided unanimously to entrust all this to Anton Prokofyevich Golopuz.[9]

But first we must acquaint the reader a bit with this remarkable person. Anton Prokofyevich was a thoroughly virtuous man in the full meaning of that word. If anyone among the worthy people of Mirgorod gave him a scarf or some underwear, he would thank him. If anyone gave him a slight fillip on the nose, he would thank him, too. If he was asked, "Anton Prokofyevich, why is your coat brown while the sleeves are blue?" he usually always answered, "You don't even have one like it! Wait a bit. It will soon get shabby, and then it will be the same all over." And sure enough: the blue cloth began to turn brown from the effect of the sun, and now it is the same color as the rest of the coat! But what is strange is that Anton Prokofyevich has the habit of wearing woolen clothes in the summer and nankeen in the winter. Anton Prokofyevich doesn't have a house of his own. He used to have one on the edge of town, but he sold it and with the proceeds he bought three bay horses and a little britska in which he used to go about visiting the landowners. But since the horses were a lot of trouble, and besides that he needed money to buy oats for them, Anton Prokofyevich traded them for a fiddle and a serf girl, getting a twenty-five-ruble note into the bargain. Then Anton Prokofyevich sold the fiddle and traded the serf girl for a morocco purse set with gold. And now he has a purse the likes of which

[9] Cf. Note 3.

nobody else has. As a price for this pleasure, he can no longer drive about the countryside but must stay in town and spend the night at various homes—especially of those noblemen who have found gratification in filliping him on the nose. Anton Prokofyevich likes to dine well, and plays a rather good game of "Fools" and "Millers."[10]

Obedience was always a natural thing for him; and so, taking his cap and walking stick, he set off at once. But on the way he began pondering how he could get Ivan Nikiforovich to come to the party. The rather stern disposition of that otherwise estimable man made his task almost impossible. And, in fact, how could he make up his mind to come, when even to get out of bed cost him such great effort? But supposing he did get up, how could he bring himself to go to a place where—as he undoubtedly knew—his irreconcilable enemy was to be found? The more Anton Prokofyevich pondered it, the more obstacles he found. The day was sultry; the sun was scorching; and he was dripping with sweat. Despite the fact that people flicked him on the nose, Anton Prokofyevich was a rather canny fellow in many matters. (It was only in swapping that he was not too lucky.) He knew very well when he had to make himself out a fool; and sometimes he was able to cope in situations and cases wherein an intelligent man is seldom able to keep his head above water.

While his inventive mind was thinking up ways to persuade Ivan Nikiforovich, and while he was going bravely forward to encounter the worst, an unforeseen circumstance somewhat discountenanced him. In this connection it might be well to inform the reader that Anton Prokofyevich had, among other things, a pair of trousers of such a strange propensity that whenever he put them on the dogs always bit him in the calf of the leg. As ill-luck would have it, he had put on those same trousers that day. So that hardly had he plunged into his ponderings, when a terrible barking from all directions assailed his ears. Anton Prokofyevich set up such an outcry—no one could shout louder than he could—that not only our friend the old serving-woman and the inmate of the immense frock coat ran out to meet him, but even the urchins from Ivan Ivanovich's yard descended upon him; and although the dogs only managed to bite one of his

---

[10]Card games.

legs, this greatly dampened his spirits, and he went up the porch steps with a certain timidity.

Chapter the Seventh
and Last

"Ah, how do you do? Why were‸ you teasing the dogs?" said Ivan Nikiforovich, when he saw Anton Prokofyevich—since no one ever spoke otherwise than in jest to Anton Prokofyevich.

"A plague on them all! I'm not teasing them!" answered Anton Prokofyevich.

"You're lying!"

"I'm not—I swear it! Pyotr Fyodorovich wants you to come to dinner."

"Hm."

"I swear it! He put it so persuasively—I simply can't tell you. 'Why is it,' says he, 'that Ivan Nikiforovich avoids me like an enemy? He never comes for a chat, or to sit a bit.' "

Ivan Nikiforovich stroked his chin.

" 'If Ivan Nikiforovich doesn't come this time,' he says, 'I won't know what to think. Most likely he has some design against me. Do me a favor, Anton Prokofyevich, and persuade Ivan Nikiforovich!' What do you say, Ivan Nikiforovich? Let's go! There's a fine company gathered there now."

Ivan Nikiforovich started to scrutinize a rooster who was standing on the porch steps and crowing with all his might.

"If only you knew, Ivan Nikiforovich," continued the zealous spokesman, "what sturgeon and fresh caviar have been sent to Pyotr Fyodorovich's!"

At those words, Ivan Nikiforovich turned his head and began to listen closely. This encouraged the spokesman.

"Let's get started right now! Foma Grigoryevich is there, too. What's the matter?" he added, when he saw that Ivan Nikiforovich was still lying in the same position.

"I don't want to."

This "I don't want to" jolted Anton Prokofyevich. He

had been quite sure that his persuasive representations had completely won over this generally worthy man, instead of which he heard a resolute "I don't want to."

"Why don't you want to?" he asked, almost with annoyance—something he displayed very rarely, even when burning paper was put on his head: an amusement that the judge and the mayor were especially fond of.

Ivan Nikiforovich took a pinch of snuff.

"Have it your way, Ivan Nikiforovich. But I really don't know what's preventing you."

"Why should I go?" Ivan Nikiforovich said at last. "That bandit will be there!"

That was what he usually called Ivan Ivanovich. Good heavens! And not so long ago. . . .

"I swear he won't be there. By all that's holy, he won't! May I be struck dead by a thunderbolt on this very spot!" replied Anton Prokofyevich, who was ready to swear an oath ten times every hour. "Let's go, Ivan Nikiforovich!"

"But you're lying, Anton Prokofyevich. He's there, isn't he?"

"I swear he isn't! I swear it! May I never leave this spot if he is! Judge for yourself. Why should I lie? May my arms and legs wither! . . . What, you still don't believe me? May I drop dead here at your feet! May neither my father nor my mother nor myself ever see the kingdom of heaven! Do you still refuse to believe me?"

Ivan Nikiforovich was completely calmed by these assurances, and he ordered his valet in the immense frock coat to bring his big, baggy pants and his nankeen Cossack coat.

I assume it is quite superfluous to describe how Ivan Nikiforovich put on his big, baggy pants, how his cravat was tied and, finally, how he was helped on with his Cossack coat, which had burst its seams under the left sleeve. Suffice it to say that during all this time he maintained a decorous composure and did not say one word in answer to Anton Prokofyevich's proposal that he should trade him something for his Turkish purse.

Meanwhile, the assembled guests were impatiently waiting the decisive moment when Ivan Nikiforovich would appear and the universal desire that these two friends should be reconciled, might at last be fulfilled. Many of them were almost certain that Ivan Nikiforovich would not come. The mayor even made a bet with the one-eyed Ivan Ivanovich that he wouldn't come; but he gave it up merely because the one-eyed Ivan Ivanovich demanded that the former stake his wounded leg against his own blind eye—at which the mayor took great offense, while the guests laughed on the sly. No one had yet sat down at the table, although it was well past one o'clock— an hour when people in Mirgorod have already been at the table for some time, even on gala occasions.

Hardly had Anton Prokofyevich appeared in the doorway, when he was instantly surrounded by everyone. In answer to all questions, he shouted one decisive phrase: "He won't come." He had scarcely said this, and a shower of reproaches and cursewords and possibly even fillips was about to come down on his head for the failure of his mission, when suddenly the door opened and . . . in walked Ivan Nikiforovich.

If Satan himself or a corpse had appeared, he would not have caused such amazement to all the assembled guests as that into which they were thrown by the unexpected entrance of Ivan Nikiforovich. As for Anton Prokofyevich, he went off into gales of laughter, holding his sides with glee at having played such a joke on the whole company.

In any case, it seemed almost incredible to everyone that Ivan Nikiforovich had managed, in so short a time, to dress as befits a nobleman. Ivan Ivanovich was not there at the moment; he had gone off somewhere. When they had recovered from their amazement, all the guests showed their interest in Ivan Nikiforovich's health, and said they were glad to see he had grown stouter. Ivan Nikiforovich exchanged kisses with all of them, and said, "Much obliged."

Meantime the smell of hot borsch drifted through the room, and pleasantly tickled the nostrils of the starving guests. They all flocked into the dining room. A line of ladies, both talkative and taciturn, fat and thin, filed in ahead, and the long table soon glittered with all possible colors. I am not going to describe all the courses on the table. I will make no mention of the dumplings in sour cream, of the sweetbreads served with the borsch, of the turkey stuffed with plums and raisins, of the course that very much resembled a pair of boots soaked in kvass, nor of that sauce which is the swan song of the ancient cook: that sauce that came to the table enveloped in flaming spirits—which greatly amused the ladies, and at the same time terrified them. I am not going to talk about these dishes because I take much greater pleasure in eating them than in discussing them at length.

Ivan Ivanovich very much enjoyed the fish prepared with horseradish sauce. He devoted himself especially to this useful and nourishing pastime. As he was picking out the smallest fishbones and laying them on his plate, he happened to glance across the table. Great God in heaven, what a strange thing! Across from him sat Ivan Nikiforovich!

At the same time, Ivan Nikiforovich also looked up . . . No, I'm not equal to it! . . . Give me another pen. Mine is flabby, dead, with too thin a nib for this scene. Their faces, with amazement reflected on them, seemed petrified. Each of them recognized a long-familiar face—a person to whom, one would have thought, he was instinctively ready to come up as to a friend who had appeared from nowhere, and proffer his snuffbox with the words, "Do me the favor," or "May I be so bold as to ask you to do me the favor?" But instead of that, the face was frightful, like an evil portent. The sweat poured off both Ivan Ivanovich and Ivan Nikiforovich.

All of the guests at the table were dumbstruck from staring, and none of them could take their eyes off the erstwhile friends. The ladies, who up to that time had been engaged in a rather interesting discussion about how to prepare capons, suddenly cut their talk short. All was stilled. It was a picture worthy of the brush of a great artist.

At length Ivan Ivanovich took out his handkerchief and began to blow his nose; meantime, Ivan Nikiforovich looked about him and fixed his eyes on the open door. The mayor immediately noticed this movement, and ordered the door closed tight. Then both of the friends began to eat, and did not look up at each other again.

The moment dinner was over, both former friends rose from their seats and began looking for their caps so they could slip away. At this point, the mayor winked, and Ivan Ivanovich—not our Ivan Ivanovich, but the one-eyed one—got behind Ivan Nikiforovich, while the mayor got behind Ivan Ivanovich, and both began shoving them from behind so as to push them together and not let them go until they had shaken hands. Ivan Ivanovich—the one-eyed one—pushed Ivan Nikiforovich, somewhat indirectly but nonetheless rather successfully, to the place where Ivan Ivanovich was standing. But the

mayor got way off course, since he could in no wise cope
with his headstrong infantry, which this time obeyed no
commands whatsoever and, as though to spite him, swung
itself exceedingly far off in the opposite direction (which
might very well have been due to the fact that there were
a great many different liqueurs on the table after dinner),
so that Ivan Ivanovich fell on a lady in a red dress who, out
of curiosity, had thrown herself into the very midst of
things. This omen boded no good. The judge, however, set
things to right, took the mayor's place and, after sniffing
up all the tobacco from his upper lip, shoved Ivan Ivanovich in the other direction. In Mirgorod, this is the custom-
ary procedure for peacemaking. It is rather like a game
of catch with a ball. As soon as the judge had shoved Ivan
Ivanovich, Ivan Ivanovich—the one-eyed one—laid on with
all his strength and shoved Ivan Nikiforovich, from whom
the sweat was pouring like rainwater from a roof. Both
friends resisted stoutly, but they were brought together
anyway, since both of the active parties received considerable support from the other guests.

Then they were closely hemmed in on all sides, and
were not let go until they had made up their minds to
shake hands.

"For heaven's sake, Ivan Ivanovich and Ivan Nikiforovich! Tell us in all honesty: What were you quarreling
about? Wasn't it over a mere nothing? Aren't you ashamed
before men and before God?"

"I don't know," said Ivan Nikiforovich, panting with
exhaustion (it was obvious that he was not at all opposed to a reconciliation). "I don't know what I did to
Ivan Ivanovich. But why did he saw down my goose-shed
and plot to destroy me?"

"I'm innocent of any evil designs," said Ivan Ivanovich,
not looking at Ivan Nikiforovich. "I swear before God
and before you, worthy noblemen, that I did nothing to
my enemy. Why, then, does he revile me and defame
my rank and title?"

"How did I defame you, Ivan Ivanovich?" said Ivan
Nikiforovich.

One more minute of explanation, and the long-standing
feud would have been on the point of extinction. Ivan
Nikiforovich had already reached into his pocket to get out
his snuff-horn and say, "Do me the favor."

"Was it not defamation," replied Ivan Ivanovich without
raising his eyes, "when you, sir, insulted my rank and

family name with a word which it would be unseemly to utter here?"

"Allow me to tell you as friend to friend, Ivan Ivanovich" (as he said this, Ivan Nikiforovich touched a finger to a buttonhole of Ivan Ivanovich's, which showed his completely favorable inclination), "that you took offense at the devil only knows what. Just because I called you a *gander*."

Ivan Nikiforovich realized immediately that he had been careless in uttering that word, but it was already too late: the word had been uttered.

Everything went to the devil.

If, when that word was uttered with no witnesses present, Ivan Ivanovich lost all self-control and flew into such a rage as God grant a person may never behold, then what now? Only judge for yourselves, gentle readers. What now, when that deadly word was uttered in an assemblage including large numbers of the fair sex, in whose presence Ivan Ivanovich liked to be especially proper? If Ivan Nikiforovich had behaved in any other way—if he had said "fowl" instead of "gander"—the situation could still have been saved.

But it was all over and finished. . . .

Ivan Ivanovich threw a look at Ivan Nikiforovich—and what a look! If that look had been endowed with effective power, Ivan Nikiforovich would have been reduced to ashes. The guests understood that look and hastened to separate them. And this man, the very model of gentleness, who never let a single beggar woman pass by without questioning her, rushed out in a terrible rage. Such violent storms do the passions produce!

For a whole month nothing was heard of Ivan Ivanovich. He locked himself in his house. His ancestral trunk was opened, and from that trunk were removed. . . . what? Silver rubles! His grandfather's old silver rubles. And those rubles passed into the soiled hands of shyster lawyers. The case was transferred to the higher court. And it was only when Ivan Ivanovich received the joyful news that it would be settled the following day, that he looked out upon the world and decided to emerge from his house. Alas! From that time onward, for the next ten years, the higher court notified him daily that the case would be settled the next day.

Five years ago I passed through the town of Mirgorod. I was traveling in a poor time of the year. It was autumn, with its cheerlessly damp weather, mud, and mist. A kind of unnatural verdure—the work of dreary, incessant rains—had spread its insubstantial network over the meadows and grain fields, to which it was as becoming as a prank to an old man or a rose to an old woman. In those days, the weather had a powerful influence on me: when it was dreary, I felt dreary. But in spite of that, when I began to draw near to Mirgorod I felt my heart beating violently. Lord, how many memories! I hadn't seen Mirgorod for twelve years. Back then, two unique persons, two unique friends, had lived here in touching friendship. And how many eminent men had died! Judge Demyan Demyanovich had already passed away, and Ivan Ivanovich—the one-eyed one—had also departed this life.

I drove into the main street. Everywhere stood poles with wisps of straw tied to the top: some new kind of surveying work was in progress. Several cottages had been torn down. The remnants of wooden and wattle fences stood there looking sad.

It was a holiday. I ordered my kibitka to stop in front of the church, and entered so quietly that no one turned around. Truth to tell, there was no one to do so. The church was empty—almost nobody there. Plainly, even the most devout worshipers were afraid of the mud. On this overcast—or, rather, sickly—day, the candles were strangely unpleasant, somehow; the darkened front part of the church was saddening; and the oblong windows with their round panes were streaming with tears of rain.

I walked into the front part of the church and addressed a venerable old man with gray hair. "Tell me, please. Is Ivan Nikiforovich still alive?"

Just then the lamp in front of an ikon flared up, and the light fell directly on his face. How surprised I was when I looked at him closely and recognized the familiar features. It was Ivan Nikiforovich himself! But how he had changed!

"Are you well, Ivan Nikiforovich? How you have aged!"

"Yes, I've aged. I'm just back from Poltova today," answered Ivan Nikiforovich.

"What? You went to Poltava in this dreadful weather?"

"I had no choice. My lawsuit. . . ."

At this I couldn't help sighing. Ivan Nikiforovich noticed my sigh, and said, "Don't worry. I have reliable information that the case will be decided next week—and in my favor."

I shrugged my shoulders and went to find out something about Ivan Ivanovich.

"Ivan Ivanovich is here!" someone told me. "He's in the choir loft."

Then I noticed a gaunt form. Was this Ivan Ivanovich? His face was all wrinkles, and his hair was completely white; but his fitted coat was still the same. After the first greetings, Ivan Ivanovich, having given me that cheerful smile which went so well with his funnel-shaped face, said, "May I tell you some good news?"

"What news?" I asked.

"My case will be decided tomorrow without fail. The high court has said so for certain."

I sighed even more deeply, made haste to say good-bye (since I was traveling on very important business), and got into my kibitka. The skinny horses, known in Mirgorod as post-horses, started off, producing with their hoofs, which had sunk into the gray mud, a sound that was unpleasant to the ear. The rain came down in torrents on the Jew sitting on the coach-box, who had covered himself with matting. The dampness went all the way through me. The town gate, with a sentry-box in which an old soldier was repairing his gray implements, passed slowly by. Again the same fields, plowed and black in some places, and green in others, the wet jackdaws and crows, the monotonous rain, the tearful sky without a streak of light. It is dreary in this world, gentlemen!

1834

THE CROCODILE

or

A Passage in the Passage[1]

> *The true story of how a gentle-
> man of a certain age and a cer-
> tain appearance was swallowed
> alive—every bit of him—by the
> crocodile of the Passage, and
> what came of it.*

> *Ohé, Lambert! Où est Lambert?
> As-tu vu Lambert?*

I

At 12:30 P.M. on January 13th of this present year of
1865, Elena Ivanovna, the wife of Ivan Matveich, my cultured friend, colleague, and more or less distant relative,
expressed a desire to go and see the crocodile being exhibited for a fee in the Passage. Since Ivan Matveich al-

---

[1] A play on two meanings of *passazh:* 1) a strange, unexpected
(and often scandalous) event; 2) an arcade. At the time of
writing, the St. Petersburg Passage, in addition to the shops usually
found in an arcade, comprised auditoriums, concert halls, and
exhibits.

ready had in his pocket a ticket for a trip abroad (not so much for reasons of health as out of scholarly curiosity) and was therefore officially on leave and completely free that morning, he did not oppose his wife's overwhelming desire but, on the contrary, was stirred to a high pitch of curiosity himself.

"A splendid idea!" he said with great satisfaction. "Let's examine the crocodile! Since I am about to leave for Europe, it would not be a bad idea to get acquainted with the indigenous inhabitants right here and now." And with these words, he took his wife by the arm and set off with her for the Passage. As was my habit, in my role as friend of the family, I went along with them.

Never before had I seen Ivan Matveich in more pleasant spirits than he was on that memorable morning. Truly, our beginnings never know our ends. The moment we entered the Passage we went into raptures over the magnificence of the building. And when we came to the shop where the monster lately brought to the capital was being exhibited, Ivan Matveich himself, in an unprecedented gesture, offered to pay my admission fee of a quarter-ruble. As we entered the small room we noticed that in addition to the crocodile there were some parrots of the foreign breed called cockatoo, plus a group of monkeys in a separate, recessed enclosure. Just inside the entrance, along the left wall, was a large tin tank that looked something like a bathtub. It was covered with a heavy iron grating, and had a few inches of water in the bottom. In this shallow pool was an immense crocodile—lying there like a log, perfectly motionless, and apparently deprived of all his faculties by our damp climate, so inhospitable to foreigners.

This monster at first aroused no particular curiosity in any of us. "So that's a crocodile!" drawled Elena Ivanovna in a disappointed tone of voice. "And there I was thinking it would be . . . you know, something different."

Most likely, she thought it would be studded with diamonds.

The shop proprietor and crocodile-owner, a German, came out and looked at us with an air of great pride.

"He's right," Ivan Matveich whispered to me, "because he knows that he's the only person in all Russia who is now exhibiting a crocodile."

This totally stupid remark I also attribute to the singularly good spirits possessing Ivan Matveich, whose usual mood was a grudging one.

"Your crocodile looks to me as though he isn't alive," Elena Ivanovna ventured, piqued by the proprietor's stolidity. And she gave him a gracious smile so as to make that boorish fellow unbend a little—a maneuver quite typical of women.

"Oh, yes he is, madame," he answered in broken Russian. And he at once raised the grating above the tank and began to prod the crocodile's head with a stick.

At this the wily monster, in order to show some signs of life, wiggled its paws and its tail a little, then raised its snout and emitted something like a prolonged snort.

"Now, now! Don't you get angry, Karlchen!" the German cooed, his vanity gratified.

"How horrid that crocodile is! He gave me a regular fright!" Elena Ivanovna babbled even more coquettishly. "Now I'll have dreams about him."

"He won't bite you in your dreams, madame," the German retorted gallantly, and laughed at his own witticism before anyone else did. But none of us responded.

"Come on, Semyon Semyonych," Elena Ivanovna continued to me, disregarding the others. "Let's look at the monkeys instead. I'm frightfully fond of monkeys—they're such darlings! And the crocodile is horrible."

"Oh, don't be afraid, my dear," Ivan Matveich called as we moved away, charmingly making a show of his manly courage. "This somnolent citizen of the realms of the Pharaohs won't do us any harm." And he remained by the tank. Not content with that, he took off one of his gloves and began to tickle the crocodile's nose with it, hoping (as he admitted later) to make him snort again. Meantime, Elena Ivanovna being the lady of the party, the proprietor followed her to the monkey cage.

And so everything was going along splendidly, and nothing could have been foreseen. Elena Ivanovna was so amused by the monkeys that she became quite frolicsome and seemed completely taken up with them. She squealed with delight, constantly turning to me as though not wanting to pay any attention to the proprietor, and giggled at the resemblances she found between these monkeys and her friends and acquaintances. I was enjoying myself, too, because the resemblance was unquestionable. The German crocodile-owner didn't know whether to laugh or not, and ended up scowling darkly.

And then suddenly, at that very moment, a terrifying— one might even say preternatural—scream shook the room.

At first, not knowing what to make of it, I froze to the spot. But noticing that Elena Ivanovna was now screaming too, I turned quickly and what did I see? Oh, heavens! I saw the hapless Ivan Matveich in the terrible jaws of the crocodile—which were gripping him by the waist—already raised horizontally in midair, with his feet kicking desperately. Then a moment later he was gone.

But I shall describe this in detail, because throughout it I was standing immobile and was able to observe the entire process that took place before my eyes, with the utmost attention and curiosity. "What," I thought in that fateful moment, "if all this were happening to me instead of Ivan Matveich? How very unpleasant it would be for me." But to return to our subject. The crocodile began as follows. Having turned poor Ivan Matveich around in his terrible jaws feet foremost, he first gulped down the legs; next, having partially belched up Ivan Matveich, who was struggling to get out and clutching at the edge of the tank, he again swallowed him up to the waist. Then, having belched once more, he gulped two more times. In this way, Ivan Matveich was visibly disappearing before our very eyes. At last, with a definitive gulp, the crocodile ingested the whole of my cultured friend, this time leaving nothing of him behind. One could follow, on the crocodile's outsides, the progress of Ivan Matveich, with all of his bodily appurtenances, through the monster's insides. I was on the point of shouting again, when fate suddenly and treacherously decided to play one more trick on us. The crocodile strained hard, no doubt feeling crammed with the immensity of the object he had swallowed, and again opened wide his hideous maw: from it, in the form of a last regurgitation, there popped out for one second the head of Ivan Matveich, with a desperate expression on his face—and his glasses fell off his nose to the bottom of the tank. It seemed as if this desperate head had popped out for the sole purpose of taking a last look at all physical objects, and mentally taking leave of all worldly pleasures. But it did not have time to carry out its intention. The crocodile again summoned up all its strength, and gulped: in a flash, the head vanished—this time forever. This appearance and disappearance of a still-living human head was so horrible, but at the same time—whether due to the rapidity and unexpectedness of the action, or as a result of the glasses' falling from the nose—had about it something so comical, that I most unexpectedly burst out laughing. But quickly realizing that, as a friend of the family, it was improper of me to laugh at such a moment, I turned at once to Elena Ivanovna with a sympathetic look and said, "Now our Ivan Matveich is kaput."

I can't even begin to describe how violently perturbed was Elena Ivanovna during this whole process. At the outset, after the first scream, she stood stock-still, as it were, and watched the commotion with seeming indifference, yet with her eyes bulging far out. Then she suddenly let out a heart-rending wail; but I grasped her hands. At that moment the proprietor, who had also gone numb with horror at the first moment, suddenly spread his hands and, looking heavenward, cried out: "Oh, my crocodile! *O mein allerliebster Karlchen! Mutter, Mutter, Mutter!*"

At this cry the back door opened and *Mutter* appeared— in a mobcap, rosy-cheeked, old but disheveled—and with a squeal threw herself on her German.

Then bedlam broke loose. Elena Ivanovna, as though in a frenzy, kept screaming over and over again: "Whip! Whip!" She threw herself at the proprietor and his *Mutter*, apparently imploring them (being almost out of her mind, no doubt) to whip somebody for something. But the proprietor and his *Mutter* weren't paying heed to any of us: both were bawling like calves around the tank. The proprietor was shouting, "He ist dead! He vill vide open shplit! He has *ganz* an official down gegulped!"

"*Unser Karlchen! Unser allerliebster Karlchen wird sterben!*" the proprietress bawled.

"Ve are orphans and have no bread!" the proprietor added.

"Whip! Whip! Whip!" howled Elena Ivanovna, clutching at the German's coat.

"He has the crocodile teased. Vot for has your husband the crocodile teased?" shouted the German, beating her off. "You vill pay if Karlchen vill vide open shplit. *Das war mein Sohn! Das war mein einziger Sohn!*"

I confess that I was terribly indignant at the selfishness of this visiting German and his disheveled *Mutter*'s cold-heartedness. Still, Elena Ivanovna's constantly repeated cries of "Whip! Whip!" upset me even more, and finally absorbed all my attention, so that I was even alarmed. I make haste to explain that I had completely misunderstood these strange cries. I had the impression that Elena Ivanovna was momentarily out of her mind; but nonetheless, being eager to take revenge for the loss of her amiable

Ivan Matveich, was proposing by way of compensation
that the crocodile be whipped. Actually, however, she
meant something quite different.

Looking around at the door (not without embarrass-
ment), I began to plead with her to calm down and, above
all, to stop using such a controversial word as "whip." To
express such a reactionary desire here, in the very center
of the Passage and of cultivated society, not two steps away
from that same hall where, at this very moment, perhaps,
Mr. Lavrov[2] was giving a public lecture—this was not
only inadmissible but downright unthinkable, and could
at any time make us the object of the derisive whistles[3] of
culture and the cartoons of Mr. Stepanov.[4] To my horror,
I was at once proved right in my anxious suspicions. The
curtain separating the crocodile room from the ticket
booth area suddenly parted, and on the threshold appeared
a bearded and moustachioed individual with cap in hand,
the upper part of his body bent very far forward while he
very carefully tried to keep his feet outside the threshold
of the crocodile room so as not to pay the admission fee.

"Such a reactionary desire, madame," said the stranger,
striving to avoid tumbling over in our direction and to
remain beyond the threshold, "does no credit to your
development, and is due to a lack of phosphorus in your
brain. You will be forthwith ridiculed in the chronicles
of progress and in our satirical leaflets. . . ."

But he didn't finish. The proprietor, coming back to his
senses and seeing to his horror that a man was talking
in the crocodile room without having paid anything for
that privilege, rushed at the progressive stranger in a
rage, set upon him with both fists, and threw him out by
the scruff of the neck.

For a moment, both were hidden from our view behind
the curtain. And it was only then I finally realized that
the whole fuss had been about nothing. Elena Ivanovna
was entirely innocent. She had had no intention—as I
mentioned earlier—of subjecting the crocodile to the
reactionary and humiliating punishment of a whipping.

---

[2]Pyotr Lavrov, the influential Populist writer who was largely
responsible, a few years later, for the movement known as "going
to the people."

[3]The satirical section of the magazine *Sovremennik* (The Contemporary) was called *Svistok* (The Whistle).

[4]N. A. Stepanov was a cartoonist for *Iskra* (The Spark) and
Budil'nik (The Alarm Clock).

She had merely wanted them to rip[5] open his belly with a knife so as to liberate Ivan Matveich from his innards.

"Vot? You vant that my crocodile die?" howled the proprietor, who had rushed back in. "No, better your husband die first, than the crocodile! . . . *Mein Vater* has crocodiles shown, *mein Grossvater* has crocodiles shown, *mein Sohn* vill crocodiles show, and I vill crocodiles show! All vill crocodiles show! I in *ganz' Europa* are known, and you in *ganz' Europa* are not known, and you vill pay me *shtraf*."[6]

"*Ja, ja!*" put in the evil-tempered German woman. "Ve von't let you. *Shtraf,* ven Karlchen vill vide open shplit."

"Besides, there's no point in cutting him open," I added calmly, wanting to get Elena Ivanovna out of there and home as quickly as possible, "because our dear Ivan Matveich, in all probability, is now soaring somewhere in the Empyrean."

"My friend," came the totally unexpected voice of Ivan Matveich at that very moment, to the great astonishment of us all, "my friend, in my opinion we should act directly through the office of the police inspector, since without the help of the police the German will not understand the truth."

These words, spoken firmly and authoritatively, and manifesting a most unusual presence of mind, so startled us at first that we all refused to believe our own ears. But of course we immediately ran over to the crocodile tank, and with as much reverence as incredulity, listened to the unfortunate prisoner. His voice was muffled, thin, and even squeaky, as though coming from a long way off. It was like the voice of a prankster who, having gone into another room and covered his mouth with a pillow, begins to shout, thereby trying to show those in the other room how two peasants call to each other in the wilderness or when they are on either side of a deep ravine—something I had the pleasure of hearing once when visiting some acquaintances over the Christmas holidays.

"Ivan Matveich, my dear! So you are alive?" Elena Ivanovna managed to get out.

---

[5] What Elena Ivanovna had said in Russian was *vsporot'*, meaning "to rip open," "to disembowel," but which could easily be understood as "to whip" or "to flog" (*cf. vsparit'*).

[6] Russian for "a fine," from the German *Strafe*.

"Alive and well," replied Ivan Matveich, "and, thanks to the Lord on high, swallowed without any injuries. I'm only worried about one thing, and that is how my superiors will view this episode. For, after getting my ticket to travel abroad, I fell into a crocodile, which is certainly not very clever—"

"But my dear, don't worry about cleverness," Elena Ivanovna interrupted. "The first thing we must do is to dig you out of there somehow."

"Dig?" shouted the proprietor. "I von't let you in the crocodile dig! Now public much more vill come, and I vill *fufzig*[7] kopecks charge, and Karlchen vill shtop vide open to shplit."

"Gott sei dank!" put in the proprietress.

"They're right," Ivan Matveich calmly observed. "The economic principle comes first."

"My friend!" I cried, "I'll go to the authorities right now and lodge a complaint, because something tells me we can't settle this mess by ourselves."

"I agree with you," said Ivan Matveich. "But in this period of trade crisis, to rip open the belly of a crocodile to no useful purpose and without payment of compensation, is not so easily done. Meantime, the unavoidable question arises: How much will the owner demand for his crocodile? And that raises still another question: Who will pay for it? Because, as you know, I am not a man of means."

"Perhaps out of your salary," I suggested shyly. But the proprietor quickly interrupted me. "I vill not the crocodile sell. I sell the crocodile tree tausend, I sell the crocodile four tausend. Now public much more vill come. I sell the crocodile fife tausend."

In short, he was intolerably arrogant. Acquisitiveness and vile greed sparkled joyously in his eyes.

"I'm going!" I shouted angrily.

"Me, too! Me, too! I'm going to see Andrey Osipych himself!" whimpered Elena Ivanovna. "I'll melt him with my tears."

"Don't do that, my dear!" Ivan Matveich quickly interposed. He had long been jealous regarding his wife and Andrey Osipych, and knew she would be only too glad to go and shed tears before such a cultivated man,

---

[7] I.e., *fünfzig.*

since tears were very becoming to her. "And I don't advise you to go either, my friend," he continued, addressing me. "There's no point in going off half-cocked. Nothing will come of it. It would be better if you went to see Timofey Semyonych today, just by way of a personal visit. He's an old-fashioned fellow, and a bit stupid; but he's reliable and, most important, he's straightforward. Give him my regards and describe the whole thing in detail. I owe him seven rubles from our last card game, so you might pay him on this convenient occasion. It will soften the stern old chap. In any case, his advice might be something useful to go by. And now, take Elena Ivanovna away. . . . Calm yourself, my dear," he said to her. "I'm tired from all this shouting and old women's squabbles, and I'd like to take a nap. It's warm and soft here, though I haven't yet had time to look over this, for me, unexpected shelter. . . ."

"Look it over? Do you mean it's light in there?" Elena Ivanovna cried out happily.

"I am surrounded by impenetrable night," replied the poor prisoner. "But I can feel and, so to speak, look things over with my hands. . . . Good-bye, now. Don't worry, and don't deny yourself any amusements. Until tomorrow! But you, Semyon Semyonych, must come back here this evening. And since you're absentminded and may forget, tie a knot in your handkerchief."

I must admit that I was glad to leave, because I was very tired and rather bored. Hastily taking the arm of Elena Ivanovna, who was disconsolate but had become even prettier from all the excitement, I escorted her quickly out of the crocodile room.

"In the evening, another quarter-ruble to come in!" the proprietor shouted after us.

"Dear me, how greedy they are!" said Elena Ivanovna, looking into every pier glass in the arcade and obviously realizing that she had become prettier.

"The economic principle," I answered, rather excited and proud to display the lady on my arm to the passersby.

"The economic principle," she drawled, in a sympathetic tone of voice. "I simply didn't understand a word of what Ivan Matveich was saying just now about that horrid economic principle."

"I'll explain it to you," I replied, and immediately began to expound the beneficial results of attracting foreign capital into our country—which I had read about earlier that morning in the *St. Petersburg News* and the *Hair*.[8]

"How strange all that is!" she interrupted, when she had listened for a while. "But stop it, you horrid man! You talk such silly stuff! Tell me: Am I very red?"

"You're not red—you're beautiful,"[9] I observed, seizing the opportunity to pay a compliment.

"You naughty boy!" she cooed, pleased with herself. "Poor Ivan Matveich!" she added a moment later, coquettishly leaning her head on my shoulder. "I'm really sorry for him. Oh, dear!" she suddenly exclaimed. "Tell me: How is he going to eat today? And . . . and . . . how is he going to . . . if he needs to do something?"

"That's an unforeseen problem," I answered, perplexed in my turn. "To tell you the truth, it hadn't occurred to me. Which just shows you how much more practical women are than men when it comes to solving the problems of everyday life."

"The poor thing—how did he ever fall into it? . . . And no entertainment, and it's dark. . . . How annoying that I don't even have a snapshot of him left. . . . And so, I'm a kind of widow," she added with a seductive smile, obviously taking an interest in her new status. "Hm. But I'm still sorry for him."

In short, she expressed the very understandable and natural grief of a young and attractive wife at the death of her husband.

I finally got her home, calmed her down, and having dined with her, after a cup of aromatic coffee I went off to see Timofey Semyonych, figuring that at that hour all family men of regular habits are sitting at home—or lying down there.

Having written this first chapter in a style appropriate to the episode recounted, I intend henceforth to employ a style which, though less lofty, is more natural; and I hereby notify the reader of that fact in advance.

---

[8] A pun on *volos* (hair) and *golos* (voice).

[9] A trite play on words: *krasny* (red) also used to mean "pretty" (*cf.* "Red Square," the original meaning of which was "pretty place"). The root meaning survives in *prekrasny* (beautiful).

II

The venerable Timofey Semyonych greeted me as though
he were in a hurry about something, and rather flustered.
He showed me into his cramped little study, and closed
the door tight. "Just so the children won't bother us," he
said with evident anxiousness. Then he gave me a chair
beside his desk. He himself sat down in an armchair, drew
the skirts of his old, quilted dressing gown together, and
just to be on the safe side, assumed a kind of official
expression even verging upon severity—although he was
by no means the superior of either myself or Ivan
Matveich and up until then had been regarded as just
another colleague, and even as a friend.

"First of all," he began, "please bear in mind that I
am not a ranking official but merely the same kind of
underling as you and Ivan Matveich. . . . I had nothing
to do with it, and I have no intention of getting involved
in anything whatsoever."

I was astonished that he already knew everything, apparently. Nevertheless, I told him the same story from
the start. I actually got quite worked up as I talked, since
at the moment I was doing my duty as a true friend. He
listened without any great amazement but with evident
suspicion.

"You know," he said, when I had finished, "I always
figured something just like that would happen to him."

"But why, Timofey Semyonych? It's really a most unusual incident."

"Agreed. But all during his career, Ivan Matveich has
been tending toward just such an end. He was frisky
and even conceited. Always talking 'progress' and all
kinds of notions. And this is what progress leads to."

"But after all, it's a most exceptional case. You just
can't lay it down as a general rule for all progressives. . . ."

"Oh, yes I can! It comes, you see, from too much
education. That you can be sure of. Because people with
too much education try to get into all kinds of places—
especially where they're not wanted. But then, maybe you
know more about it than I do," he added, as though in a
huff. "I'm an old man, and don't have much education.

I started out as a soldier's son, and I completed my fiftieth year of service this year."

"Oh, that's not it at all, Timofey Semyonych! On the contrary. Ivan Matveich craves your advice—your guidance. He even craves it with tears, so to speak."

" 'With tears, so to speak.' Hm. Well, those are crocodile tears, and they're not entirely to be trusted. Tell me, now: Why did he have that urge to go abroad? And what was he going to use for money? Surely he doesn't have any means?"

"The money he saved, Timofey Semyonych, from the last bonuses," I replied dolefully. "He only wanted to go for three months. To Switzerland . . . to the land of William Tell."

"William Tell? Hm."

"He wanted to greet the spring in Naples—to look over the museums, the local customs, the animals. . . ."

"Hm! The animals? In my opinion it was just out of pride. The animals? Don't we have plenty of animals here? We have zoos, museums, and camels. There are even bears living near Petersburg itself. And he goes and gets himself into a crocodile. . . ."

"For goodness' sake, Timofey Semyonych! The man is in distress. He appeals to you as a friend or an older relative. He's frantic for your advice. And you reproach him! At least have pity on poor Elena Ivanovna!"

"You mean his wife? A winsome little lady," said Timofey Semyonych, obviously mellowing. He took a pinch of snuff with gusto. "A subtle creature! So buxom! And always tilting her pretty little head to one side, like that. . . . Very fetching! Andrey Osipych was mentioning her just the other day."

"Was mentioning her?"

"Yes, and in very complimentary terms. 'Her bust,' he said. 'The way she looks at you. Her coiffure. . . . She's not a woman, she's a bonbon,' he said. And then he laughed. He's still a young man." Timofey Semyonych blew his nose loudly. "Still young, but he's making quite a career for himself."

"But you've strayed a long way from the subject, Timofey Semyonych."

"Of course. Of course."

"So what do you say, Timofey Semyonych?"

"But what can I do?"

"Give advice and guidance as a man of experience—like

a relative! What should we do? Should we go to the authorities, or—"

"To the authorities? By no means!" Timofey Semyonych said quickly. "If you want my advice, the thing of first importance is to hush the matter up and act, so to speak, as a private person. It's a suspicious case, and unprecedented. That's the main thing: unprecedented—no examples of it before. And besides, it doesn't look good. . . . So, caution above all. . . . Let him lie there for a bit. He'll have to wait it out—just wait it out."

"But how can he wait it out, Timofey Semyonych? What if he suffocates?"

"Why should he? You yourself said, I believe, that he was actually settled quite comfortably."

I went over the whole thing again. Timofey Semyonych grew thoughtful.

"Hm," he said, toying with his snuffbox. "In my opinion it's actually a good thing for him to stay there a while, instead of going abroad. Let him meditate at his leisure. Naturally, he mustn't suffocate, and therefore appropriate steps must be taken to safeguard his health. You know—making sure not to catch a cold, and so on. . . . As far as the German is concerned, in my personal opinion he is within his rights, and even more so than the other party; because it was *his* crocodile that was entered without permission, and not he who entered without permission into the crocodile of Ivan Matveich—who, so far as I can recall, never had a crocodile of his own, anyway. Besides, a crocodile constitutes private property, and hence he may not be cut open without payment of compensation."

"It's to save a human life, Timofey Semyonych!"

"Well, then, that's a case for the police. It should be reported to them."

"But after all, Ivan Matveich may be needed at the office. He may be called for."

"Ivan Matveich *needed?* Heh, heh. Besides, he's officially on leave. Consequently, we can ignore him and let him look over the countries of Europe from in there. Of course, if he fails to show up when his leave has expired, that will be something else. Then we'll have to make inquiries and investigate."

"But three months! For pity's sake, Timofey Semyonych!"

"It's his own fault. Did anybody shove him in there? We may have to hire a nurse for him at government expense, though that's not in the personnel regulations. But the main thing is that the crocodile is private property; therefore, the so-called economic principle applies. And the economic principle comes before everything else. Just the other night, at Luka Andreyich's, Ignaty Prokofich was saying . . . Do you know Ignaty Prokofich? He's a capitalist—a big businessman. And he speaks very well, you know. . . . 'What we need,' he was saying, 'is industry. We have almost no industry. It must be created. We must create capital; therefore, we must create a middle class— a so-called bourgeoisie. And since we have no capital, we must attract it from abroad. First of all, we must encourage foreign companies to buy up tracts of land in Russia, as they are now doing in all other countries. Communal ownership is poison,' he said. 'It is ruin!' And he speaks with such heat, you know! Well, that's fine for him—he's a capitalist, and not in the government service. 'With the village commune,' he was saying, 'neither industry nor agriculture develops. It is essential,' he said, 'that foreign companies buy up all of our land that they possibly can, in large units, and then break it, break it, break it up into the smallest tracts possible.' And, do you know, it was very forceful the way he said it. 'B-b-break it up!' he said, 'and then sell it as private property. Or rather, not sell it but simply rent it out. When,' he said, 'all the land is in the hands of the foreign companies we have attracted, they can charge whatever rent they like. And so the peasants will work three times as hard for the same amount of daily bread, and they can be fired at any time. So they will feel the effect; they will be docile and industrious, and will turn out three times as much work for the same wages. But today, with the village commune, what do they care? They know they won't starve to death, so they just loaf around and get drunk. But the other way, money will be attracted into Russia, and capital will be created, and a bourgeoisie will develop. Just the other day the English political and literary newspaper, the *Times,* in an analysis of our finances, stated that the reason our finances aren't improving is that we don't have any middle class, we don't have any large fortunes, we don't have any compliant proletarians. . . .' Ignaty Prokofich speaks very well. He wants to write a report on the subject himself for the authorities, and then get it published in the *News.* That's something very different from Ivan Matveich's verses—"

"But what about Ivan Matveich?" I interposed, after letting the old man ramble on. (Timofey Semyonych sometimes liked to ramble on like that, to show he wasn't lagging behind the times but knew everything that was happening.)

"What about Ivan Matveich, you say? That's just what I've been leading up to. Here we are, fussing about trying to attract foreign capital into our country, and just look what happens! No sooner has the capital of the foreign crocodile-owner been doubled through Ivan Matveich than we, instead of protecting the foreign capitalist, try to rip open the belly of his fixed capital. Does that make sense? In my opinion, Ivan Matveich as a true son of the fatherland should be glad and proud of the fact that through him the value of the foreign crocodile has been doubled, perhaps even trebled. That's just what we need to attract foreign capital! If one man succeeds, before you know it another will come with a crocodile, and then still another with two or three all at once, and capital will build up around them. Then we'll have a bourgeoisie! It must be encouraged."

"Have some pity, Timofey Semyonych!" I cried. "The sacrifice you're demanding from Ivan Matveich is almost superhuman!"

"I'm not demanding anything. And I ask you, above all— as I have asked before—to bear in mind that I am not a ranking official and therefore cannot demand anything of anybody. I speak not as the *Son of the Fatherland*[10] but simply as *a* son of the fatherland. Once again I ask you: Who ordered him to get into the crocodile? Here we have a solid citizen, a married man with a decent rank, and suddenly he makes a move like that! Is that any way to behave?"

"But after all, that move was an accident."

"Who knows for sure? And furthermore, where is the money coming from to compensate the crocodile-owner? Just tell me that!"

"Why, from his salary I suppose, Timofey Semyonych."

"Will it be enough?"

"No, it won't, Timofey Semyonych," I replied sadly. "You see, at first the crocodile-owner was afraid that the beast would burst. But later, when he was sure everything

[10]A St. Petersburg newspaper.

was all right, he got on his high horse and was delighted that he could double his price."

"He's likely to treble it or quadruple it. The public will come flocking in, now, and crocodile-owners are a clever breed. Then, too, this is the festive season, and people want to be entertained. So I say again: above all, Ivan Matveich must remain incognito and not be in any hurry. It's probably all right to let everybody know he's in the crocodile, but they shouldn't know it *officially*. In this respect, the circumstances are in fact favorable, since officially he is abroad. They'll say he's in the crocodile, but we won't believe it. It can be managed that way. The main thing is—he should sit it out. For that matter, what's his hurry?"

"But if—"

"Don't worry. He's strong as an ox."

"And then? After he has sat it out?"

"Well, I won't conceal from you the fact that the case is most complicated. There's just no way of coping with it. And the most troublesome thing is that there never has been such a case before. If we had a precedent, we'd have something to go by. But as it is, what can we do? You start pondering, and the thing just drags on and on."

A happy thought flashed through my mind. "If he's doomed to remain in the bowels of the monster, and if Providence wills that his life be spared, can't we arrange for him to put in a request to be considered as still in the service?"

"Hm. . . . You mean on leave without pay?"

"Not that. Can't he be kept on salary?"

"On what basis?"

"On the basis of a special mission."

"What kind of mission, and where to?"

"Why, into the crocodilean interior . . . to investigate, so to speak. To study the facts on the spot. Of course, it will be something new. But after all, it's progressive, and at the same time it shows a concern for enlightenment. . . ."

Timofey Semyonych pondered this. "In my opinion," he said, "to send a particular official into the bowels of a crocodile on a special mission, is absurd. It's not in the personnel regulations. For that matter, what would his mission be?"

"Why, to make a scientific study, so to speak, of nature on the spot, *in vivo*. The natural sciences are all the rage now—like botany. . . . He could live there and report on

. . . well, on digestion, for instance, or simply on local customs, for the sake of accumulating facts."

"You mean in the field of statistics? Well, I'm no expert on that, and I'm not a philosopher, either. Facts, you say. But we're already up to our ears in facts, and we don't know what to do with them. Besides, statistics are dangerous. . . ."

"How so?"

"They're just dangerous. Anyway, you must admit that he'll be reporting his facts while he's just lying there loafing.[11] And can a person perform official duties when he's just lying there loafing? That's another new thing, and a dangerous one. And once again, there's no precedent. If we had just any kind of precedent, then in my opinion he could probably be assigned to a special mission."

"But after all, Timofey Semyonych! Before now, no living crocodiles have been imported here."

"Hm. True enough. . . ." And he pondered again. "No doubt your objection is well taken, and it might even serve as grounds for proceeding further. But then you must also bear in mind that if, with the appearance of living crocodiles, civil servants begin to disappear; and if then, on the basis that it is soft and warm in there, they start requesting special missions there and proceed to loaf, it would set a bad example, you must admit. Then everybody would probably want to crawl in there and get paid for doing nothing. . . ."

"Please, Timofey Semyonych! Please do what you can for him. Incidentally, he asked me to give you the seven rubles he owes you from your last card game."

"Ah, yes! I remember. He lost the other night at Nikifor Nikiforovich's. How gay he was then—how he laughed! And now. . . ." The old man was genuinely moved.

"Please help him, Timofey Semyonych!"

"I'll do what I can. I'll make inquiries in my own name, on a private basis. And you be sure to find out, unofficially and indirectly, how much the proprietor is willing to take for his crocodile."

Plainly, Timofey Semyonych was now in a kindlier mood.

"I'll be sure to," I answered. "And I'll come back here immediately and report."

"And what about his wife? Is she alone now? Is she in low spirits?"

<hr>

[11]Literally, "lying on his side." *Cf.* Note 19.

"You should pay her a visit, Timofey Semyonych."

"I will. Just the other day I was thinking I'd do that, and now is a convenient time. . . . But why, oh why, did he get that urge to go and see the crocodile? But then I'd like to have a look at it myself."

"Go and visit the poor chap, Timofey Semyonych."

"I will. Of course, I don't want to build up his hopes with such a gesture. I'll go as a private person. . . . Well, good-bye. I'm off to Nikifor Nikiforovich's again. Will you be there?"

"No, I'm going to see the prisoner."

"Yes, now he's a prisoner! Ah, that's what comes of being irresponsible!"

I took my leave of the old fellow. All kinds of thoughts passed through my mind. Timofey Semyonych was a kindhearted man, and a most honest one. But as I left him I was glad that he had already completed fifty years of service, and that the Timofey Semyonychs are a rarity these days.

It goes without saying that I immediately rushed back to the Passage to report everything to that poor man, Ivan Matveich. Besides, I was bursting with curiosity. How was he getting on there inside the crocodile? And how was he managing to live inside the crocodile? For that matter, was it really possible to live inside a crocodile? Actually, at times it seemed to me that the whole thing was a monstrous dream—especially since it involved a monster.

III

And yet, it was no dream but an actual, indubitable reality. Otherwise, would I be telling this story? But to continue.

I got back to the Passage rather late—about nine o'clock —and had to use the rear entrance to get into the crocodile room, since that evening the German had closed up shop earlier than usual. He was pacing about in at-home attire (a greasy old frock coat of some sort), but he was at least three times as pleased with himself as he had been that morning. It was plain to see that he was no longer afraid of anything, and that "public much more" had come. The *Mutter* came out a moment later, obviously so as to keep an eye on me. The German and his *Mutter* kept whispering together. In spite of the fact that the place was closed, he collected his quarter-ruble from me. What needless exactitude!

"You vill effery time pay. The public vill one ruble pay, but you vill only one quarter pay, because you are goot friend uhff your goot friend, ant I haff for friends—"

"Is he alive? Is my cultured friend alive?" I shouted loudly, walking toward the crocodile so that my words, even from a distance, would reach Ivan Matveich and tickle his vanity.

"Alive and well," he answered as if from a long way off or from under a bed, although I was standing quite near him. "Alive and well. But we'll speak of that later. How are things going?"

As though I had deliberately not heeded his question, I began to query him rapidly and with solicitude. How was he? How were things there inside the crocodile? And what were the insides of a crocodile like? This was required of me by both friendship and common politeness. But he interrupted me—arbitrarily and with annoyance.

"How are things going?" he shouted, ordering me about, as usual—this time in a squeaky voice which was most disgusting.

I recounted my entire conversation with Timofey Semyonych, down to the last detail. As I told him this, I tried to show by my tone of voice that I was offended.

"The old fellow is right," Ivan Matveich decided, just as abruptly as always in his conversations with me. "I like practical people. I cannot abide wishy-washy milksops. I must admit, however, that your idea about the special mission is not altogether absurd. For in fact I *can* report a good deal of information, as regards both science and local customs. But now all this is assuming a new and unforeseen aspect, and it is not worthwhile to fuss about merely the salary. Listen carefully. Are you sitting down?"

"No, I'm standing."

"Well, sit down on something—on the floor, if you have to—and listen carefully."

Peeved, I got a chair, and as I was setting it in place I slammed it on the floor in a fit of temper.

"Listen," he began imperiously. "Today a great horde of people came. By evening there was no room left, and the police showed up to keep order. By eight o'clock—earlier than usual, that is—the proprietor even found it necessary to close up shop and discontinue the exhibit so that he could count all the money he had taken in, and have more time to make preparations for tomorrow. We'll have a regular fair here tomorrow—I'm sure of that. Thus it can be assumed that all the most cultivated people of the capital will come: the ladies of high society, the foreign ambassadors, the judges and lawyers, and so on. Not only that, but they will start coming in from the diverse provinces of our far-flung and curious empire. The result: I am everyone's favorite; and, although hidden from view, I prevail over all.[12] I shall begin to instruct the pleasure-seeking crowd. Taught by experience, I shall serve as an example of greatness and the humble acceptance of fate. I shall be, so to speak, the rostrum from which I shall begin to instruct mankind. Of itself alone, the biological information I can report concerning the monster I inhabit, is priceless. And so not only do I desist from bewailing the recent incident: I have high hopes for a more brilliant career."

"Won't it become boring?" I asked sarcastically.

What irked me most of all was that he had become so pompous that he had almost entirely stopped using personal pronouns.[13] And yet all this confused me. "Why, just tell me why, is that frivolous nitwit swaggering?" I whispered to myself through gritted teeth. "He ought to be weeping, not swaggering."

"No!" he replied sharply to my question. "For I am totally imbued with great ideas. Only now do I have the leisure to meditate on improving the lot of all mankind. Now, from the crocodile, truth and light will come forth. I shall undoubtedly develop a new and unique theory of economic relations of which I shall be proud—something I have heretofore been unable to do, owing to the time consumed by my official duties and in petty worldly distractions. I shall disprove everything and be a new Fourier. By the way, did you return the seven rubles to Timofey Semyonych?"

---

[12]There is a rather horrendous pun in the Russian at this point (which, incidentally, has confused more than one translator). Literally, we get: "I am on view to everyone; and, although hidden from view. . . ." But the idiomatic sense of the first phrase (*u vsekh na vidu*) is "everyone's favorite."

[13]A phenomenon not, of course, reproducible in our English text. Curiously, the pronoun most often omitted by Ivan Matveich, in order to sound impressive, is *ya* (I).

"Out of my own pocket," I answered, trying to stress that fact by my tone of voice.

"We'll settle up," he replied haughtily. "I fully expect a raise in pay. Because who is entitled to a raise, if not I? I am now infinitely valuable. But to business. The wife?"

"I take it you are asking about Elena Ivanovna?"

"The wife?" he shouted—this time with a kind of screech.

There was nothing for it. Docilely, but again gritting my teeth, I told him how Elena Ivanovna was when I left her. He didn't even hear me out.

"I have special plans for her," he began impatiently. "If I am to be famous *here*, I want her to be famous *there*. Scientists, poets, philosophers, visiting mineralogists, and statesmen, after having conversed with me in the morning, will visit her salon in the evening. Beginning next week, she must hold an informal reception every evening. My salary, having been doubled, will provide the funds for those receptions. And since all that will be required for them is tea and some hired footmen, that takes care of that. Both here and there, they will talk about me. I have long yearned for something to happen that would make everyone talk about me; but I was never able to bring it about, fettered as I was by my insignificance and low rank in the service. Now, however, all this has been achieved merely through the most ordinary gulp of a crocodile. Every word of mine will be carefully heeded; each aphorism will be pondered on, passed on to others, and published. I shall let the world know what I am! They will finally understand what kind of abilities they allowed to disappear into the bowels of a monster! Some will say, 'This man might have been Foreign Minister and ruled a kingdom.' Others will say, 'And to think that this man never ruled a foreign kingdom!' I ask you: In what way am I inferior to some Garnier-Pazhesishky[14] or whatever he's called? . . . My wife must become my *pendant*. I have the brains, and she has the beauty and charm. 'She is beautiful, and that's why she is his wife,' some will say. But others will correct them: 'She is beautiful *because* she is his wife.' Just to be on the safe

[14]Garnier-Pagès (Etienne-Joseph-Louis): a prominent participant in the July Revolution in France; later, a deputy to the National Assembly and, as a leader of the *parti républicain,* a universally popular figure.

side, Elena Ivanovna must buy, tomorrow, the encyclopedia being published under the editorship of Andrey Krayevsky[15] so that she will be able to talk on all subjects. But what she should read most frequently is the political editorials in the *St. Petersburg News,* comparing them every day with the *Hair.*[16] I assume as a matter of course that the crocodile-owner will be willing occasionally to transport me, together with the crocodile, to my wife's brilliant salon. I shall stand there in the tank, in the middle of that magnificent drawing room, and I shall spout forth those witticisms that I shall have prepared that morning. To the statesmen I shall impart my projects; to the poets I shall talk in rhyme; and with the ladies I shall be amusing and charming in a way that is strictly moral, since I shall not be a threat to their husbands. To everyone else I shall serve as an example of submission to fate and the will of Providence.

"I shall make of my wife a brilliant literary figure. I shall bring her into prominence and explain her to the public. As my wife, she must abound in the greatest virtues. And if people are right when they call Andrey Aleksandrovich[17] our Russian Alfred de Musset, they will be even more right when they call her our Russian Evgeniya Tur."[18]

I must confess that even though all this blather was quite like our old Ivan Matveich, I couldn't help thinking he was feverish and raving. It was the same ordinary, everyday Ivan Matveich, but seen through a magnifying glass and enlarged twenty times.

"My friend," I asked him, "are you counting on a long life? And, just in general, tell me: Are you well? How are you eating? How are you sleeping? How are you breathing? I am your friend, and you must agree that the situation is most supernatural, so that my curiosity is most natural."

"Idle curiosity, and nothing more!" he answered sententiously. "But it shall be satisfied. You want to know how

---

[15]The *Encyclopedic Dictionary Prepared by Russian Scientists and Men of Letters,* published at government expense in 1861. Quite a furor was raised over Krayevsky's appointment as general editor, since his competence was largely confined to the field of publishing.
[16]*Cf.* Note 8.
[17]I.e., Krayevsky.
[18]Countess Elizaveta Vasilyevna Salios de Tournemir, a novelist and journalist, wrote under the pen name of Evgeniya Tur. She was a rabid feminist.

I am getting on in the bowels of the monster? In the first place the crocodile proved, to my amazement, to be completely hollow. His innards consist of a kind of huge empty rubber bag like those rubber articles sold on Gorokhovaya Street, on the Morskaya and, if I mistake not, on Voznesensky Prospect. Otherwise, how could I have found room there? Just figure it out for yourself."

"Is it possible?" I cried. "Is the crocodile really quite hollow?"

"Quite," Ivan Matveich assured me sternly and authoritatively. "And in all probability he is so constructed in accordance with the laws of nature. The crocodile possesses only a set of jaws equipped with sharp teeth and, in addition to the jaws, a very long tail. Nothing more, actually. In the middle, between these two extremities of his, is a hollow space encased in something like rubber. Most likely it actually is rubber."

"But," I interrupted, positively angry with him, "how about the ribs, the stomach, the intestines, the liver, and the heart?"

"Nothing. There is absolutely none of that, and most likely there never has been. All that is the idle fancy of featherbrained explorers. In the same way as one inflates a hemorrhoidal air cushion, I am now with my person inflating the crocodile. He is incredibly elastic. In fact, you yourself, as a friend of the family, could get in here beside me—if you were really big-hearted—and even with you here there would still be room. As a matter of fact, I am thinking that if worse comes to worst, I might send for Elena Ivanovna to join me in here.

"Incidentally, this hollow construction of the crocodile is completely in accord with the natural sciences. Let us assume, for example, that you were called upon to construct a new crocodile. The question would naturally arise: What is the basic characteristic of the crocodile? The answer is obvious: gulping down people. But how to design the crocodile that he will gulp down people? The answer is even more obvious: make him hollow. It was long ago established by physics that nature abhors a vacuum. Accordingly, the interior of the crocodile must be hollow, so that it abhors a vacuum: hence he will be constantly gulping down and filling himself up with whatever is within reach. And this is the only intelligible reason why all crocodiles swallow us humans. Such is not the case with the constitution of man. For example, the emptier a man's head, the less eager he is to fill it; and that is the sole exception to the general rule.

"All this is clear as day to me now. All this I have come to understand through my own intelligence and experience—being, so to speak, in the bowels of nature, in its retort, and listening to its pulse. Even etymology supports me, for the very name 'crocodile' means 'voracity.' Crocodile—*Crocodillo*—is evidently an Italian word, perhaps dating back to the ancient Egyptian pharaohs, and evidently derived from the French root *croquer,* meaning 'to gobble up,' 'to eat,' and in general 'to take food.' All this I intend to present as my first lecture to the audience assembled in Elena Ivanovna's salon when I am taken there in the tank."

"My friend, don't you think you should take a laxative now?" I cried out unwittingly. ("He has a fever! A fever!" I repeated to myself, horrified. "He's feverish!")

"Nonsense!" he replied scornfully. "Besides, in my present position it would be most awkward. I had a notion, though, that you would bring up the subject of laxatives."

"But, my friend, how . . . how do you manage to eat now? Have you dined today, or not?"

"No, but I am surfeited, and in all probability I shall never take food again. And that is quite understandable. Since with my person I fill up the whole interior of the crocodile, I make him forever full. Now he won't have to be fed for several years. On the other hand, being surfeited with me, he naturally communicates to me all the vital juices of his own body. It is rather like the way certain subtle coquettes envelop themselves and all their bodily appurtenances in raw ground meat at night, and then, when they have taken their baths in the morning, become fresh, supple, juicy, and seductive. Thus while nourishing the crocodile with myself, I in turn obtain nourishment from him, so that we mutually feed each other. But since it is difficult, even for a crocodile, to digest a man like me, he is of course bound to feel a certain heaviness in the stomach—which, by the way, he does not possess. And that is why—so as not to cause needless pain to the monster—I seldom turn over from one side to the other. I *could* turn over, but I refrain from it out of humane considerations. This is the only drawback to my present position; and in an allegorical sense, Timofey

Semyonych was right when he called me a loafer.[19] But
I shall prove that even when lying idly on one's side—
nay, *only* when lying idly on one's side—one can revolu-
tionize[20] the fate of mankind. Obviously, all the great ideas
and trends of thought in our newspapers and magazines
have been conceived by people lying idly on their sides.
That is why they call them 'ivory tower' ideas. But who
cares what they call them?

"Now I shall invent an entire social system—and you
would never believe how easy it is! All you have to do is
get off by yourself in some corner—or, for that matter,
get into a crocodile—close your eyes, and immediately you
invent a complete paradise for all mankind. Just a few
hours ago, when you left, I at once set about inventing;
and I have already invented three systems and am now
working on my fourth. True, you have to begin by refuting
everything. But refuting things from within a crocodile is
easy! Besides, seen from inside a crocodile, everything becomes much clearer, somehow.

"By the way, in my position there *are* a few other
drawbacks, though they are trivial ones. The interior of
the crocodile is rather damp and more or less coated with
mucus. Moreover, there is a rather strong smell of rubber—just like the smell from my last year's galoshes. But
that's all. There are no other drawbacks."

"Ivan Matveich," I broke in, "all these things are
marvels in which I can scarcely believe! Is it really true that
you intend never to dine again for the rest of your life?"

"What trivial tripe you worry about, you light-minded,
foolish fellow! I tell you about my great ideas, and you . . .
You are to understand that I am very well fed, merely
on the great ideas that light up the darkness enveloping
me. Just a short time ago, however, the good-natured
owner of the monster, after consulting with his kindhearted *Mutter,* decided with her that every morning they
would insert into the crocodile's mouth a bent metal tube
something like a whistle pipe, through which I can imbibe
coffee or broth with white bread soaked in it. The pipe has
already been ordered in the neighborhood, but I consider it a needless luxury. I hope to live for at least a
thousand years, if it is true that crocodiles live that long—

---

[19]Literally, "lie-on-the-side." *Cf.* Note 11.
[20]The root meaning of the Russian word is "to turn over" (from
one side to the other).

which (good thing I remembered) you will please check on tomorrow in some natural history book and let me know, because I may have made a mistake and confused the crocodile with some other excavated monster.

"There is only one thing that rather disturbs me. Since I am dressed in cloth, and am wearing boots, the crocodile obviously cannot digest me. Moreover, I am alive and am therefore resisting with all my willpower the digestion of myself, it being quite understandable that I don't want to become what all food becomes, since that would be most humiliating to me. But there is one thing I fear. In the course of a thousand years, the cloth of my coat (of Russian make, unfortunately) may rot. And then, left without clothing, I may in spite of my indignation begin to be digested. Although in the daytime I would never let this happen, at night, when asleep—when a man's willpower deserts him—I may suffer the very humiliating fate of a potato, or pancakes, or veal. Just to think of it makes me furious. This alone is reason enough to revise the tariff and encourage the importing of English cloth, which is stronger and will therefore hold out longer against nature if one happens to get into a crocodile. At the first opportunity I shall pass on this idea of mine to some statesman and, at the same time, to some of the political columnists on our Petersburg dailies. Let them spread the word. I trust this will not be the only idea they will borrow from me. I foresee that every morning a whole crowd of them, supplied with quarter-rubles from the editorial offices, will throng around me to hear my views on the dispatches of the day before. In short, the future looks very rosy to me."

"A raging fever!" I whispered to myself.

"But what about freedom, my friend?" I asked, wishing to hear his opinion in full. "After all, you're in a dungeon, so to speak, whereas man should enjoy freedom."

"You are stupid," he answered. "Savages love independence, but wise men love order. And there is no order—"[21]

"Spare me, Ivan Matveich! Please!"

"Hold your tongue and listen!" he screeched, irked that I had interrupted him. "Never before have my spirits

<hr>

[21] A distorted quotation from a story by Nikolai Karamzin, a well-known historian and influential writer of the later eighteenth and early nineteenth century. The actual passage reads: "Savage peoples love independence, but wise peoples love order; and there is no order without autocracy."

soared so high as now. In my cramped shelter I fear only one thing: the literary criticism of the thick monthly journals and the boos of our satirical newspapers. I am afraid I may be ridiculed by nitwit visitors, fools, and envious people, and nihilists in general. But I shall take steps. I am impatiently awaiting the public's reaction tomorrow—and especially the opinion of the press. Give me an account of the papers tomorrow."

"All right. Tomorrow I'll bring a whole batch of papers."

"Tomorrow will be too soon to expect reports in the papers, since it takes four days for notices to be printed. But from now on, come every evening by the rear entrance through the yard. I intend to employ you as my secretary. You will read the papers and magazines to me, and I shall dictate my ideas to you, and give you instructions. Be particularly careful not to forget the telegrams. I want all the European dispatches here every day. But enough. You probably want to get some sleep now. Run along home, and pay no heed to what I said just now about the critics. I am not afraid of them, because they themselves are in a critical position. All one has to do is to be wise and virtuous, and one is certain to be put on a pedestal. If not Socrates, then Diogenes—or perhaps the two of them together. There you have my future role among mankind."

Such was the scatterbrained and insolent manner in which Ivan Matveich (though to be sure, he was feverish) sounded off to me—like those irresponsible women of whom the proverb says that they can't keep a secret. Besides, everything he had told me about the crocodile struck me as highly suspicious. For instance, how could the crocodile possibly be completely hollow? I would have bet he was only bragging—out of vanity, and partly to belittle me. True, he was sick, and sick people must be humored. But I must frankly confess that I could never abide Ivan Matveich. All my life, since my earliest childhood, I have wanted to escape from his tutelage, and have never been able to. A thousand times I tried to call it quits with him; and each time I was drawn back to him, as though I still hoped to prove something to him and take my vengeance for something. A strange thing, that friendship! I can say definitely that nine-tenths of my friendship for him was made up of spite.

"Your friend is a very shmart man," the German said

to me in a loud whisper as he made ready to see me out. (He had been listening assiduously to our conversation all this time.)

"A propos," I said, "before I forget. How much would you take for your crocodile in case someone wanted to buy it?"

Ivan Matveich, who had heard my question, was awaiting the answer with curiosity. At any rate, he gave a special kind of grunt when I put the question, making it obvious that he didn't want the German to ask too little.

At first the German would hear nothing of it, and even became very angry. "Nobody vill dare my own crocodile to buy!" he shouted furiously, getting red as a boiled lobster. "I not vant my crocodile to sell. I vould not a million thaler take for my crocodile. Today haff I one hundert thirty thaler got from the public. Tomorrow vill I ten tausend thaler get; and then vill I effery day one hundert tausend thaler collect. I not vant to sell!"

Ivan Matveich actually tee-heed with satisfaction.

Keeping my self-control—for I was doing my duty as a true friend—I coolly and reasonably pointed out to the crazy German that his calculations were not altogether accurate; that if he took in a hundred thousand every day, in four days' time all Petersburg would have visited his place and there would be nobody left to collect from; that life and death were in God's hands; that the crocodile might somehow burst; that Ivan Matveich might get sick and die; etc., etc.

The German grew thoughtful. "I vill him drops from the pharmacy give," he said, after pondering, "and your friend vill not die."

"Drops are all very well," I said, "but also bear in mind that you may be in for a lawsuit. Ivan Matveich's wife may demand to get her lawful spouse back. You intend to get rich, but do you intend to provide any kind of pension for Elena Ivanovna?"

"No, I intend not!" the German replied resolutely and sternly.

"No, he intend not!" put in the *Mutter,* downright spitefully.

"Well, then, wouldn't it be better for you to accept something right now in a lump sum—something moderate, perhaps, but secure and solid—rather than be a prey to chance? I believe I should add that I am not asking you this out of idle curiosity."

The German led his *Mutter* off to consult with her in a corner next to the cage that had in it the biggest and ugliest monkey of the entire collection.

"Now you'll see!" Ivan Matveich said to me.

As for me, at that moment I was burning with the desire, first, to give the German a good, hard beating; second, to give the *Mutter* an even harder beating; and, third, to give the biggest and hardest beating of all to Ivan Matveich, for his boundless conceit.

But all this was as nothing compared to the answer given by the greedy German.

After consulting with his *Mutter,* he demanded for his crocodile fifty thousand rubles in notes on the last domestic loan with lottery tickets; a brick house on Gorokhovaya Street with his own pharmacy included; and to boot, the rank of a Russian colonel.

"See?" Ivan Matveich cried out triumphantly. "I told you so! Except for that last insane hankering to be made a colonel, he's perfectly right, because he fully understands the current value of the monster he is exhibiting. The economic principle above all!"

"For heaven's sake!" I shouted in fury at the German. "Why should you be made a colonel? What exploits have you performed? What service have you rendered? What military glory have you reaped? You really *are* crazy, aren't you?"

"Crazy!" screeched the insulted German. "No, I am very shmart man, but you are very shtupid. I haff the colonel deserved because I haff the crocodile shown, and in him a live *Hofrat* sits. But the Russian a crocodile cannot show, and in him a live *Hofrat* sitting! I am very shmart man and very much vant colonel to be!"

"Well then, good-bye, Ivan Matveich," I called out, shaking with fury, and rushed out of the crocodile room almost at a run. I felt that in one more minute I wouldn't be able to answer for myself. The insane hopes of those two blockheads were unbearable.

The cold air refreshed me and somewhat tempered my indignation. Finally, after vigorously spitting fifteen times on both sides, I got a cab, went home, undressed, and threw myself on the bed. What irked me worst of all was that I had fallen into his clutches as his secretary. Now I would die of boredom there every evening, doing my duty as a true friend. I was ready to beat myself for this; and as a matter of fact, when I had put out the

candle and pulled the blanket up over me, I did punch
myself several times on the head and other parts of my
body. This gave me some relief, and at last I fell asleep—
and rather soundly, at that—because I was very tired.
All night long I dreamed of nothing but monkeys; but
well along toward morning I dreamed of Elena Ivanovna.

IV

I suppose I dreamed of the monkeys because they were
shut up in the cage at the crocodile-owner's shop; but
Elena Ivanovna was something quite different.

I'll say it right now: I loved the lady. But I make
haste—post-haste—to qualify that. I loved her as a father:
no more and no less. I draw this conclusion because I
very often felt an overwhelming desire to kiss her little
head or rosy cheek. And though I never actually did it,
I swear I would not have declined to kiss even her lips.
And not only her lips, but her teeth, which were always
displayed so charmingly when she laughed—like a row
of pretty, well-matched pearls. For that matter, she
laughed amazingly often. In moments of fondness, Ivan
Matveich used to call her his "darling absurdity"—an
epithet that was eminently right and apt. She was a sugar-
plum lady, and that was all. That is why I simply could
not understand what possessed Ivan Matveich to imagine
his wife as our Russian Evgeniya Tur.

At any rate, my dream (if we leave the monkeys out
of it) produced a most pleasant impression on me; and
mentally rehearsing all the events of the previous day as
I drank my morning cup of tea, I decided to go at once
to see Elena Ivanovna on my way to the office—which,
for that matter, I was obliged to do as friend of the
family.

In a tiny room just off the bedroom—their so-called
little drawing room, though their big drawing room was
also little—on an elegant little sofa before a little tea
table, Elena Ivanovna was sitting in a kind of semi-
transparent morning wrapper, sipping coffee out of a
little cup into which she was dipping a tiny biscuit. She

was ravishingly pretty, but at the same time she seemed to me rather pensive.

"Ah, so it's you, naughty boy!" she greeted me with a preoccupied smile. "Sit down, sillyhead, and have some coffee. Well, what did you do last night? Were you at the masquerade ball?"

"You mean you were there? I don't go to those things, you know. Besides, last night I went to see our prisoner. . . ." I sighed, and assumed a pious expression as I drank my coffee.

"Who? What prisoner? Oh, yes! The poor chap! Well, how is he? Bored? You know, I've been meaning to ask you. . . . I can sue for a divorce now, can't I?"

"A divorce!" I exclaimed in indignation, and almost spilled my coffee.

"It's that swarthy fellow!" I thought to myself. There was a certain swarthy individual with a little moustache who had something to do with architecture, who came much too often to visit them and was extraordinarily skillful at amusing Elena Ivanovna. I must admit that I hated him; and there was no doubt that he had managed to get together with Elena Ivanovna the evening before— either at the masquerade or perhaps even here—and had talked all kinds of rubbish to her.

"After all," Elena Ivanovna started off suddenly, as though she had been coached, "if he's going to stay there in the crocodile and perhaps not come back all his life, am I supposed to wait for him here? A husband should live at home, and not in a crocodile."

"But it was an unforeseen occurrence," I began, perturbed in a way that was quite understandable.

"No, no! Don't talk to me! I won't listen, I won't!" she cried out, in a spasm of anger. "You're always against me, you wicked man! There's no doing anything with you! You'll never give me any advice! Even strangers tell me I can get a divorce because Ivan Matveich won't be getting his salary."

"Elena Ivanovna! Is this you I hear talking? What villain could have put such a notion into your head? Anyway, a divorce on such flimsy grounds as salary is completely impossible. And poor, miserable Ivan Matveich is, so to speak, all aflame with love for you, even in the bowels of the monster. Not only that—he is melting with love, like a lump of sugar. Just last night, while you were enjoying yourself at the masquerade, he was saying that

if worse came to worst he might send for you, as his
lawful wife, to join him in there—especially as it turns
out that the crocodile is very capacious: roomy enough
not only for two people but even for three."

At this point I immediately related to her all that
interesting part of my talk with Ivan Matveich the night
before.

"What?" she cried out in amazement. "You want me
to crawl in there with Ivan Matveich? The very idea!
Anyway, how would I get in there, with my hat and
crinoline? Good heavens, what foolishness! And what
kind of a figure will I cut when I'm crawling in there—
probably with somebody watching me, too? It's ridiculous!
And what will I eat in there? And . . . and what will I
do in there when. . . . Goodness gracious! What an idea!
And what kind of amusements will I have there? You say
it smells of rubber? And what will I do if we have a
quarrel? Would we lie side-by-side just the same? Ugh,
how disgusting!"

"I agree. I agree with all those arguments, my dearest
Elena Ivanovna," I interposed, striving to express myself
with that natural enthusiasm that always possesses a person
when he feels he is in the right. "But there is one thing
in all this that you haven't appreciated. You haven't
appreciated the fact that if he is inviting you there, it
means he can't live without you. It means love: passionate,
true, ardent love. It was love that you failed to appreciate,
dear Elena Ivanovna. Love!"

"I won't do it! I won't! And I don't even want to hear
anything more about it!" She waved me away with her
pretty little hand with the pink nails that had just been
cleaned and polished. "You're horrid! You're making me
cry. Crawl in there yourself, if you like the idea so much.
You're his friend, aren't you? Well then, lie down in there
next to him out of friendship, and spend your whole life
arguing about some boring science or other."

"You are wrong to make fun of these proposals," I
said with dignity, checking the giddy woman. "Ivan
Matveich has already invited me. Of course it is duty
that bids you go there, while with me it is sheer magnanimity. But in telling me last night of the remarkable
elasticity of the crocodile, Ivan Matveich hinted very
plainly that there would be room enough not only for the
two of you but for all three of us—for me, too, as friend
of the family, especially if that's what I wanted. And so—"

"What do you mean, 'all three'?" Elena Ivanovna exclaimed, looking at me in astonishment. "You mean we. . . . So all three of us will be in there together? Ha, ha, ha! What ninnies you are! Ha, ha, ha! I'll make sure to be pinching you all the time in there, you wicked man! Ha, ha, ha! Ha, ha, ha!" And throwing herself back on the sofa, she laughed till she cried.

All this, with the tears and the laughter, was so enchanting that I couldn't restrain myself; and seizing her little hands, I started kissing them passionately—which she did not oppose, though she tweaked my ear lightly as a sign of reconciliation.

Then we both grew very gay, and I told her in detail of all Ivan Matveich's plans of the day before. The idea of her having a salon and evening receptions pleased her very much.

"But I shall need a great many new dresses," she observed, "and so Ivan Matveich must send me as much of his salary as possible, and as quickly as possible. . . . Only . . . only, how will they. . ." she added, her thoughts troubled by something, "how will they bring him to me in the tank? That's ridiculous. I don't want my husband being carried around in a tank. I'd feel awfully ashamed in front of my guests. . . . No, I don't want that. I just don't."

"By the way, while I think of it. Did Timofey Semyonych come to see you last evening?"

"Oh, yes. He did. He came to console me, and just imagine—we played cards all the time! His stakes were candy, and if I lost he could kiss my hands. What a wicked man! And just imagine—he almost went to the masquerade with me! Really!"

"He was carried away by his feelings," I remarked. "But then, who wouldn't be carried away by you, you temptress!"

"Oh, get along with your compliments! Just you wait— I'll give you a pinch when you leave! I've learned to pinch frightfully well lately. What do you say to that? By the way, were you saying that Ivan Matveich spoke of me very often last night?"

"Well, no, not really often. . . . I must admit he is more taken up, now, with the fate of mankind, and he wants—"

"Well, then let him! Don't tell me any more! Really, it's frightfully boring. I'll manage to visit him there somehow. I'll definitely go tomorrow. But not today—I have a headache. And besides, there'll be so many people there. They'll say, 'That's his wife!' and I'll feel embarrassed. . . . Good-bye. You'll be there this evening, won't you?"

"To see him? Yes. He told me to come and bring the newspapers."

"Now that's really splendid! Run along and read to him. But don't come back to see me tonight. I'm not feeling well, and I may go out visiting. Well, good-bye, naughty boy!"

"It's that swarthy fellow who's coming to see her tonight," I thought.

At the office I of course gave no sign of being consumed by these worries and troubles. But I soon noticed that some of our most progressive newspapers, that morning, were being passed from hand to hand among my colleagues with a kind of special rapidity, and were being read with an extremely serious facial expression. The first one to reach my hands was the *Leaflet*,[22] a paper of no particular shade of opinion but just generally humanitarian—for which it was held in contempt by the majority of us, although we all read it. It was not without astonishment that I read the following in it:

Yesterday, in our far-flung capital city, ornamented with its magnificent buildings, most unusual rumors were circulating. A certain Mr. X, a well-known gourmet of high society, no doubt weary of the cuisine at Borel's[23] and at the —— Club, went into the building of the Passage to the place where a huge crocodile, only recently brought to the capital, was being exhibited, and demanded that it be prepared for his dinner. Having come to terms with the owner, he at once set about devouring him (that is, not the owner—a most unassuming German with a penchant for exactitude—but his crocodile) while he was still alive, slicing off juicy morsels with his penknife, and gulping them down in great haste. Little by little the entire crocodile disappeared into his corpulent belly, so that he was even ready to start in on a mongoose,

---

[22]The *Peterburgskiy listok*, a newly founded tabloid reporting on "events about town."
[23]An expensive restaurant in St. Petersburg.

the crocodile's constant companion, no doubt assuming that it would be equally tasty.

We are by no means averse to this new food product, which has long been familiar to foreign gourmets. We even predicted this in advance. In Egypt, English lords and travelers catch crocodiles in whole batches; and they consume the back of the monster in the form of beefsteaks, with mustard, onions, and potatoes. The French who accompanied De Lesseps prefer the paws baked in hot ashes—which, incidentally, they do to spite the English, who laugh at them. Both methods will no doubt find favor among us.

For our part, we welcome a new branch of industry preeminently lacking in our mighty and variegated fatherland. Following this first crocodile, who disappeared into the belly of a Petersburg gourmet, hundreds of them will no doubt be brought here before so much as a year has passed.

And why not acclimatize the crocodile here in Russia? If the waters of the Neva are too cold for these interesting foreigners, there are ponds in the capital and rivers and lakes outside the city. Why not, for example, breed crocodiles in Pargolov or Pavlovsk, in the Presnensky Pond and the Samotek in Moscow? While providing tasty and healthful food for our fastidious gourmets, they could at the same time entertain the ladies who stroll beside these ponds, and serve to instruct the children in natural history. Crocodile skin could be used to manufacture cases for jewels or musical instruments, valises, cigarette cases, and wallets; and perhaps more than one Russian merchant's roll of a thousand rubles (in those greasy bills especially preferred by the merchants) would come to rest in a crocodile skin.

We hope to return more than once to this interesting topic.

Even though I had had a premonition of something like this, the rash irresponsibility of the news item upset me. Finding no one with whom to share my impressions, I turned to my desk-neighbor, Prokhor Savvich, and noticed that he had been watching me for a long time, and was holding a copy of the *Hair* as though ready to pass it on to me. He took the *Leaflet* from me without saying a word; and as he handed me the *Hair* he heavily

marked with his thumbnail an article he apparently wished
to bring to my attention. This Prokhor Savvich was a
very strange man. A taciturn old bachelor, he never
entered into any relationships with any of us; spoke to
almost no one in the office; and always had his own
opinions about everything, but could not bear to import
them to anyone. He lived alone. Hardly any of us had
ever been to his lodgings.

Here is what I read in the indicated place in the *Hair:*

As everyone knows, we are progressive and humanitarian and want to catch up with Europe in
this respect. But despite all our endeavors and the
efforts of our newspaper, we still have by no means
"matured,"[24] as witness the alarming incident that
occurred yesterday in the Passage—one that we had
previously predicted.

A foreign entrepreneur comes to our capital, bringing with him a crocodile, which he begins exhibiting
in the Passage. We immediately hasten to welcome a
new branch of useful industry basically lacking in
our mighty and variegated fatherland. Then suddenly,
at 4:30 yesterday afternoon, an exceptionally corpulent individual in an inebriated condition comes to
the foreign entrepreneur's establishment, pays his
admission fee, and immediately, without any warn-
ing, gets into the maw of the crocodile, who is of
course obliged to swallow him, if only from an
instinct of self-preservation to avoid choking. Having
tumbled into the crocodile's belly, the stranger at
once falls asleep. Neither the shouts of the foreign
proprietor nor the wailings of his terrified family,
nor threats to send for the police, make the slightest
impression. From within the crocodile is heard only
a laugh and a threat to whip him with scourages
(*sic*); while the poor mammal, compelled to swallow
such a mass, vainly sheds tears. "An uninvited guest
is worse than a Tartar." But in spite of this proverb,
the insolent visitor refuses to leave.

We have no idea of the explanation for such bar-
barous incidents, which testify to our immaturity and
disgrace us in the eyes of foreigners. The sweep and

---

[24] "We have by no means matured" was a much-mooted phrase
in the Russian press of the day.

recklessness of the Russian temperament have found worthy employment.

Just what, it may be asked, was the uninvited visitor in quest of? Warm and comfortable lodgings? But our capital city has numerous handsome houses with cheap and very comfortable apartments, with water piped in from the Neva and gas-lit staircases—often with a porter employed by the landlord.

We would also like once again to call our readers' attention to the great barbarity in the treatment of domestic animals. It is, of course, difficult for the visiting crocodile to digest such a mass all at once. And now he lies there, swollen up to the size of a mountain, awaiting death in unbearable agonies. In Europe, persons who treat domestic animals inhumanely have long been subject to punishment by law. But in spite of our European lighting systems, our European sidewalks, and our European architecture, we are still far from letting go of our traditional prejudices.

The buildings are new, but the prejudices old. . . .[25]

And not even the buildings are new—at least not the staircases. Several times heretofore we have reported in our pages that in the house of the merchant Lukyanov, on the Petersburg Side, the lower steps of the wooden stairs have rotted and fallen through, and have long constituted a hazard for the soldier's wife Afimya Skapidarova, who is employed in the house and must frequently climb the stairs carrying water or an armful of wood. At last our prediction has proven right. At 8:30 yesterday evening, the soldier's wife Afimya Skapidarova, while carrying a bowl of soup, fell and broke her leg. We do not know whether Lukyanov will now have his staircase repaired. Russians are gifted at hindsight. But the victim of the Russian "Who knows?" has already been taken to the hospital.

Similarly, we shall never cease to maintain that the house-porters who clear away the mud from the wooden sidewalks on the Viborgsky Side,[26] should

---

[25] A much-quoted line from Griboyedov's classic comedy, *Gore ot uma*, perhaps best known in English under the title of *Woe from Wit*.
[26] A distinctly unfashionable district of St. Petersburg, situated "on the wrong side of the river."

not spatter the legs of passersby but should heap up
the mud in little mounds, as is done in Europe when
cleaning boots. . . etc, etc.

"What's this?" I asked, looking at Prokhor Savvich in
some puzzlement. "What's this all about?"

"How do you mean?"

"Why, for heaven's sake! Instead of feeling sorry for
poor Ivan Matveich, they feel sorry for the crocodile!"

"Well, and what of that? They even have pity for a
beast—a *mammal*. We have to catch up with Europe,
don't we? They have a great deal of pity for crocodiles
there, too. Hee, hee, hee!"

With that, the eccentric Prokhor Savvich buried his
nose in his documents and wouldn't say one word more.

I put the *Hair* and the *Leaflet* in my pocket and, in
addition, gathered up as many old copies of the *News*
and the *Hair* as I could find, for Ivan Matveich's evening
entertainment. And though evening was still a long way
off, I slipped out of the office early (for once) so as to
be at the Passage and watch—if only from a distance—
what was going on there, and pick up various opinions
and trends of thought. I had a feeling there would be a
tightly packed crowd there; and just in case, I pulled my
coat-collar up more closely around my face, because I
somehow felt a bit shy—so unaccustomed are we to
publicity. But I feel that I am not entitled to report my
own prosaic reactions in the face of such a remarkable
and unprecedented event.

1865

A TALE OF HOW ONE MUZHIK

LOOKED AFTER TWO

GENERALS[1]

BY MIKHAIL SALTYKOV

Once upon a time there were two generals. They were
both nitwits, and so in no time at all, by a wave of some
magic wand, they found themselves on a desert island.

The two generals had spent all their lives in some kind
of registry office: there they had been born and brought up,
and there they had grown old. Consequently, they didn't
understand anything at all. They didn't even understand
any words except: "With assurance of the highest esteem,
I remain, Your Most Humble Servant. . . ."

The registry office had been abolished as superfluous,
and the two generals had been let go. They had settled
down to retirement in Petersburg, on Podyacheskaya
Street, in separate apartments. Each of them had a woman
to cook for him, and each collected a pension. But then
suddenly they found themselves on a desert island. They
woke up and lo! they were both lying under the same
blanket.

"I had a strange dream just now, Your Excellency,"
said one of the generals. "It was just as if I was living on
a desert island."

---

[1]These are "civilian generals"; i.e., civil servants whose grade
in the civil service was the equivalent of a general's rank in the
military. *Cf.* the Table of Ranks and Note 8.

Having uttered these words, up he jumped. So did the other general.

"Good heavens! What's going on here?" they both cried out in amazement. And they began pinching each other to find out whether this strange thing had happened to them in reality, or only in a dream. But no matter how hard they tried to convince themselves that it was all nothing more than a dream, they had to acknowledge the sad reality.

Before them, the sea stretched away on the one hand; on the other lay a small clump of earth beyond which the same boundless sea stretched away again. The generals wept for the first time since the registry office had been closed.

They began looking each other over, and noticed that they were in their nightshirts, and that each had an order[2] hung around his neck.

"I'd certainly give a lot for a cup of coffee right now!" said one of the generals. But then he recalled what an outlandish thing had happened, and began to weep again. "What are we going to do?" he continued through his tears. "If we wrote a report right now, what earthly good would it do?"

"I'll tell you what, Your Excellency," the other general said. "You go east, and I'll go west, and toward evening we'll both come back here. Who knows? Perhaps we'll find something."

They started trying to find out which direction was east and which was west. They remembered that their departmental chief had once said: "If you want to find the east, stand so that you're facing north, and the east will be on your right." So they started trying to find which was north. They faced this way and that, they tried every country in the world; but since they had spent all their lives in the registry office, they didn't find anything.

"I'll tell you what, Your Excellency. You go to the right and I'll go to the left—that's the best." This was said by the general who, in addition to his service at the registry office, had been a penmanship teacher at a school for soldiers' sons, and was consequently a bit less stupid than the other.

No sooner said than done. One of the generals set off

---

[2] I.e., an official decoration of the kind worn on a ribbon around the neck.

to the right, and came upon some trees with all kinds of fruit on them. He wanted to pick at least one apple, but they were all so high above the ground that he would have to climb the tree. He tried to climb it, but without success: all he managed to do was tear his nightshirt.

Next he came to a brook, and saw it was teeming with fish—just like the fish farm on the Fontanka.[3]

"How fine it would be to have fish like that and be back home on Podyacheskaya Street!" he thought, his mouth watering so much that it changed the very expression on his face.

He went on into the woods: the hazel grouse were whistling, the black grouse were drumming, and the hares were scampering about.

"Good Lord, just think of all that food!" he said, so hungry by now he was starting to feel sick to his stomach.

But there wasn't a thing he could do about it, and he had to return empty-handed to the rendezvous point. When he got there the other general was waiting for him.

"Well, how did it go, Your Excellency? Did you get anything?"

"Just this old copy of the *Moscow News*[4] that I came across. Nothing more."

The generals again lay down to sleep, but they were too hungry. First they would fret over who might be getting their pensions; then they would remember the fruit, fish, grouse, and hares they had seen that day.

"Who would have thought, Your Excellency, that human food, in its original form, flies, swims, and grows on trees?" said one of the generals.

"Yes," answered the other, "I must confess that until now I always thought that breakfast rolls came into the world in the very same shape in which they are served with the morning coffee."

"Hence it follows that if, for example, a person wants to eat a partridge, he must first catch it, kill it, pluck it, and roast it. . . . But how does one do all that?"

"But how does one do all that?" the other general repeated, just like an echo.

They lapsed into silence and tried to fall asleep; but

---

[3] The "left branch" of the Neva River (upon whose delta St. Petersburg was built). The residential district along the Fontanka was very fashionable.

[4] An archconservative paper.

hunger had driven off sleep for good. Grouse, turkeys, and suckling pigs kept flashing before their mind's eye. succulent, done to a turn, garnished with pickles, relish, and other fixings.

"Right now I think I could eat one of my own boots!" said one general.

"Gloves can be tasty, too," sighed the other general, "when they've been worn a long time."

Suddenly the two generals looked at each other: there was an evil gleam in their eyes, their teeth were snapping, and a low growl issued from their chests. They began slowly to creep toward each other, and the next instant both were raging with bloodlust. Handfuls of hair and rent clothing swirled about in the air, which resounded with squeals and groans. The general who had been a teacher of penmanship bit off his colleague's decoration and gobbled it up. But the sight of blood seemed to bring them back to their senses.

"God help us!" they both cried out at once. "Why, at this rate we'll be eating each other!"

"But how do we happen to be here? Who was the villain that played such a trick on us?"

"The thing to do, Your Excellency," said one of the generals, "is to keep our minds occupied with some kind of conversation. Otherwise, murder will be done here."

"Commence!" said the other.

"Well, just for example. Why is it, do you think, that the sun first rises and then sets, instead of the other way around?"

"You're a droll fellow, Your Excellency! Don't you yourself first rise, then go to the office and do your paperwork, and not until then lie down to sleep?"

"But why not a different arrangement of things? Why don't I lie down first, have various kinds of dreams, and *then* rise?"

"Hm . . . yes, I suppose. . . . And yet I must confess, when I was still working at my office I always thought of it like this: 'Now it's morning, next will come the day, then they'll serve dinner, and then it will be time to go to bed.'"

But the mention of dinner threw them both into despondency and nipped that little conversation in the bud.

"I was told by a doctor I know, that a man can nourish

himself on his own juices for a long time," one of the generals resumed.

"But how?"

"It's simple. It seems that your own juices produce other juices, and these in turn produce still other juices, until finally you run out of juices."

"And then what?"

"Then you have to eat something."

"Oh, damnation!"

In short, no matter what the generals started to talk about, it always ended up by reminding them of food; and this whetted their appetites even more. They decided to break off the conversation; and, remembering the copy of the *Moscow News* they had found, they began avidly to read it.

In a voice vibrant with emotion, one of them read:

> Yesterday the venerable mayor of our ancient capital gave a banquet. The table was set with dazzling splendor for a hundred persons. The tributes of all lands had made and kept, as it were, a rendezvous at this marvelous gala. They included "the golden sterlet from Sheksna,"[5] the pheasant bred in the forests of the Caucasus, and strawberries—which are so rare in our northern clime in the month of February—

"Damn it all, anyway!" the other general exclaimed in despair. "Can't you find something else to read about?" And snatching the paper from his colleague, he read the following:

> From our correspondent in Tula. Yesterday, on the occasion of the catching of a sturgeon in the Upa River (an event unprecedented in the memory of the oldest local inhabitants, and all the more so since the sturgeon bore a distinct resemblance to the district police inspector), a banquet was held at the local club. The hero of the festivities was brought in on a huge wooden platter, garnished with gherkins and

---

[5] The first line of "Invitation to a Dinner" by Gabriel Derzhavin, the chief Russian poet of the eighteenth century.

holding in its mouth a piece of membrane.[6] Dr. P—,
who acted as master of ceremonies on this occasion,
took care to see that each of the guests got a morsel.
The sauces were most varied and, one might even
say, fanciful—

"Pardon me, Your Excellency," the first general cut in,
"but it seems that you yourself are not very prudent in
your choice of reading matter." And seizing the paper in
his turn, he began to read:

From our correspondent in Vyatka. One of the
oldest of the local inhabitants has devised the following original recipe for making fish soup. Take a live
burbot, and first of all give it a lashing. Then when,
as a result of its sorrows, its liver has become enlarged. . . .

The generals' heads drooped. Whatever their eyes fell
upon reminded them of food. Even their own thoughts
contrived mischief against them; for no matter how hard
they tried to keep thoughts of steak from their minds,
those thoughts forced their way in.

But suddenly the general who had been a teacher of
penmanship was struck by an inspiration. "How about
it, Your Excellency?" he said joyously. "Let's find ourselves a muzhik!"

"What do you mean, 'a muzhik'?"

"Why, just an ordinary muzhik—one of the usual kind.
He could serve us rolls right away, and catch grouse and
fish for us."

"Hm. . . . A muzhik. . . . But where are we going to
find this muzhik when there's no muzhik here?"

"What do you mean, 'no muzhik'? There's always a
muzhik—everywhere! You just have to look for him.
Most likely he's hiding somewhere so he won't have to
work."

This idea heartened the generals so much that they

---

[6]This little piece of membrane has caused infinite difficulties
for editors and translators. Saltykov had originally written *kusok
zeleni,* meaning a piece of parsley (or other greens), but later
changed it to *slen',* meaning (Dahl) "a hard membrane resembling
translucent skin, with which a fish covers himself in the winter."
"Our correspondent from Tula" must have confused the sturgeon
with a lungfish!

jumped up in fine fettle and went off looking for a muzhik.

They wandered around the island for a long time without having any success. But at last the pungent odor of bran bread and sour-smelling sheepskin put them on the right track. Lying under a tree, belly up, with his hands under his head, a colossal muzhik was sleeping—avoiding work in the most brazen manner. The indignation of the two generals knew no bounds.

"So you're sleeping, lazybones!" they fumed at him. "Probably you don't care at all that there are two generals right in front of you who have been starving for two days. Hop to work this instant!"

The muzhik got up. He saw that the two generals were stern. He would have liked to show them a clean pair of heels, but they grabbed him and held on for dear life.

And so, with them watching him, he got to work. First thing, he climbed a tree and picked ten of the ripest apples for each of the generals. For himself he picked only one, and it was green. Next he dug around in the ground and got some potatoes. After that, he took two sticks of wood, rubbed them together, and made a fire. Then, using some of his own hair, he made a snare and caught a hazel grouse. Finally, he kindled the fire into a hot blaze, and over it he cooked so much food of all kinds that the generals even began to wonder whether they shouldn't give a little of it to this loafer.

The generals observed the muzhik's exertions, and their hearts leapt for joy. They had already forgotten that they had almost starved to death the day before. Instead, they thought: "What a splendid thing it is to be a general! Wherever you are, you're secure!"

Meantime, the huge muzhik kept asking them, "Will that do, masters?"

"Oh, yes, dear friend. We can see you're industrious," the generals replied.

"Then is it all right if I rest a little?"

"By all means, dear friend. But first make up a rope."

The huge muzhik promptly gathered some wild hemp, soaked it in water, pounded and dressed it; and by evening the rope was ready. With this rope the generals tied the big muzhik to a tree so he could not run away, and then they lay down to sleep.

One day went by, then another, and the huge muzhik proved so clever that he even cooked soup in his cupped hands. The generals were happy, plump, well-fed, and pampered-looking. They began telling each other that it wasn't costing them anything to live here, and meantime their pensions were piling up higher and higher.

"What do you think, Your Excellency?" one general would say to the other after breakfast. "Was there ever really a Tower of Babel? Or is it just some kind of allegory?"

"I think, Your Excellency, that it really happened. Otherwise how explain the existence of different languages on earth?"

"And so the Flood really happened too?"

"Yes, it really happened too. Otherwise, how explain the existence of antediluvian animals? Besides, the *Moscow News* says—"

"How about reading the *Moscow News* now?"

So they would find the copy of the newspaper, sit down in the shade, and read it from the front page to the last: about how people were eating in Moscow, eating in Tula, eating in Penza, eating in Ryazan. And everything was fine—they didn't even feel queasy.

But after a while—maybe a short one, maybe a long one—[7] the generals got bored. More and more often they would remember the cooks they had left behind in Petersburg; and they even shed a few tears on the sly.

"What do you suppose is happening now on Podyacheskaya Street, Your Excellency?" one general would ask the other.

"Oh, don't even talk about it, Your Excellency!" the other would reply. "My heart is so heavy with homesickness!"

"No two ways about it: the living is really good here. But still, you know, the young ram misses his yearling ewe, as they say. And one misses one's uniform, too."

"I should say so! Especially if it's an actual state councillor's uniform.[8] Why, the gold braid alone is enough to dazzle you!"

And so they began nagging at the muzhik to get them back to Podyacheskaya Street. And what do you think? It turned out that the muzhik actually knew his way around Podyacheskaya Street. He had "been there, and

---

[7] A formula recurrent in Russian folk and fairy tales.
[8] Literally, "of the fourth grade."

drunk mead and beer, but it had run down his beard and never got into his mouth."[9]

"Why, we're Podyacheskaya Street generals!" they exclaimed joyously.

"And me?" replied the muzhik. "Maybe once you happened to see a man on a scaffolding hung by a rope on the outside of a building, slapping paint on the wall, or crawling along the rooftop like a fly. If you did, that was me!"

And the muzhik began to ponder how to pleasure his two generals because they had been so kind to a loafer like him and had not scorned his lowly labors. So he built a ship—well, not really a ship but a vessel of sorts that would take you across the ocean-sea and clear to Podyacheskaya Street.

"Just be careful you don't drown us, you scum!" said the generals, when they saw the boat bobbing on the waves.

"Don't worry, masters—this ain't the first time for me," the muzhik replied, and began making ready for their departure.

He gathered some swansdown of the softest kind and lined the boat's bottom with it. This done, he had the generals lie down in the bottom and, crossing himself, he shoved off.

How great was the generals' fright at the storms and various gales during that voyage, and how they berated that big muzhik for his laziness—this was something no man could write with a pen or tell in a tale.[10] But the muzhik just kept on rowing and rowing, and feeding the generals herring.

Then at last they sighted old Mother-Neva, then the glorious canal named for Catherine, and finally Great Podyacheskaya Street.

When the cooks saw how well-fed their generals were, how pampered-looking, and how happy—they threw up their hands in amazement. The generals drank their fill of coffee, stuffed themselves on sweet rolls, and put on their uniforms. Then they went to the Treasury; and the money they raked in there is something no man could write with a pen or tell in a tale.

---

[9] A very common signature in Russian folk and fairy tales, indicating that the storyteller has become thirsty in the telling of his tale and wouldn't object to a drink.

[10] Another fairy-tale formula.

Nor did they forget the muzhik. They sent him a small glass of vodka and a five-kopeck piece.

Make merry, Muzhik!

1869

THE EAGLE AS
PATRON OF THE ARTS[1]

BY MIKHAIL SALTYKOV

Poets have written many verses about eagles, always in their praise: the eagle's features are beautiful beyond description, his glance is swift, and his flight majestic. He does not fly, like other birds: he either soars or "spread-eagles." Moreover, he stares straight at the sun, and he contends with the thunderclaps. Some poets even endow him with a magnanimous heart. If, for example, they want to sing the praises of a policeman, they invariably compare him to an eagle. They say, "Like an eagle, the officer wearing Badge Number Such-and-Such located the suspect, seized him, and, having heard his statement, pardoned him."

For a long time, I myself believed these panegyrics. I used to think: "Why, now, that's really fine! 'He seized him . . . and pardoned him'!" *Pardoned* him! That's what I found especially fascinating. Whom did the eagle pardon? A mouse. And what is a mouse? So I'd run off hurry-scurry to one of my poet friends and tell him about this latest act of magnanimity on the part of the eagle. And my poet friend would strike a pose, breathe deeply for a moment, and then start belching out verses.

But one day it occurred to me: "Just why did the eagle 'pardon' the mouse? The mouse was scampering across the road on his own business when the eagle saw him, swooped down, crushed him into a bloody lump, and . . .

---

[1]The double-headed eagle was of course the national emblem of the Russian Empire.

pardoned him! Why did *he* pardon the mouse, and not vice versa?

The more I thought about it, the more doubts I had. I began to keep my eyes peeled and my ears perked up. Plainly, something was wrong. In the first place, an eagle certainly doesn't catch mice just in order to pardon them. In the second place, even supposing that the eagle did "pardon" the mouse, it really would have been much better if he had just left him alone. And finally, in the third place, even though he's an eagle—or, for that matter, an arch-eagle—he's still a bird. He is in fact so much a bird that only through a gross misunderstanding could a comparison to him be found flattering—even by a policeman.

And today my ideas on eagles are as follows: eagles are eagles, and that's all they are. They are predatory and carnivorous; but it can be said by way of justification that nature herself fitted them out to be antivegetarians. And since they are, at one and the same time, powerful, long-sighted, swift, and merciless, it is only natural that at the sight of them, all other denizens of the air make haste to hide. But this is owing to fright, and not to rapture—as some of the poets would have it. Also, eagles always live in isolation, in inaccessible places. They do not spend their time dispensing hospitality but in plundering; and when they are not plundering, they doze.

There was once, however, an eagle who got bored with living in isolation, so he said to his eagless, "This is a damned dull life—just the two of us, always together! And you can get feeble-minded from staring at the sun all day."

So he began to ponder. And the more he pondered, the more it seemed to him that it would be good to lead the kind of life the landowners did in the old days. He would assemble a household of menials and live like a king. The crows would report all the nasty gossip; the parrots would turn somersaults for him; the magpie would cook his porridge; starlings would sing paeans in praise of him; the common owls, owlets, and great horned owls would fly night patrols; and the hawks, vultures, and falcons would catch game for him. And he himself would have nothing else to do but be bloodthirsty.

He thought and thought, and finally made up his mind. So one day he summoned a hawk, a vulture, and a falcon, and said to them: "Assemble for me a household of menials such as the landowners had in the old days. They will provide amusement for me, and I will tyrannize over them. That is all."

Having received their orders, these birds of prey flew off in different directions. They got things off to a fast start, with no playing around. First of all, they drove in a whole horde of crows. They herded them in, registered them in the census lists, and gave them tax forms. Now, crows are fertile birds, and docile. But the best thing about them is that they so well represent the "muzhik" class of society. And everybody knows that if the "dear little muzhiks" are on hand, the job is as good as done— except for a few details that are easily managed. And the latter were managed. The corncrakes and loons were organized into a brass band; the parrots were dressed up as buffoons; the magpie, seeing that he was a thief, was given the keys to the Treasury; and the owlets and great horned owls were assigned to fly night patrol. In short, they set up an establishment that no nobleman would have been ashamed of. They didn't even forget the cuckoo: they appointed him soothsayer to the eagless, and built a foundling home for cuckoo orphans.

But scarcely had they put the regulations of the establishment into effect, when they realized that something was lacking. For a long time they puzzled their heads over what it was, and finally they hit on it. In every nobleman's establishment the arts and sciences should be represented; but the eagle's had neither.

Three birds in particular considered this oversight personally offensive: the bullfinch, the woodpecker, and the nightingale. The bullfinch was a clever fellow, and had been whistling since adolescence. He had got his primary education at a school for soldiers' sons, and then become a regimental clerk. Once having learned how to use punctuation marks, he began to publish—without prior censorship—a newspaper called the *Forest Herald*. But he just couldn't make a go of things. Whatever subject he brought up was one he shouldn't have. Whatever he *didn't* bring up was something he not only could have but should have. And for this he kept getting his ears boxed. So he decided: "I'll join the eagle's establishment. What do I care if he orders me to proclaim his fame every morning, so long as I don't get hurt?"

The woodpecker was a modest scholar, and led a strictly solitary life. He never associated with anyone at all. (He was even thought by many to be a hard drinker, like all serious scholars.) Instead, he would sit for whole days on the branch of a pine tree, pecking away. And he pecked out a whole batch of historical articles: "The Genealogy of the Wood-Sprite." "Was Baba-Yaga[2] Married?" "Under Which Sex Should Witches Be Registered in the Census Lists?" and so on. But, peck as he would, he couldn't find a publisher for his pamphlets. And so he decided: "I'll enter the eagle's service as one of his court historians. Maybe he'll have my articles published at the crows' expense!"

As for the nightingale, he couldn't complain about how life had treated him. From time immemorial, he had sung so sweetly that not only the tall, straight pines but even the merchants in the Moscow bazaar had been stirred upon hearing him. All the world loved him, and all the world held its breath and listened as, perched in some thicket, he poured forth his sweet songs. But he was sensual and vain beyond all measure. It was not enough that he made the woods resound with his untrammeled song. It was not enough that he drenched grieving hearts in his music. He kept thinking of how the eagle would hang a necklace of ant eggs around his neck, or decorate his whole breast with live cockroaches;[3] and of how the eagless would arrange secret trysts with him in the moonlight. To make a long story short, the three birds kept pestering the falcon to plead their cause to the eagle.

The eagle listened closely—right through to the end— to the falcon's report on the necessity of introducing the arts and sciences, but he didn't understand it right away. He just sat there clacking his beak and flexing his talons; and his eyes glittered in the sunlight like polished gems. He had never so much as seen a newspaper; he had no interest in Baba-Yaga or other witches; and as for the nightingale, he had heard only one thing about it: that it was a small bird, and not worth soiling one's beak on.

"I dare say you don't know that Bonaparte is dead?" asked the falcon.

"Who is this Bonaparte?"

---

[2]Baba-Yaga, in the Russian fairy tales, is the archetypal witch.

[3]Cf. Note 2 to the preceding story. One type of decoration awarded by the Imperial Government was worn on a ribbon around the neck, another on a broad band across the chest, and so on.

"See what I mean? And that's something worth knowing, too. Some of these days you'll be having guests, and they'll start up a conversation. They'll say, 'That was in Bonaparte's time,' and you'll just look blank. That's not good."

The common owl was called in for advice, and he reaffirmed that the arts and sciences should be introduced into the establishment, since life would then be made interesting for the eagles. And besides, said he, there was nothing shameful about taking an objective view of things. Knowledge is light, but ignorance is darkness. Anybody can eat and sleep. But just try to solve the problem that begins "A flock of geese were flying . . . ," and you're in trouble. In the old days the clever landowners always figured one man who could read and write was worth two illiterates. In other words, they realized that education was useful. Just take the siskin, for example. All his education consists in knowing how to carry a pail of water. But what money they pay for that! I can see in the dark, and for this they have called me wise. You stare at the sun for hours on end without blinking, and what they say about you is: "The eagle is skillful, but he's a nitwit."

"Well, I'm not downright *against* education!" clacked the eagle.

No sooner said than done. The next day a "Golden Age" began in the eagle's establishment. The starlings memorized the anthem, "Education Nourishes Youth." The corncrakes and loons practiced on the trumpet; the parrots worked up some new stunts. Another tax was levied on the crows, under the name of "educational tax"; a cadet corps was founded for the young falcons and young hawks; an *Académie des Sciences* was established for the common owls, the great horned owls, and the owlets; and a penny primer was purchased for each of the young crows. Finally, the oldest starling was made poet laureate under the name of Vasily Kirilych Tredyakovsky,[4] and instructed to make ready for a contest with the nightingale on the following day.

The eagerly awaited day arrived. The new recruits were brought before the eagle and ordered to display their talents.

---

[4] After the famous eighteenth-century poet Vasily Kirillovich Tredyakovsky, one of whose duties as secretary of the Russian Academy of Sciences was to compose odes, paeans, etc., for public ceremonies.

The bullfinch was most successful. Instead of making a speech of welcome, he read a humorous sketch from a newspaper—one so frothy that even the eagle thought he understood it. The bullfinch said that the best thing to do was live high on the hog; and the eagle approved with "That's right!" He said that his retail sales were good, and he didn't care about anything else; and the eagle approved with "That's right!" He said that the servant had a better life than the master, because the master has many worries but the servant doesn't have to worry about the master; and the eagle approved: "That's right!" He said that back when he still had a conscience he went around with no pants, but now that he hadn't one iota of conscience left, he wore two pairs of pants at once; and the eagle approved: "That's right!"

Finally the bullfinch became a bore. "Next!" clacked the eagle.

The woodpecker began by saying that the genealogy of the eagle went back to the Sun; and the eagle confirmed this on his own part, saying, "I heard something like that from my Pop."

"The Sun," said the woodpecker, "had three children: a daughter, the Shark; and two sons, the Lion and the Eagle. The Shark was a harlot; and for this her father imprisoned her in the depths of the ocean. The Lion forsook his father; so the Sun made him sovereign of the wastelands. But the Eagle was a respectful son, so the father established him closer to himself, making him ruler over the realms of the air."

But the woodpecker had hardly pecked his way through the introduction to his learned paper, when the eagle screamed impatiently, "Next! Next!"

Then the nightingale began to sing, and right away he got into trouble. He sang of the joy of the servant upon learning that God has sent him a landowner for a master; he sang of the generosity of the eagles who don't begrudge their servants an occasional tip. But no matter how hard he tried to sound fashionably servile, he couldn't make it jibe with his innate "artistry." He himself was every inch a flunkey (he had even come up with a second-hand white cravat from somewhere, and had his hair tightly curled), but his "art" couldn't be kept within the bounds of servility: it kept bursting out into the open. Sing as he might, the eagle didn't understand him; and that was that.

"What is that nincompoop mumbling about?" he yelled finally. "Call Tredyakovsky!"

Vasily Kirilych was there in a hop, skip, and a jump. He took up the same servile themes, but he spelled them out so plainly that the eagle kept repeating: "That's right! That's right! That's right!" When the contest was over the eagle hung a necklace of ant eggs around Tredyakovsky's neck and, his eyes flashing with wrath at the nightingale, he screamed, "Get that bum out of here!"

This put an end to the nightingale's ambitious efforts. Quickly, they bundled him off to the market and sold him to the Parting Friends Tavern, where to this day he pours his sweet poison into the hearts of those customers so soused that they are feeling "meteoric."

Nevertheless, the pursuit of enlightenment was not abandoned. The young hawks and falcons continued to attend school; the *Académie des Sciences* undertook to publish a dictionary and vanquished half of the letter "A"; and the woodpecker completed the tenth volume of his *History of Wood-Sprites*. But the bullfinch lay low. From the very first day he had sensed that all this commotion about culture would come to a speedy and ungracious end; and apparently his premonitions were well-founded.

The thing was that the common owl and the falcon, who had assumed the direction of these educational activities, had made a big mistake: they had conceived the idea of teaching the eagle himself to read and write. They used the phonetic method, which is easy and interesting; but for all their strenuous efforts, after a year the eagle was still signing his name "Easel" instead of "Eagle," with the result that no self-respecting creditor would accept a promissory note with that signature on it. But an even bigger mistake was this: following the general pattern of pedagogues, neither the owl nor the falcon gave the eagle any time off. The owl was constantly breathing down his neck and screeching, "A. . . , B. . . , C. . . ." And the falcon, just as constantly, kept harping that if the eagle didn't learn the first four rules of arithmetic, he couldn't divide up the game plunder.

"Let's suppose you steal ten goslings. If you give two to the police clerk and eat one, how many are left?" the falcon would ask reproachfully.

The eagle could never figure it out, and so he kept still. But with each passing day he harbored more and more wrath in his heart against the falcon.

Relations became strained, and a group of intriguers were quick to take advantage of the situation. The vulture headed up the plot, and he soon got the cuckoo to join him. The latter started whispering to the eagless, "They're undoing our lord and master with all this teaching. They're torturing him."

And the eagless began to taunt the eagle, "Oh, you scholar! You professor, you!"

Then, by means of their joint efforts, they aroused "dark desires" in the hawk.

And one morning at daybreak, when the eagle had just waked up, the owl crept up on him from behind, as usual, and began buzzing: "R. . . , S. . . , T—"

"Go away, you pest!" the eagle growled—but rather gently.

"Your Eagleship, please be so kind as to repeat after me: 'U. . . , V—' "

"Go away, I said."

"W. . . , X. . . , Y—"

In one instant the eagle turned on the owl and ripped him in two.

An hour later, knowing nothing of what had happened, the falcon came back from his morning's hunting. "Here's a problem for you," he said. "Supposing the night's plunder comes to seventy-two pounds of game. If we divide it into two equal parts—one for you and one for all your menials—how much will you get as your share?"

"All of it," answered the eagle.

"Come, now—be serious," objected the falcon. "If the answer had been 'all of it,' I wouldn't even have asked you the question."

It wasn't the first time the falcon had given him such a problem to solve; but this time the tone he adopted struck the eagle as intolerable. It made his blood boil to think that when he had said "all of it," his servant had dared to contradict him. Now, it is well known that an eagle, when his blood starts to boil, can't tell the difference between pedagogical methods and a treasonous plot. And this eagle acted accordingly.

However, after liquidating the falcon, he stipulated, "But the *des Sciences Académie* will remain as before."

Once again the starlings sang "Education Nourishes Youth," but it was plain to everybody that the Golden Age was drawing to a close. Up ahead loomed the darkness of ignorance, with its inseparable companions: civil discord and strife of all kinds.

The strife began with the appearance of two claimants, the vulture and the hawk, for the position of the deceased falcon. And since both rivals concentrated their attention exclusively on their own interests, public affairs were relegated to second place and gradually fell into neglect. In a month's time, not a trace of the recent Golden Age remained. The starlings got lazy; the corncrakes began to play out of tune; the magpie stole left and right; and the crows got so far behind on their taxes that mass floggings had to be resorted to. Things even reached the point where the eagle and eagless were being served spoiled meat.

In order to clear themselves of any responsibility for this mess, the hawk and the vulture teamed up temporarily, and put all the blame on enlightenment. Education, said they, is no doubt useful, but only when times are right for it. Our grandfathers got along without education, and so can we.

By way of proving that all the harm came from education, they began discovering plots; and those plots always involved a book of some kind—if only a prayer book. Then came a spate of searches, investigations, and trials. . . .

"That's all!" rang out from on high. It was the eagle. Enlightenment had run its course.

Such a silence now reigned all through the establishment that one could even hear the slanderous whisperings as they crawled along the ground.

The first victim of the new climate of ideas was the woodpecker. God knows the poor little bird was innocent! But he knew how to read and write, and that was ample grounds for his indictment.

"Do you know how to use punctuation marks?"

"Yes, not only the usual ones but such rare ones as quotation marks, hyphens, and parentheses. I always use them conscientiously."

"And can you tell the feminine gender from the masculine?"

"Yes, I can. I wouldn't confuse them even in the darkness of night."

That settled it. They put him in chains and imprisoned him in a hollow tree for life. And the next day he died there, having been eaten alive by ants.

This business of the woodpecker was scarcely over when

it was followed by a pogrom in the *Académie des Sciences*. However, the owlets and great horned owls defended themselves stoutly; they didn't like the idea of giving up the well-heated apartments provided for them by the government. They said they weren't pursuing the sciences in order to popularize them but rather to protect them from the evil eye. But the vulture at once punctured this subterfuge by asking, "Why have science at all?" This question took them by surprise, and they couldn't answer it. So they were sold off separately to truck gardeners, who stuffed them as scarecrows and set them out to protect their vegetable gardens.

At the same time the penny primers were taken away from the young crows and mashed into a pulp from which playing cards were made.

The longer it went on, the worse it got. The owls were followed by the starlings, the corncrakes, the parrots, the siskins. . . . Even the deaf black grouse was suspected of "having opinions" because he kept quiet all day and slept at night.

The establishment dwindled. There remained only the eagle and eagless, together with the hawk and the vulture, while in the distance was the horde of crows, who kept on multiplying quite shamelessly. And the more they multiplied, the higher their back taxes piled up.

Then the hawk and the vulture, not knowing whom else to destroy (the crows didn't count), set out to destroy each other, and all on the grounds of education. The hawk informed on the vulture, reporting that he was reading a prayer book in secret; and the vulture falsely accused the hawk of keeping a songbook concealed in a hollow tree.

The eagle was quite at a loss what to do.

But at that moment, History itself stepped up its flow in order to put an end to all this turmoil. Something most extraordinary occurred. The crows, noticing they had been left untended, suddenly wondered: "Let's see. What was it the penny primer said on this subject?" But before they could rightly remember, the whole flock instinctively took off and flew away.

The eagle started after them, but it was no go: the easy life in the style of the landowners had made him so flabby he could scarcely flap his wings.

Then he turned to his wife and said, "Let this be a lesson to all eagles!"

But just what the word "lesson" meant in this case—whether education was bad for eagles, or eagles were bad for education, or both at once—he didn't say.

1886

THE DEATH OF A
CIVIL SERVANT

By Anton Chekhov

One fine evening an equally fine administrative clerk, Ivan Dmitrich Chervyakov, was sitting in the second row of the orchestra and watching a performance of *The Chimes of Normandy* through his opera glasses. He watched, and felt that he was at the very height of bliss. But suddenly. . . . (In stories, one often encounters this "But suddenly. . . ." The authors are right: life is so full of surprises!) But suddenly his face wrinkled up, his eyes rolled, his breathing stopped. . . . He lowered the opera glasses, bent forward, and . . . *Kerchoo!* He sneezed, as you have seen.

Now, sneezing is not forbidden to anybody anywhere. Muzhiks sneeze, and police chiefs, and sometimes even privy councillors. Everybody sneezes. Chervyakov was not at all embarrassed. He wiped his face with his handkerchief and, like the polite man he was, looked around to see whether he had disturbed anyone with his sneezing. But then he found reason enough to be embarrassed. He noticed that the little old man sitting in front of him, in the first row, was vigorously wiping his bald pate and the back of his neck with his glove, and muttering something. Chervyakov recognized the little old man as Civil Service General Brizzhalov, of the Ministry of Railroads.

"I splattered him!" Chervyakov thought. "He's not my boss, but it's still awkward. I'll have to apologize."

He coughed, leaned forward in his seat, and whispered into the general's ear, "Pardon me, Your Excellency, for splattering you. . . . It was an accident. . . ."

"No harm done. Forget it."

"Please forgive me! I . . . I didn't mean to."

"Oh, *do* sit back! I can't hear what they're saying!"

Chervyakov became flustered. He smiled stupidly, and
went back to watching the play. He watched, but he felt
no more bliss. Anxiety began to torment him. During
intermission he approached Brizzhalov, stalled around
until he had conquered his shyness, and then mumbled,
"Your Excellency, I splattered you. . . . Forgive me. . . .
Honestly. . . . I didn't mean. . . ."

"Oh, leave off it! I'd already forgotten it, but you keep
harping away!" said the general, his lower lip twitching
with impatience.

"He says he's forgotten, but there's a mean look in his
eye," thought Chervyakov, glancing at the general suspi-
ciously. "He doesn't even want to talk about it. I ought to
explain to him that I hadn't the slightest intention of . . .
that it was just a law of nature. If I don't, he'll think I
intended to spit on him, as the saying goes. He may not
think so right now, but he will later. . . ."

When he got home, Chervyakov told his wife about his
stupid behavior. She took the incident too lightly, it
seemed to him. She was merely startled; and then, when
she found out that Brizzhalov was "somebody else's boss,"
she relaxed.

"But you should still go and apologize," she said, "or
he'll think you don't know how to behave in public."

"But that's just it! I did apologize! But he acted strange
—didn't say one sensible word. Besides, there was no
time to talk it over."

The next day Chervyakov put on a new uniform dress
coat, got a haircut, and went to Brizzhalov's to explain.
. . . As he entered the general's reception room, he saw
a whole lot of petitioners, and in their midst the general
himself, who had already begun to hear requests. When
he had dealt with several petitioners, the general looked
up and noticed Chervyakov.

"Last night at the Arcadia Theater," the clerk began to
report, "if Your Excellency will recall, I sneezed and
accidentally splattered you. . . . Please for—"

"Such stupid trifles! What is this, anyway?" And the
general turned to the next petitioner. "What can I do for
you?"

"He doesn't want to talk about it!" thought Chervyakov,
growing pale. "That means he's angry. . . . No, I can't
leave things like this. . . . I'll explain to him. . . ."

When the general had concluded his audience with the last petitioner and was headed for his private chambers, Chervyakov followed him and mumbled, "Your Excellency! If I dare to disturb you, Excellency, it is only, I can assure you, out of a feeling of repentance. . . . What I did was not done on purpose—please take note of that!"

The general made a face as if about to cry, and waved his hand. "Why, sir, you're simply mocking at me!" he said, and vanished behind the door.

"What kind of mockery does he mean?" thought Chervyakov. "I'm not mocking him in the slightest! He may be a general, but he doesn't understand. And if that's the way it is, I won't make any more explanations to that braggart. The devil with him! I'll write him a letter, but I won't try to see him in person. Never again!"

Such were Chervyakov's thoughts as he went home. But he didn't write any letter to the general. He thought and thought, but he couldn't think up a letter. So the next day he had to go in person to explain.

"The reason I came and bothered you yesterday, Your Excellency," he mumbled, when the general looked up at him with questioning eyes, "was not, as you deigned to say, to mock at you. I was apologizing because, when I sneezed, I splattered you. I had no idea of mocking at you. Would I dare mock at you? If people like me started mocking at others, there would be no respect for . . . for persons of—"

"Get out!" barked the general, who had suddenly turned purple and started to tremble.

"W-what, sir?" Chervyakov asked in a whisper, going faint with fright.

"Get out!" repeated the general, stamping his feet.

In Chervyakov's stomach, something broke loose. Seeing nothing and hearing nothing, he back-pedaled to the door, went out into the street, and shuffled away. . . . Arriving home like a sleep-walker, he lay down on the sofa without taking off his dress coat, and died.

1883

A CALCULATED MARRIAGE

(A Novel in Two Parts)

BY ANTON CHEKHOV

Part One

At the widow Mymrina's house, in Five Dogs Lane, a wedding supper is in progress. Twenty-three people are at the table, eight of whom are passing up the food, complaining of feeling "urpy," and nodding their heads drowsily. The candles, the lamps, and a twisted chandelier borrowed from a tavern are blazing so brightly that one of the guests sitting at the table, a telegrapher, squints affectedly and keeps bringing up, apropos of nothing, the subject of electrical lighting. He prophesies a great future for this kind of illumination, and for electricity in general; but the others are nonetheless rather disdainful toward what he has to say.

"Electricity. . . ." mutters the nuptial godfather, staring stupidly at his plate. "In my opinion electric lighting is only a swindle! They stick a little piece of coal in there and think they're fooling us! No, friend, if you're going to give me lighting, don't make it a little piece of coal. Give me something substantial, something you can light up, something a man can get hold of! Give me flame—understand? Flame that's natural, not mental!"

"If you'd ever seen an electric battery and what it's made of," says the telegrapher, showing off, "you'd think different."

"I don't even want to see one. It's a swindle. . . . They're

149

bilking us ordinary folks—squeezing the last drop out of us. Oh, we know them and their kind! . . . But as for you, Mr. Young Man—I don't have the honor of knowing your name—instead of taking sides with swindlers, you'd do better to drink up and pour drinks for others."

The bridegroom, Aplombov, a young man with a long neck and bristly hair, says in a raspy tenor voice, "I entirely agree with you, Papa. Why start these intellectual conversations? Me, I can talk about all kinds of discoveries in a scientific way! But that's for another time, after all. And what is your opinion, *ma chère?*" the bridegroom asks the bride, sitting next to him.

Dashenka, the bride, on whose face are inscribed all the virtues but one—a capacity for thinking—flushes, and says, "He wants to show off his education, and he's always talking about things a body can't understand no how."

"Praise be to God we've lived all our lives without education, and now, thank the Lord, we're marrying off our third daughter to a decent man," says Dashenka's mother from the other end of the table, sighing and turning to the telegrapher. "But if to your way of thinking we act uneducated, why come here? Better you should go visit some of your educated friends!"

Silence descends. The telegrapher is flustered. He had never expected the talk about electricity to take such an unlikely turn. The silence is of a hostile kind. It seems to him a symptom of general displeasure, and he thinks he must justify himself.

"Tatyana Petrovna," he says, "I have always respected your family. And if I mentioned electric lighting, that still doesn't mean I did it out of pride. I'll be glad to drink up. . . . With all my heart I have always hoped Dashenka would get a good husband. In these times, Tatyana Petrovna, a good husband is hard to find. Today everybody is out to get married for material gain—for money."

"You're insinuating!" says the bridegroom, getting red in the face and blinking his eyes.

"I'm not insinuating at all," says the telegrapher, feeling a bit frightened. "I'm not speaking of present company. I just meant . . . in general . . . oh, good Lord! Everybody knows you married for love! The dowry was a mere trifle. . . ."

"No! It was not a mere trifle!" the insulted mother

of the bride objects. "Talk away, but watch what you say! Along with the thousand rubles, we're giving three coats, bed linen, and all this furniture! Just you try and find a dowry like that anywhere else!"

"But I didn't mean anything. . . . Certainly the furniture is good. . . . I just said that because he was offended, as if I had insinuated—"

"Just make sure you *don't* insinuate!" says the bride's mother. "We've always had a regard for you because of your parents. And we invited you to the wedding, and now you're saying all kinds of insulting things. . . . Besides, if you knew Yegor Fedorych was marrying for money, why did you keep quiet about it? You should have come to us like one of the family, and said, 'The thing is, he just wants to feather his nest.' As for you, *batyushka"*— and she turns to the bridegroom, her tearful eyes blinking—"It's a sin! I raised her and reared her the best way I could. She's been the apple of my eye, this dear little child of mine. And now you . . . just to feather your nest. . . ."

"And you believed that slander?" says Aplombov, getting up from his side of the table and nervously plucking at his bristly hair. "My most humble thanks! *Merci* for such an opinion! And you, Mr. Blinchikov!" He turns to the telegrapher. "For all that you are an acquaintance of mine, I won't allow you to commit such outrages in somebody else's home. Kindly get out!"

"What's that you said?"

"Kindly get out! I want you to be as honorable a man as I am. In a word, kindly get out!"

"Lay off it! That's enough!" The bridegroom's friends try to cool him down. "Is it worth it? Sit down! Lay off it!"

"No! I want to prove he has no real right on his side! It was for love that I entered into the state of matrimony. Why are you still sitting there? I don't understand! Kindly get out!"

"I didn't mean anything. . . . Why, I . . ." says the bewildered telegrapher, getting up from the table. "I just don't understand. . . . All right, then, I'll go. . . . But first give me back the three rubles you borrowed from me to buy the piqué vest. I'll have one more quick one, and then go. But first pay me what you owe me."

There is prolonged whispering among the bridegroom and his friends. The latter give him three rubles in small change. He indignantly throws it at the telegrapher. And he, after a long search for his uniform cap, bows, and leaves.

Such is the way a harmless discussion of electricity can sometimes end up. However, the supper is now almost over. . . . Night is falling. The well-bred author curbs his fantasy with a strong bit, and throws a dark veil of mystery over immediate events.

Rosy-fingered Dawn finds Hymen still in Five Dogs Lane. But now the gray morn arrives, and gives the author abundant material for

The Second and Final Part

A gray morning in autumn. It is not yet eight o'clock, but there is unusual commotion in Five Dogs Lane. Perturbed policemen and doormen are running along the sidewalks; kitchen maids, chilled to the bone, are crowding about at the gates, with expressions of great bewilderment on their faces. . . . From all the windows, inhabitants look out. And women's heads crane out from the open window of the laundry, with temples and chins squeezed against other temples and chins.

"Either it's snow, or it's . . . no telling what it is!" voices are saying.

Something white that looks very much like snow is swirling in the air, from the ground to the rooftops. The pavement is white. The streetlamps, the roofs, the doormen's benches by the gates, the shoulders and caps of passersby—all are white.

"What happened?" a laundrywoman asks some doormen as they run by.

By way of an answer, they wave their hands and keep running. . . . They themselves don't know what it is. But finally one doorman comes slowly along, gesticulating and talking to himself. Obviously, he has been at the scene of the incident and knows everything. "What happened, dearie?" the laundrywomen ask him from the window.

"Disgruntlement," he replies, "at Mymrina's house, where they had the wedding yesterday. They cheated the bridegroom. Instead of a thousand, they only gave him nine hundred."

"And what did he do?"

"Blew his top. 'I'll this and I'll that,' says he. Then he ripped up the featherbed in a rage, and shook the eiderdown out the window. . . . Just look how much down there is! Just like snow!"

"They're coming! They're coming!" voices cry out.

The procession is moving away from the widow Mymrina's house. First come two policemen with worried expressions. Behind them strides Aplombov in a knitted woolen overcoat, and a top hat. On his face is written, "I am an honorable man, but I don't let anybody swindle me!"

"The law will soon show you what kind of a man I am!" he mutters, turning from time to time to look back.

He is followed by Tatyana Petrovna and Dashenka, both in tears. Bringing up the rear is a doorman carrying a book, who is trailed by a crowd of small boys.

"Why are you crying, young wife?" the laundrywomen ask Dashenka.

"The eiderdown—such a pity!" her mother answers for her. "A hundred pounds of it, my dears! And what beautiful down! Hand-picked bit by bit, and not one feather in it!"

The procession rounds the corner, and quiet descends upon Five Dogs Lane. The eiderdown drifts through the air until evening.

1884

THE CULPRIT

BY ANTON CHEKHOV

A short, exceedingly skinny little peasant in patched pants and a shirt made of mattress ticking stands before the investigating magistrate. His hairy, pockmarked face and his eyes, almost concealed by thick, overhanging brows, have an expression of grimness. A mop of tangled hair that has not been combed for ages makes him look even grimmer in a spiderish way. He is barefoot.

"Denis Grigoryev!" the magistrate begins. "Come up closer and answer my questions. On the morning of the seventh of July—that is, this month—the railroad watchman Ivan Semyonov Akinfov, while walking the tracks, came upon you, at the 141st milepost, unscrewing a nut by which the rails are fastened to the crossties. I have the nut here. It was on your person when he arrested you. Is all that true?"

"Whas'at?"

"Did all this happen just as Akinfov stated?"

"Sure enough."

"Very well. Now, why were you unscrewing the nut?"

"Whas'at?"

"Stop saying 'Whas'at?' and answer the question. Why were you unscrewing the nut?"

"If I didn't need it, I wouldn't've unscrewed it," Denis says in a rasping voice, glancing up at the ceiling.

"What need did you have for it?"

"For the nut? We make sinkers out of 'em."

"Who is 'we'?"

"Us folks. . . . The Klimovo muzhiks, I mean."

"Listen, fellow! Don't try playing dumb with me! Just talk sense. No use making up lies about sinkers."

"I never lied in my whole life, and now you say I'm lying," mutters Denis, blinking his eyes. "Could a man do without a sinker, Your Honor? If you put live bait or a worm on the hook, would it go down to the bottom without a sinker? . . . Sure, I'm lying!" Denis smiles sarcastically. "What damned good is bait if it floats on the surface? Perch and pike and burbot will always go for a baited hook on the bottom. But if it's floating on top, a bullhead's about the only fish that'll take it, and not much of the time at that. . . . Anyway, we don't have no bullheads in our river. . . . That's a fish likes plenty of room."

"Why are you telling me all this about bullheads?"

"Whas'at? On account of you asked me yourself. Up our way the gentlemen fish that way too. Even a little boy wouldn't try to catch fish without a sinker. 'Course a man with poor wits might go fishing without a sinker. There's no rules for fools. . . ."

"So you are saying you unscrewed this nut in order to make a sinker out of it?"

"What else? Not to play knucklebones with!"

"But for a sinker you could have used a piece of lead, a bullet . . . perhaps a nail of some kind."

"You don't just find lead on the road—you have to buy it. And a nail's no good. No, you won't find nothing better than a nut. It's heavy, and it's got a hole in it."

"He's still playing dumb! As though he'd been born yesterday, or had dropped out of the sky! Don't you understand, you numskull, what this unscrewing can lead to? If the watchman hadn't kept a sharp eye out, the train might have gone off the tracks, and people would have been killed! You would have *killed* people!"

"God forbid, Your Honor! Why kill people? Are we unbaptized, or some kind of criminals? Glory be to God, sir! We've lived all our lives and never once had such a thought—much less kill anybody? Save us, Queen of Heaven, and have mercy on us! What are you saying, sir?"

"And what do you think causes train wrecks? Just unscrew two or three nuts, and you'll have your train wreck!"

Denis laughs sarcastically and squints at the magistrate in disbelief. "Humph! All these years all of us in the village have been unscrewing nuts, and the Lord's protected us. And now you talk about train wrecks and killing people! . . . If I'd hauled off a rail, say, or laid a log 'crossways on the tracks, maybe then the train would've gone off 'em. . . . But a nut, pshaw!"

"But the nuts hold the rails to the crossties! Try to get that through your head!"

"Oh, we understand that. . . . After all, we don't unscrew all of 'em. . . . We leave some. . . . We use our heads. . . . We understand."

Denis yawns and makes the sign of the cross over his mouth.

"Last year a train was derailed here," the magistrate says. "Now it's plain to see why it was."

"Beg pardon?"

"I said it is now plain to see why the train was derailed last year . . . Now I understand it."

"That's why you're educated—you who protect us— so you can understand. . . . The Lord knew who to give understanding to. . . . Here you've gone and figured out how and what. . . . But the watchman, who's just a muzhik like us without any understanding at all, he grabs a man by the collar and drags him in. . . . A person should figure it out first and then do the dragging. But, as the saying goes, a muzhik's got a muzhik's brains. . . . Your Honor, write down that he hit me in the jaw twice—and in the chest, too."

"When your house was searched, one more nut was found. . . . Where did you unscrew it, and when?"

"You mean the one that was under the little red clothes chest?"

"I don't know where you were keeping it, but they found it. When did you unscrew it?"

"I didn't. Ignashka—that's cross-eyed Semyon's son— he gave it to me, I'm talking now about the one that was under the clothes chest. But the one in the sledge out in the yard—me and Mitrofan unscrewed that one together."

"What Mitrofan?"

"Mitrofan Petrovich. Didn't you ever hear tell of him? He makes fish nets and sells 'em to the gentlemen. He needs lots of nuts for that—figure about ten for a net."

"Listen . . . Article 1081 of the Penal Code states that any willful damage to a railroad that might expose to danger the trains traveling on said railroad, provided the perpetrator was aware that such damage might cause an accident. . . . Do you understand? 'Was aware!' And you could not help being aware of what this unscrewing leads to . . . is punishable by hard labor in a prison camp."

"Well, you know best. . . . We're just ignorant folks. . . . How could we understand?"

"You understand the whole thing! You're lying, faking!"

"Why should I lie? Just ask in the village, if you don't believe me. . . . A bleak's the only fish you can catch without a sinker. A gudgeon, now, that's the worst fish of all. But even a gudgeon won't bite if you don't have a sinker."

"And now tell me about bullheads," the magistrate says with a smile.

"We don't have no bullheads in our river. . . . If we cast our lines without any sinker, right on top of the water with a butterfly for bait, maybe a chub will nibble, but mostly not."

"All right, now. Be quiet."

There is a silence. Denis shifts from one foot to the other, stares at the desk covered with green baize, and blinks his eyes hard, as though he were looking at the sun instead of the cloth. The magistrate writes rapidly.

"Can I go now?" Denis asks, after being quiet for a while.

"No. I must take you into custody and send you to prison."

Denis stops blinking and, raising his shaggy eyebrows, looks doubtfully at the official. "What do you mean, 'prison'? Your Honor! I can't spare the time! I have to go to the fair. And I have to get three rubles from Yegor for lard. . . ."

"Be quiet! Don't bother me!"

"To prison! . . . If I'd done something, I'd go. But just like that . . . for no reason at all! . . . For what? I didn't steal anything—not that I know—and I wasn't fighting. If you're thinking I'm behind in my taxes, Your Honor, don't believe the elder. . . . Ask the permanent member of the board. . . . That elder, he's not a Christian at all. . . ."

"Be quiet!"

"I'm being quiet as it is," Denis mutters. "The elder lied in the assessment—I swear he did! There're three of us brothers: Kuzma Grigoryev, then Yegor Grigoryev, and me—Denis Grigoryev. . . ."

"You're bothering me. . . . Hey, Semyon!" the magistrate shouts. "Take him away!"

"There're three of us brothers," Denis is muttering, as

two husky soldiers seize him and take him out of the room. "A brother's not supposed to answer for his brother . . . Kuzma don't pay, so you, Denis, have to answer for him . . . Judges! Our master, the late general, he died—God rest his soul! If he hadn't, he'd show you judges what's what! . . . You should use some brains when you judge people—not do it any which way. . . . Flog a man if you like, but for some reason—when it's right and fair. . . ."

1885

THE EXCLAMATION MARK

A Christmas Story

BY ANTON CHEKHOV

On Christmas Eve, Yefim Fomich Perekladkin, a collegiate secretary, went to bed feeling insulted and even
abused. "Get thee behind me, Satan!" he roared at his
wife, when she asked why he was so gloomy.

The fact was that he had just returned from a party
where many things had been said that were unpleasant and
insulting to him. At first the guests had begun talking about
the usefulness of education in general. Next they had
passed naturally to the educational qualifications of the
confraternity of government clerks, making a great many
pitying remarks, criticisms, and even gibes with respect
to the low echelons. And then, as so often happens at
social gatherings among Russians, they went from general
matters to personalities.

"Take yourself, for example, Yefim Fomich," said one
young man, turning to him. "You have a rather good
position. . . . But what kind of education do you have?"

"None, sir. But our work doesn't require an education,"
Perekladkin replied meekly. "You have to use correct penmanship, that's all."

"And where did you learn to use correct penmanship?"

"I just got into the habit, sir. . . . In forty years of
service you can pick up a knack of a thing. Of course it
was hard at first, and I made mistakes. But then I got
into the habit, and it went along fine. . . ."

"And how about the punctuation marks?"

"They don't give me any trouble. I put them in correctly."

159

"Hm," said the young man, somewhat at a loss. "But a habit is by no means the same thing as an education. It's not enough that you put in the punctuation marks correctly—not enough, sir! You must be fully aware of what you're doing when you put them in. Oh, yes, sir! As for your unconscious, reflexive penmanship, it's not worth a tinker's damn! It's mechanical production, and nothing more."

Perekladkin remained silent, and even smiled meekly. (The young man was the son of a state councillor, and was himself entitled to the tenth rank.) But now, as he went to bed, he became all anger and indignation.

"For forty years I've served," he thought, "and nobody ever called me a simpleton. But now—is it possible? —what criticisms! 'Unconscious'! 'Irreflexive'! 'Mechanical production'! . . . Oh, the devil take you! But it just may be that I still understand more than you, even if I didn't go to your universities!"

When he had mentally poured out upon his critic all the curses he knew, and had warmed himself under his blanket, Perekladkin began to calm down. "I know . . . I understand," he thought as he began to grow drowsy. "I don't put in a colon where a semicolon is needed. Therefore, I am fully aware. I understand. Yes, I do. . . . So there, young man! . . . First you have to live and work a while, *then* you can judge your elders. . . ."

Perekladkin was almost asleep. Before his closed eyes, through a throng of dark, smiling clouds, a fiery comma sped like a meteor. After it came another, and then another. Soon the entire background, extending without bounds in his imagination, was covered with thick clusters of whizzing commas. . . .

"Just take those commas, for example," thought Perekladkin, feeling in his limbs the sweet numbness of imminent sleep. "I understand them very well indeed. . . . I can find a place for each one of them, if you want, and . . . with full awareness, not just any which way. . . . Just test me, and you'll see. . . . Commas are put in various places, both where they are needed and where they are not. The more muddled the document is, the more commas it needs. Commas are placed before 'which' and 'that.' If the document lists the names of officials, each of them must be set off by a comma. . . . I *know!*"

The golden commas began to spin around and drifted away. Fiery periods sped in to replace them.

"And a period is put at the end of a document. . . . A period is also placed where it's necessary to take a long breath and look up at the person who is listening. After all long passages, there must be a period, so that the secretary, when he reads it aloud, doesn't drool. . . . In no other places are periods used."

The commas came skittering back. . . . They mixed in with the periods, swirled about, and Perekladkin saw before him a huge throng of semicolons and colons. . . .

"I know them, too," he thought. "When a comma isn't enough, and a period is too much, a semicolon is required. Also, a semicolon is always put before 'but' and 'consequently.' . . . And colons? Colons are used after the words 'decreed' and 'resolved.' . . ."

The semicolons and colons faded. It was now the turn of the question marks. They emerged from the clouds and began to dance the can-can. . . .

"That's a fine thing, indeed—the question mark! But even if there were a thousand of them, I'd find a place for all of them. They are always used when an inquiry must be made, or a question is asked about a document. 'What disposition was made of the sums remaining on hand for such-and-such a year?' Or 'Does not the police department find it possible, with regard to the said Ivanov, to . . . ?' And so on."

The question marks nodded their hook-shaped heads in approval, and then promptly—as though by command—straightened themselves up and became exclamation marks.

"Hm! . . . That punctuation mark is often used in letters. 'Dear Sir!' or 'Your Excellency—Father and Benefactor!' . . . But when is it used in documents?"

The exclamation marks stretched themselves even taller and stood there waiting. . . .

"In documents they are used when . . . er . . . uh. . . . How is that again? Hm! . . . Come to think of it, when *are* they used in documents? Wait. . . . Just let me think. . . . Hm!"

Perekladkin opened his eyes and rolled over on his other side. But no sooner had he closed his eyes again, than the exclamation marks reappeared against the dark background.

"The devil take them! . . . When *is* it they're supposed to be used?" he thought, trying to drive the uninvited guests out of his imagination. "Is it possible I have forgotten? Either I have forgotten, or . . . or I never used any of them. . . ."

Perekladkin began to review in his memory the contents of all the official documents he had copied in his forty years of service. But no matter how hard he thought, or how he wrinkled his brow, in his whole past he could not find a single exclamation mark.

"Now what do you think of that? I've been writing for forty years, and I've never once used an exclamation mark. . . . Hm. . . . But, damn it all, when *are* they used?"

From behind the row of fiery exclamation marks, the evilly grinning mug of his young critic appeared. . . . The exclamation marks themselves smiled, and merged into one big exclamation mark.

Perekladkin shook his head and opened his eyes. "What the devil!" he thought. "I have to get up for early mass to-morrow morning, and I can't get that damned foolishness out of my head! . . . Phooey! . . . But when *is* it used? There's habit for you! There's 'getting the knack'! A whole forty years, and not one exclamation mark, eh?"

Perekladkin crossed himself and closed his eyes, but immediately opened them again: the big exclamation mark was still standing there against the dark background. . . .

"Confound it, I won't get any sleep at all tonight! Marfusha!" he asked his wife, who often bragged of the fact that she had completed boarding school. "Do you happen to know, *dushenka*, when exclamation marks are used in official documents?"

"Of course I know! I didn't study seven years at boarding school for nothing! That punctuation mark is used after salutations, exclamations, and expressions of rapture, indignation, joy, wrath, and other feelings."

"So that's it," thought Perekladkin. " 'Rapture, indignation, joy, wrath, and other feelings.' . . ."

The collegiate secretary brooded. . . . For forty years he had copied documents—he had copied thousands and tens of thousands of them—but he couldn't remember one line expressing rapture, indignation, or anything of the sort. . . .

" 'And other feelings,' " he thought. "But are feelings necessary in official documents? Documents can be written by a person with no feelings at all. . . ."

The mug of his young critic once again looked out

from behind the fiery exclamation mark and grinned evilly. Perekladkin got up and sat on the edge of the bed. His head was aching, and cold sweat came out on his brow. . . . In the corner, the ikon lamp glowed affectionately, the furniture had a polished, festive appearance—everything exuded warmth and the presence of a feminine touch. But the poor clerk felt cold and comfortless, as though he were coming down with typhus.

And now the exclamation mark was no longer in his mind's eye but standing right there in front of him in the bedroom near his wife's vanity table, and winking at him in mockery.

"A writing machine! A machine!" the phantom whispered, blowing a draught of cold air at him. "A block of wood with no feelings!"

The clerk pulled the blanket over his head; but even under the blanket he could still see the phantom. He buried his face in his wife's shoulder; but it loomed up from behind her shoulder. . . . Poor Perekladkin was tormented all night. And even in the morning, the phantom did not go away. He saw it everywhere: in his boots, as he was putting them on; in a saucer of tea; and in his Order of Stanislaus. . . .

"And other feelings. . . ," he thought. "It's true that I've never experienced any feelings. Right now, for instance, I'm going to my chief's house to sign the guest book by way of Christmas greetings. . . . But is *that* done with feeling? . . . It's all meaningless. . . . A greeting machine. . . ."

When Perekladkin went out into the street and hailed a cab, it seemed to him that instead of a cabbie an exclamation mark came driving up.

When he walked into his chief's antechamber, he saw the same exclamation mark in place of a doorman. . . . And all these things kept speaking to him of rapture, indignation, wrath. . . . The penholder also looked like an exclamation mark. Perekladkin picked it up, dipped the pen in the inkwell, and signed: "Collegiate Secretary Yefim Perekladkin!!!"

And as he wrote those three exclamation marks, he was rapturous, he was indignant, he was joyous, and he boiled with wrath. "That for you! Take that!" he muttered, bearing down hard on the pen.

The fiery exclamation mark was satisfied, and vanished.

1885

THE SPEECHMAKER

BY ANTON CHEKHOV

One fine morning they were burying Collegiate Assessor
Kirill Ivanovich Vavilonov, who had died from those two
diseases so widespread in our country: a venomous wife,
and alcoholism. As the funeral cortege was proceeding from
the church to the cemetery, one of the deceased's colleagues, a certain Poplavsky, got into a cab and rushed
to the lodgings of his friend Grigory Petrovich Zapoykin,
a young man but already rather popular. Zapoykin, as
many of my readers know, possesses a rare talent for
making impromptu speeches at weddings, anniversaries,
and funerals. He can speak at any old time at all: when
he's half-awake, half-starving, dead drunk, or feverish.
His words flow smoothly and evenly (like water from a
drain pipe) and in great abundance. There are far more
pathetic terms in his oratorical vocabulary than there are
cockroaches in any tavern. He always speaks eloquently
and at great length, so that sometimes—especially at
merchants' weddings—the assistance of the police must be
sought in order to stop him.

"I've come to fetch you," began Poplavsky, having
found him at home. "Get dressed right now, and let's
be on our way. One of the bunch from my office has died,
and we're just now seeing him off to the Great Beyond.
Somebody has to say a few words of farewell—some kind
of rubbish—and we're counting on you, old boy. If
somebody unimportant had died, we wouldn't bother you.
But this one was a departmental secretary—a pillar of the
office, so to speak."

"Oh, the secretary!" Zapoykin yawned. "You mean that
drunk?"

"Yes, the drunk. There'll be pancakes and hors d'oeuvres, and you'll get cab fare. Come along, old chap! Give us some kind of fancy Ciceronian claptrap at the graveside, and you'll get a hearty thanks."

Zapoykin readily agreed. He tousled his hair, assumed a melancholy mien, and went out with Poplavsky.

"I knew that secretary friend of yours," he said, as they got into the cab. "He was one of the foxiest old scoundrels you could find anywhere, God rest his soul!"

"Come now, Grisha. You mustn't sling mud at the dead."

"*Aut mortuis nihil bene,* of course. But he was still a swindler."

The two friends caught up with the funeral procession and joined it. The deceased was being carried along slowly, so that before reaching the cemetery they managed three times to duck into a tavern and grab a quick drink for the repose of his soul.

At the cemetery, the prayer for the dead had already been recited. In obedience to the custom, the deceased's mother-in-law, his wife, and his sister-in-law wept copiously. When the coffin was lowered into the grave, his wife even cried out, "Let me in with him!" But she didn't follow her husband into the grave, apparently having bethought herself of his pension.

Zapoykin waited until everything had quieted down. Then he stepped forward, cast a glance over all his listeners, and began: "Can we believe our own eyes and ears? Is it all not just a bad dream—this coffin, these tear-stained faces, this weeping and wailing? Alas, it is not a dream, and our eyes do not deceive us. He who, only a short time ago, looked so hearty, so youthfully fresh and pure; he whom only a short while ago we watched as, like unto the indefatigable bees, he brought his honey to the communal hive of the national order and harmony; he who . . . that same one has now become dust—a material mirage. Implacable Death laid its stiffening hand on him at a time when, despite his stooping age, he was still full of the bloom of strength and radiant hopes. An irreplaceable loss! Who can ever take his place? We have many good civil servants, but Prokofy Osipych was unique. To the very bottom of his soul he was dedicated to his honorable duty. He never spared his strength, he never slept at night, he was selfless and incorruptible. . . . How he scorned those who, to the prejudice of the national interest, attempted to bribe him—those who tried by means of seductive creature comforts to lure him into betraying his duty! Yes, before our very eyes Prokofy Osipych distributed his salary among his most needy comrades. And just now, you yourselves have heard the wails of the widows and orphans supported by his alms. Dedicated to his official duty and to good works, he partook of no joys in his lifetime, and even denied himself the happiness of a family life. As you are all aware, he was a bachelor until the end of his days. And who will take his place among us as a comrade? As though it were right now, I can see his compassionate, clean-shaven face turned toward us with a kindly smile. As though it were right now, I can hear his gentle, tender, friendly voice. Peace to thy ashes, Prokofy Osipych! Rest in peace, noble and honorable toiler!"

Zapoykin continued, but his listeners had begun to whisper. They all liked the speech, and it had wrung a few tears out of them; but there was a good deal in it that seemed strange. In the first place, it was incomprehensible why the speaker called the deceased Prokofy Osipych, whereas his name was Kirill Ivanovich. In the second place, everybody knew that the deceased had battled all his life with his wife, to whom he had been married in proper form; hence he could not be called a bachelor. In the third place, he had had a bushy red beard, and had never shaved in all his life, so that it was incomprehensible why the speaker referred to his face as "clean-shaven."

"Prokofy Osipych!" the speechmaker continued. "Your face was unattractive—even ugly. You were gloomy and stern. But we all knew that beneath that visible exterior there beat an honest, friendly heart!"

Soon the listeners began to notice something strange in the speaker himself. He kept staring in one direction, shifted about nervously, and his shoulders began to jerk.

"I say!" he said, looking about him in terror. *"He's alive!"*

"Who's alive?"

"Why, Prokofy Osipych! He's standing over there by the headstone!"

"But *he* wasn't the one that died! It was Kirill Ivanovich!"

"What? You yourself told me the secretary had died!"

"Kirill Ivanovich *was* the secretary. It's true that Prokofy Osipych used to be the secretary. But two years ago he was transferred to the second department as head clerk."

"Oh, only the devil can understand you!"

"Why did you stop? Keep on talking—it's getting embarrassing!"

Zapoykin turned toward the grave again, and with all his former eloquence, resumed his interrupted speech. Sure enough, standing there near the headstone was Prokofy Osipych, an old civil servant with a clean-shaven face. He was looking at the speechmaker and frowning angrily.

On the way back from the burial ceremony, the other civil servants asked Zapoykin with a laugh, "What on earth made you do that? You buried a living man."

"That was not good, young man," grumbled Prokofy Osipych. "Your speech may have been all very well for a dead man, but for a live one it was a jeer. For goodness' sake, what were you saying? 'Selfless, incorruptible, never takes bribes.' Why, things like that can be said about a living man only in mockery! And besides, sir, no one asked you to expatiate upon my face! Unattractive and ugly it may well be—but why put my physiognomy on public display? It's insulting, sir!"

1886

WHO IS TO BLAME?

By Anton Chekhov

My uncle, Pyotr Demyanych, a skinny, bilious collegiate assessor very much resembling a stale smoked salmon with a stick struck through it, was getting ready to go to the high school where he taught Latin, when he noticed that the binding of his grammar book had been nibbled by mice.

"I say there, Praskovya," he said, going into the kitchen and addressing the cook. "How do we happen to have mice around here? For heaven's sake! Yesterday they chewed holes in my top hat, and now they've desecrated my grammar book. The next thing you know, they'll start eating my clothes!"

"What am I supposed to do about it?" answered Praskovya. "I didn't bring them into the house."

"*Something* has to be done! You could get us a cat, couldn't you?"

"We already have one, but what's he good for?" And Praskovya pointed to a corner, where a white kitten, thin as a sliver, was curled up asleep beside a twig broom.

"Why isn't he good for anything?" asked Pyotr Demyanych.

"He's still young and stupid. He can't be as much as two months old yet."

"Hm . . . Then he should be taught. It would be better for him to be learning than just lying there."

Having said that, Pyotr Demyanych sighed a care-worn sigh and walked out of the kitchen. The kitten raised his head lazily, watched him leave, and again closed his eyes.

The kitten was awake, though, and thinking. About

168

what? Being unfamiliar with real life, and having no store of impressions, he could think only instinctually, and envision life only according to those notions he had inherited, together with his flesh and blood, from his tiger ancestors. (*Vide* Darwin.) His thoughts were on the order of daydreams. His feline imagination pictured something like the Arabian desert, across which moved shadows very much resembling Praskovya, the stove, the broom. Among the shadows there suddenly appeared a saucer of milk. The saucer grew paws, and began to move and manifest an inclination to flee. The kitten pounced and, in a swoon of bloodthirsty voluptuousness, sank his claws into it. . . . When the saucer had vanished into the mist, a piece of meat appeared, dropped by Praskovya. With a cowardly squeak, the meat started to run away; but the kitten pounced, and sank his claws into it. . . . Each one of the young daydreamer's visions had as its starting point pounces, claws, and teeth. . . .

The soul of another is a mystery, and a cat's soul even more so. Nonetheless, just how close the foregoing images are to the truth, is evident from the following incident. Under the spell of his daydreams, the kitten suddenly gave a start, looked with glittering eyes at Praskovya and, his fur bristling, pounced, sinking his claws into the hem of her skirt. Obviously, he was a born mouser, fully worthy of his bloodthirsty ancestors. Fate had intended him to be the terror of cellars, pantries, and granaries. And had it not been for education. . . . But let us not get ahead of the story.

On his way home from the school, Pyotr Demyanych went into a variety store and bought a mousetrap for fifteen kopecks. After dinner he put a piece of chopped meat on the hook and placed the trap under the sofa, where there was a pile of students' assignment papers that Praskovya used for household purposes. Exactly at six o'clock in the evening, when the venerable Latinist was sitting at his desk and correcting papers, a sudden *clunk!* came from under the sofa—so loud that my uncle started and dropped his pen. Without delay, he went to the sofa and retrieved the trap. A neat little mouse about the size of a thimble was sniffing the wire of the cage and trembling with fright.

"Aha!" muttered Pyotr Demyanych. And he glared so balefully at the mouse that you'd have thought he was about to give him an "F." "You're caught, you vile creature! Just you wait! I'll show you how to eat grammar books!"

Having had his fill of glaring at his victim, Pyotr Demyanych put the mousetrap on the floor and shouted, "Praskovya! I've caught a mouse! Bring the kitten here!"

"R-r-right away!" Praskovya called back. And a moment later she came in, holding in her arms the descendant of tigers.

"Fine!" muttered Pyotr Demyanych, rubbing his hands. "We're going to teach him. . . . Put him down by the mousetrap. . . . That's it. . . . Let him smell it and look at it. . . . That's the way. . . ."

The kitten looked with astonishment at my uncle, then at his armchair; sniffed the mousetrap with a baffled air; and then—no doubt having been frightened by the bright lamplight and all the attention being paid to him—took off in terror toward the door.

"Stop!" shouted my uncle, seizing him by the tail. "Stop, you scoundrel! You've been frightened by a *mouse*, you idiot! Look: it's a mouse. Come, look! Well? *Look, I tell you!*"

Pyotr Demyanych grabbed the kitten by the scruff of the neck and shoved his nose against the mousetrap.

"Look, you little bastard! Pick him up, Praskovya, and hold him. . . . Hold him against the door of the trap. . . . When I let the mouse out, you let him go at the same time, understand? Let him go at exactly the same time. All right?"

My uncle assumed a conspiratorial expression and raised the door. . . . The mouse emerged hesitantly, sniffed the air, and then darted under the sofa. The liberated kitten hoisted his tail in the air, and ran under the desk.

"It got away! It got away!" shouted Pyotr Demyanych, making a ferocious face. "Where is he, the villain? Under the desk? Just you wait. . . ."

My uncle dragged the kitten out from under the desk and shook him in the air. . . .

"You scum!" he muttered, pulling him by the ear. "Take that! And that! Will you ever flunk like that again? You s-s-scum!"

The next day, Praskovya once again heard the shout: "Praskovya, I've caught a mouse! Bring the kitten here!"

After his humiliation of the day before, the kitten had gone to hide under the stove, and had not come out all night. When Praskovya had dragged him out and, carrying him by the scruff of the neck into the study, had deposited him in front of the mousetrap, he trembled all over and meowed plaintively.

"All right," Pyotr Demyanych commanded. "Let him get the lay of the land first. Let him look and sniff. Look and learn, you! Stop, damn you!" he shouted, noticing that the kitten was backing away from the mousetrap. "I'll thrash you! Hold on to him by the ear. That's it. . . . Now put him down in front of the door."

My uncle slowly raised the door. . . . The mouse whisked right under the kitten's nose, ricocheted off Praskovya's arm, and ran under the bookcase. The kitten, meanwhile, sensing that he was at liberty, made a desperate leap and hid under the sofa.

"He's let another mouse go!" bellowed Pyotr Demyanych. "Do you call that a cat? He's an abomination! Just plain trash! He needs to be thrashed—thrashed right in front of the mousetrap!"

When the third mouse was caught, the kitten trembled all over at the sight of the mousetrap and its tenant, and scratched Praskovya's hand. . . . After the fourth mouse, my uncle lost all self-control and gave the kitten a kick. "Get rid of this nasty thing!" he said. "I want him out of the house today! Just dump him somewhere. He isn't worth a tinker's damn!"

A year went by. The thin, sickly kitten developed into a solid, sagacious tomcat. One night he was prowling through the backyards on his way to a lovers' tryst. He was already near his destination when suddenly he heard a rustling sound, and then saw a mouse scampering from the horse-trough toward the stables. . . . Our hero bristled, arched his back, began to hiss and, shaking all over, pusillanimously took to flight.

Alas! Sometimes I feel that I'm in the ludicrous position of the fleeing tomcat. Like the kitten, I had the honor in my time of studying Latin with my uncle. Today, whenever I chance to see some work of classical antiquity, instead of going into wild raptures about it I begin to recall the *ut consecutivum*, the irregular verbs,

the sallow-gray face of my uncle, and the ablative absolute. . . . I go pale, my hair stands on end, and like
the tomcat, I take off in ignominious flight.

1886

A DEFENSELESS CREATURE

BY ANTON CHEKHOV

No matter how bad his attack of gout had been during
the night, nor how raw it left his nerves, Kistunov always
went to his office in the morning and began promptly to
receive the petitioners and clients of the bank. But he
looked enfeebled and weary, and spoke in a scarcely
audible voice, like a dying man.

"What can I do for you?" he said (one such morning)
to a layd petitioner in an antediluvian coat who from the
rear resembled a large dung beetle.

"Just consider, Your Excellency!" she began very
rapidly. "My husband, Collegiate Assessor Shchukin, was
sick for five months. And while he was lying in bed—if
you will pardon the expression—and taking treatments,
Your Excellency, he was retired for no reason at all.
And when I went to get his pay, understand, they deducted
twenty-four rubles and thirty-six kopecks from it. 'For
what?' I asked them. 'Because,' said they, 'he borrowed
from the employees' fund, and other clerks cosigned for
him.' How could that be? As if he could borrow any
money without my approval! That's impossible, Your
Excellency! And why, I ask you? I'm a poor woman. I
barely make a living by taking in boarders. I'm weak and
defenseless. . . . I take insults from everybody, and don't
hear a kind word from anybody. . . ."

The lady began to blink and reached into her coat
pocket for her handkerchief. Kistunov took her petition
and began to read it. "Excuse me," he said with a shrug,
"but what's this all about? I simply don't understand.
It is obvious, Madame, that you have come to the wrong
place. Actually, your petition has nothing whatsoever

173

to do with us. You'll have to go to the agency where
your husband was employed."

"What do you mean, my good sir? I've been to five
places already," said Madame Shchukina, "and they
wouldn't even look at my petition. I was about ready to
lose my mind. But my son-in-law, Boris Matveich—my
thanks to him, and may God give him health!—suggested
that I come to see you. *'Mamasha,'* he said, 'go to see Mr.
Kistunov. He's a man of influence. He can do everything
for you! . . . Help me, Your Excellency!"

"I'm sorry, Madame, but there's nothing at all we
can do for you. You must try to understand. Your husband, so far as I can make out, was an employee of the
Department of Military Medicine. But our institution is
completely private and commercial. We run a bank. Surely
you can understand *that* much!"

Kistunov shrugged again, and turned to a gentleman
in military uniform with a swollen cheek.

"Your Excellency!" Madame Shchukina cried out plaintively. "I have a doctor's certificate to prove that my
husband was sick. Here it is. Please look at it!"

"Wonderful!" Kistunov said irritably. "I quite believe
you. But I must repeat: this has nothing to do with us.
It's strange—even ridiculous! Can it be possible that your
husband doesn't know what agency you should go to?"

"He doesn't know anything, Your Excellency. He just
kept saying, 'It's none of your business! Get out of here!'
That's all he said. . . . But then, whose business is it? After
all, it's my back that's bearing the burden. Mine!"

Kistunov once again turned to Madame Shchukina and
began explaining the difference between the Department
of Military Medicine and a private bank. She listened
to him attentively, nodded her head in agreement, and then
said, "Yes, yes. I understand, sir. In that case, Your Excellency, have them pay me only fifteen rubles. I don't
have to have all of it right away."

"Oof!" sighed Kistunov, throwing his head back.
"There's just no way to get it into your head! If you'd
just realize that to come to us with this kind of claim
is as strange as, let us say, trying to get a divorce at
a drugstore or an assay office. You may have some money
coming to you, but what do we have to do with it?"

"Your Excellency, I'll be eternally grateful to you!
Have pity on me, an orphan!" Madame Shchukina im-
plored him tearfully. "I'm a weak, defenseless woman. . . .

I'm exhausted to the point of death. I'm suing my boarders and fussing over my husband and running this way and that taking care of the household, and on top of it all I'm fasting and my son-in-law is out of work. . . . It's a wonder I can still eat and drink. I can hardly stand on my own two feet. . . . I didn't get a wink of sleep last night."

Kistunov's heart began to flutter. With an expression of acute suffering, and with his hand on his heart, he once again began to explain to Madame Shchukina. But his voice failed him. . . .

"You must excuse me," he said, with a wave of the hand, "but I can't speak to you any longer. My head is spinning. You are holding us up, and wasting your own time. *Oof!* Aleksey Nikolaich," he said, turning to one of his assistants, "please explain things to Madame Shchukina."

When he had dealt with all his other petitioners, Kistunov returned to his private office and signed some dozen documents; meantime, Aleksey Nikolaich was still trying to cope with Madame Shchukina. Sitting in his office, Kistunov listened for a long time to the two voices: the monotonous, restrained bass of Aleksey Nikolaich, and the plaintive, whining voice of Madame Shchukina.

"I'm a weak, defenseless woman," Madame Shchukina was saying, "a sick woman. And if the truth be told, there's not a healthy bone in my body. I can hardly stand on my own two feet, and I don't have any more appetite. I drank some coffee this morning, but I didn't enjoy it at all."

Aleksey Nikolaich, for his part, went on explaining the difference among agencies, and the complex system of routing documents. But he soon wore out, and a bookkeeper replaced him.

"An amazingly headstrong woman!" Kistunov exclaimed, nervously twisting his fingers and repeatedly going to the water decanter. "She's an idiot! A nitwit! She wore me clear out, and now she's wearing them out, damn her! *Oof!* My heart is fluttering!"

A half-hour later he rang, and Aleksey Nikolaich came in.

"How is it going?" Kistunov asked wearily.

"Can't get a thing into her head, Pyotr Aleksandrych! I'm simply exhausted. We're at sixes and sevens."

"I just can't stand the sound of her voice. . . . I'm ill. . . . I can't bear it."

"Call the doorman, Pyotr Aleksandrych, and tell him to get her out of here."

"Oh, no!" exclaimed Kistunov in alarm. "She'd start screaming. There are lots of apartments in this building, and the Lord only knows what people might think we were up to. . . . Just try once more to explain it to her somehow, my boy."

A minute later the low hum of Aleksey Nikolaich's voice could again be heard. A quarter of an hour later, it was replaced by the strong tenor of the bookkeeper.

"R-r-remarkably vile!" exclaimed Kistunov in exasperation, his shoulders jerking convulsively. "As stupid as they come, damn her! It feels like my gout is kicking up again. . . . And my headache. . . ."

In the next office, Aleksey Nikolaich, having finally reached the breaking point, rapped his finger on his desk and then against his forehead. "In short," he said, "what you have on your shoulders is not a head but a block of—"

"Well, I must say!" exclaimed the lady, insulted. "Go beat on your own wife, you . . . you nothing! Don't be so free with your hands!"

Giving her a wrathful look, enraged enough to swallow her, Aleksey Nikolaich said in a quiet, smothered voice: "Get out!"

"W-w-what?" Madame Shchukina suddenly screeched. "How dare you? I'm a weak woman—defenseless. I won't allow it! My husband is a collegiate assessor. You pipsqueak! I'll go to Dmitry Karlych, the lawyer, and you'll have no position left! I've had three boarders sentenced! You'll fall on your knees to me for those impudent words! I'll go to see your general! Your Excellency! Your Excellency!"

"Get out of here, you plague!" hissed Aleksey Nikolaich.

Kistunov opened the door and looked into the office. "What is it?" he asked in a querulous voice.

Madame Shchukina, red as a lobster, was standing in the middle of the room and, her eyes rolling, was poking her fingers into the air. Some bank clerks were standing along the sides of the room and, also red, and obviously embarrassed, were looking at one another in confusion.

Madame Shchukina threw herself on Kistunov. "Your Excellency! That one there—that very one—that one" (she pointed to Aleksey Nikolaich) "rapped with his finger on his forehead, and then on the desk. . . . You

ordered him to look into my case, but he is mocking at me!
I'm a weak woman, defenseless. . . . My husband is a
collegiate assessor. And I myself am a major's daughter!"

"All right, Madame," Kistunov sighed. "I'll take care
of it. I'll take steps. . . . Just go on out, now. Later. . . ."

"But when will I get it, Your Excellency? I need the
money now!"

With a trembling hand, Kistunov wiped his brow, sighed,
and once again began to explain. "Madame, I have already
told you: this is a bank—a private commercial establishment. So what do you want of us? And please *do* get it
through your head that you're bothering us!"

Shchukina listened to him and sighed. "All right, all
right," she agreed. "But you, Your Excellency, do me
the favor—I'll be eternally grateful to you. Be my benefactor and protect me. If the doctor's certificate isn't
enough, I can get one from the police station. Make them
pay me my money!"

Kistunov's head began to swim. He blew out all the
air that was in his lungs, and sat down on a chair, exhausted. "How much do you want?" he asked in a weak
voice.

"Twenty-four rubles and thirty-six kopecks."

Kistunov reached into his pocket and took out a
wallet, from which he took a twenty-five-ruble bill and gave
it to the old lady. "Take this, and leave!"

She wrapped the money up in a little handkerchief, hid
it, and, crinkling her face into a saccharine, delicate, even
coquettish smile, asked: "Your Excellency, can't my husband return to his job?"

"I'm leaving . . . I'm sick," said Kistunov in a faint
voice. "My heart is fluttering badly."

When he left, Aleksey Nikolaich sent Nikita for laurel
cherry drops; and all of them, having taken twenty drops
apiece, went back to work. But Madame Shchukina sat
in the waiting room for another two hours, talking with
the doorman and waiting for Kistunov to return.

She was back again the next day.

1887

THE TALE OF
IVAN THE FOOL

*and His Two Brothers, Semyon the
Soldier and Taras the Big-Belly, and
of His Sister, Malanya the Deaf-
Mute, and of the Old Devil and the
Three Imps*

BY LEO TOLSTOY

In a certain kingdom in a certain land there once lived a
rich peasant. And the rich peasant had three sons—
Semyon the Soldier, Taras the Big-Belly, and Ivan the
Fool—and one daughter, Malanya the Deaf-Mute. Semyon the Soldier went to war to serve the Tsar, Taras the
Big-Belly went to a merchant's in the city to become a
trader, and Ivan the Fool stayed home with his sister to
work in the fields.

Semyon the Soldier won high rank and an estate, and
married a nobleman's daughter. His pay was big and his
estate was big, but he still couldn't make ends meet.
Whatever he took in, his high-born wife squandered it
all, and they never had any money.

When Semyon went to his estate to collect the income, his steward said to him, "We don't have anything
to earn money with. We don't have any horses, or milk

cows, or other livestock, or tools, or a plow or harrow. We must get these first—then there'll be an income."

So Semyon the Soldier went to his father. "You are rich, Father," he said, "but you have never given me anything. Give me a third of what you have, and I'll add it to my estate."

But the old man said, "You never made any contribution when you were here at home. Why should I give you a third? It wouldn't be fair to Ivan and the girl."

Semyon said, "But after all, he's a fool and she's deaf and dumb. What good is it to them?"

Then the old man said, "It's up to Ivan."

And Ivan said, "Well, why not? Let him take it."

So Semyon the Soldier took the portion of his father's property and added it to his own estate, and then went off to serve the Tsar again.

Taras the Big-Belly also acquired a lot of money, and married a merchant's daughter. But his income still wasn't enough; so he came to his father and said, "Give me my share."

But the old man was not willing to give Taras his portion, either. "You never contributed anything when you were here at home. Everything in this house was brought in by Ivan. Besides, it wouldn't be fair to him and the girl."

But Taras said, "What good is it to him? He's a fool. He'll never get married, because nobody will have him. And a girl who's a deaf-mute doesn't need anything, either. Come on, Ivan," he said. "Give me half of the grain, and as for the livestock, all I want to take is the big gray stallion. You can't use him for plowing, anyway."

Ivan laughed. "Well, why not?" he said. "I'll go and put a halter on him."

So they gave Taras his portion too. He hauled the grain into town, and led away the gray stallion. Ivan was left with one old gray mare to go on with his farming as before—and to feed his father and mother and Malanya.

II

Now the Old Devil was most annoyed that the three brothers had not quarreled over the divvying-up, but had parted affectionately. So he summoned the three imps.

"Now listen to me," he said. "There are three brothers: Semyon the Soldier, Taras the Big-Belly, and Ivan the Fool. They all should have quarreled, but instead they're living in peace and on good terms. The Fool upset all of my plans. I want the three of you to go out and take on the three of them. Get them so worked up they'll tear each other's eyes out. Can you do that?"

"We can do it," the three imps said.

"How will you go about it?"

"Like this," they said. "First we'll make them so poor they won't have a crust of bread to nibble on. Then we'll throw them together in a heap, and they'll start fighting."

"All right," the Old Devil said. "I see you know your business. Get going. And don't come back until all three of them are at loggerheads. Otherwise I'll skin all three of you alive."

The imps went off to a swamp to discuss how they should go at this business. They argued and argued, each one trying to get the easiest job. Finally they decided to draw straws to determine who would take on whom. And if one finished his job first, he was supposed to help the others. They drew straws, and then set a time when they would again meet in the swamp to find out who had finished his job, and whom he should help.

When the time came, the imps assembled in the swamp as agreed. Each one began to explain how things were going with him. The first imp started telling about Semyon the Soldier.

"My job is coming along fine," he said. "Tomorrow Semyon will be going home to his father."

His brothers began to question him. "How did you manage it?" they asked.

"Well," he said, "the first thing I did was to instill so much bravery into Semyon that he promised his Tsar he would conquer the whole world. So the Tsar made him a commanding general and sent him to do battle with the king of India. The battle lines were drawn up. But during the night I dampened all the gunpowder that Semyon's army had. Then I went to the king of India, and for him I made more straw soldiers than can possibly be imagined. When Semyon's soldiers saw the straw soldiers coming at them from every side, they took fright. Semyon gave orders to fire, but the artillery and the rifles wouldn't discharge. Semyon's soldiers panicked and fled like sheep, and the king of India defeated them.

"Now Semyon the Soldier is in disgrace; the people have taken away his estate, and they intend to execute him tomorrow. I have only one day's work left—to get him out of prison so he can run home. My job will be finished then. Now tell me, which one of you two needs help?"

The second imp—the one assigned to Taras—began telling about his work. "I don't need any help," he said. "My job has come along very well, too. Taras won't hold out for more than another week. The first thing I did was to make his belly still bigger and fill him with envious greed. He developed so much envy for the things other people had, that he wanted to buy whatever he saw. He spent all his money buying immense quantities of things, and he's still buying—except that now it's with borrowed money. By this time he has a load of debts. A week from now his payments will be due, but I'll turn all his merchandise into manure. He won't be able to pay, and he'll go home to his father."

Then they began to question the third imp about Ivan. "How is your work coming along?" they asked.

"To tell the truth," he said, "it isn't going very well. The first thing I did was to spit in his jug of kvass so he'd have a stomach-ache. Then I went to the field he was plowing, and pounded the earth until it was as hard as stone, so he wouldn't be able to plow it. I was sure he couldn't. But, fool that he is, he came with his wooden plow and began making a furrow. He groaned with the pain in his stomach, but he kept right on plowing. I broke that one plow, but the idiot went home, rigged up another one, and started plowing again. I crawled under the ground and grabbed onto the plowshare, but there was no holding it back: the Fool leaned hard on the plow, and the plowshare was sharp—it cut my hands all over. By now he's plowed almost the whole field; there's only one little strip left. Come and help me, fellows," he said, "because if we don't get the better of him, all our labor will be lost. If that fool keeps on farming, none of them will be really up against it, because he'll feed both of his brothers."

III

Ivan had plowed almost all of the fallow land. Only one little strip was left, and he went out to finish it. His stomach ached, but the plowing had to be done.

Ivan let the harness ropes go slack, flipped the plow over, and started plowing. He had just made one furrow and headed back when the plow began to drag as if it was caught on a root. Actually, it was the imp, who had twined his legs around the plowshare and was holding it back. That's funny, Ivan thought. There wasn't any root there before, but now there is.

He reached down into the furrow and felt something soft. He grabbed it, and pulled it out. It was black, like a root; but on that root something was wriggling. Lo and behold! a live imp!

"Just look at you!" said Ivan. "How disgusting!"

He raised his hand, and was about to smash the imp on the plow handle, but the imp squealed: "Don't hit me! I'll do whatever you want!"

"What will you do for me?"

"Anything you want—just tell me."

Ivan scratched himself. "My belly aches," he said. "Can you fix it?"

"Yes," said the imp.

"Well then, fix it."

The imp bent over and scratched around in the furrow with his claws. He scratched around some more, then he pulled out a little three-pronged root and handed it to Ivan. "Here," he said, "Whenever anybody eats one of these little roots, all his pains go away."

Ivan took it, tore it apart, and swallowed one of the rootlets. His stomach-ache vanished immediately.

The imp began to plead again. "Let me go," he said. "If you do, I'll jump into the earth and never walk on top of it again."

"Well, why not?" said Ivan. "I don't care what you do, God knows."

No sooner had Ivan mentioned God than the imp sank down into the earth like a stone into water, and nothing remained but a hole. Ivan stuck the other two roots in his cap and set about finishing his plowing. When he had plowed the rest of the strip, he flipped the plow over and went home.

He unharnessed the mare, and went into the hut. There sat his older brother, Semyon the Soldier, and his wife— eating supper. Semyon's estate had been taken away from him; he had barely managed to escape from prison; and he had come running home to live with his father.

When Semyon saw Ivan he said, "I've come to live with you. Feed me and my wife until a new position opens up for me."

"Well, why not?" said Ivan. "You're welcome to live here."

He was about to sit down on the bench, but the high-born lady objected to his smell. "I simply cannot eat," she said, "at the same table with a stinking peasant."

And Semyon the Soldier said, "My lady says you don't smell good. You'd better go eat in the hallway."

"Well, why not?" said Ivan. "Anyway, it's time for the night watch. I have to put the mare out to pasture."

He took some bread, picked up his coat, and went out for the night watch in the pasture.

IV

Semyon the Soldier's imp, having finished his job that night, came looking for Ivan's imp to help him get the better of the Fool. He came to the plowed field and looked and looked for his brother, but found only a hole in the ground. Well, he thought, it looks as though my brother ran into trouble, so I'll have to take his place. And the plowing is all done, so I'll have to get the better of the Fool while he's mowing the hay.

The imp went to the meadow and flooded the entire crop of hay so that it was all covered with mud. At day-break, Ivan returned from his night watch, sharpened a scythe, and went to the meadow to mow. He had only swung the scythe a couple of times when it became dull and in need of sharpening again. Ivan struggled and struggled, but finally he said, "Enough of this. I'll go home and get the whetstone and bring it out here with me. And I'll bring along a loaf of bread. Even if it takes me a week of hard work, I'm not leaving until this hay is mowed."

The imp heard him, and thought, "This fool is a tough nut to crack. I'll have to try some other tricks."

Ivan came back, whetted the scythe, and began to mow. The imp crawled into the uncut hay and began grabbing the scythe by the heel, driving the tip of the blade into the ground. It was hard going for Ivan, but he mowed all of the hay except one small patch in a bog. The imp crawled into the bog, thinking to himself, "Even if I get my paws cut off, I won't let him finish mowing."

Ivan went into the swamp. He could see that the grass there wasn't thick; and yet he couldn't cut through it. He grew angry and started swinging with all his might. The imp began to give up—he just couldn't get out of the way fast enough on the backswing. Seeing it was no use, he hid himself in a bush. Ivan swung the scythe and grazed the bush, cutting off half the imp's tail.

When he had finished mowing the hay, Ivan told his sister to rake it while he went to mow the rye.

He went to the rye field with his sickle; but the bobtailed imp had got there first and tangled up the rye so badly that the sickle wouldn't cut. Ivan went back, brought a reaping-hook, and started cutting down the rye with that. He reaped all of it.

"Now," he said, "it's time to go to work on the oats."

The bobtailed imp heard him and thought, "I didn't get the better of him on the rye, but I will on the oats. Just wait till morning!"

The next morning the imp hurried out to the oat field, but the oats were already cut. Ivan had harvested them at night. The imp was furious. He said to himself, "That Fool has cut me up and worn me out. Not even in war did I ever see such calamities. He never sleeps, damn him! You just can't keep up with him. But now I'll get into the shocks and rot all of them for him."

So the imp went up to a shock of rye, crawled in among the sheaves, and began rotting them. He warmed them up, but he warmed himself at the same time, and dozed off.

Meantime, Ivan harnessed the mare and went with his sister to bring in the rye. He came to that particular shock where the imp was sleeping and began pitching the sheaves onto the cart. He pitched up two of them, stuck his fork in again—and jabbed the imp right in the rear end! He raised up the fork, and lo and behold! on the prongs was a live imp—and a bobtailed one at that—

wriggling, making horrible faces, and trying to get off the hook!

"Just look at you!" Ivan said. "How disgusting! Are you back again?"

"I'm not the same one," the imp said. "That was my brother. And I used to be with your own brother Semyon."

"Well," said Ivan, "whoever you are, you're going to get the same thing he got." And he was about to smash him on the edge of the hayrack when the imp began to plead with him.

"Let me go!" he said. "I won't bother you any more, and I'll do whatever you want me to."

"And what can you do?"

"Well," he said, "for one thing I can make soldiers out of almost anything."

"But what are they good for?"

"Why, for whatever you want. They can do anything."

"Can they play tunes?"

"Oh, yes!"

"Well then, make some."

Then the imp said, "Take that sheaf of rye there and shake it over the ground, bottom down, and then say: *By my bondman's decree, let his sheaf cease to be. And let there be as many soldiers as there are straws in thee.*"

Ivan took the sheaf and shook it over the ground, uttering the words the imp had told him to say. The sheaf burst apart and turned into soldiers, with a drummer and buglers marching in front.

Ivan laughed. "Just look at that!" he said. "How clever! Just dandy! The girls will enjoy it."

"Well, then," the imp said, "let me go now."

"No," said Ivan, "I'll make them out of straw. That way, the grain won't be wasted. Show me how to turn them back into a sheaf. Then I'll thresh it."

So the imp told him: "Just say: *Let there be as many straws as there are soldiers now. By my bondman's decree, let this sheaf once more be.*"

Ivan said the words, and the sheaf reappeared.

"Now let me go," the imp said.

"Well, why not?"

Ivan hooked him onto the edge of the hayrack, took hold of him with one hand, and pulled him off the pitchfork. "God be with you," he said.

As soon as he mentioned God, the imp sank into the

ground like a stone into water, and nothing remained but a hole.

Ivan went home, and there he found his other brother, Taras, sitting at supper with his wife. Taras the Big-Belly hadn't managed to pay his debts, and had run home to his father. When he saw Ivan he said, "What do you say, Ivan? Can you feed me and my wife until I get back on my feet?"

"Well, why not?" said Ivan. "You're welcome to live here."

He took off his coat and sat down at the table. But the merchant's daughter said: "I can't eat at the same table with the Fool. He reeks," said she, "of sweat."

And Taras the Big-Belly said, "Ivan, you smell bad. You'd better go eat in the hallway."

"Well, why not?" said Ivan. He took some bread and headed out the door. "Besides," he said, "it's time to pasture the mare for the night."

V

That night Taras's imp came to help his brothers get the better of Ivan the Fool. He came to the plowed field and looked and looked for them, but there wasn't anyone there—just a hole in the ground. He went to the hayfield, and in the bog he found a tail, and near a shock of rye he found another hole. "Well," he told himself, "it's plain to see that they ran into trouble. I'll have to take their place and get to work on the Fool."

The imp went looking for Ivan. But Ivan had already finished up the work in the harvest fields and was in the grove cutting down trees. (Ivan's two brothers had begun to feel cramped living together, so they had told the Fool to keep the hut for himself and go out and fell some trees and build new houses for them.)

The imp hurried to the grove, crawled up into the branches of a tree, and began to hinder Ivan at his work. Ivan had undercut a tree so it would fall clear, and then chopped through it. But it fell the wrong way and got caught in some branches. He cut off a pole, pried the tree loose, and finally managed to bring it down. He started felling another tree, and the same thing happened: he struggled and struggled, and barely managed to free it. He went to work on a third tree, and again the same thing happened.

Ivan had intended to cut down about fifty young trees; but night settled over the farm before he had even brought down a dozen. And he was exhausted. Steam rose from him and spread through the woods like a fog, but still he would not quit. He undercut one more tree, but then his back began to ache so painfully that he couldn't stand it. He drove his axe into the tree and sat down to rest.

When the imp saw that Ivan had stopped working, he was delighted. Well, he thought, he's worn out—he'll give up now, and I can get a rest, too.

He sat down astride a branch, rejoicing. But Ivan got up, pulled out his axe, and hauled off and hit the tree from the other side with such force that it immediately began to sway, and then crashed down. The imp was caught off guard; he couldn't get his leg free in time. The branch broke off, and trapped the imp by his paw.

Ivan had begun stripping the tree when, lo and behold! a live imp!

Ivan was amazed. "Just look at you!" he said. "How disgusting! Are you back again?"

"I'm not the same one," he said. "I was with your brother Taras."

"Well, whoever you are, you're going to get the same thing he got!"

Ivan brandished his axe, and was about to beat the imp with the butt end.

"Don't hit me!" he pleaded. "I'll do whatever you want."

"And what can you do?"

"Well," he said, "for one thing I can create money for you—as much as you want."

"Well, then," said Ivan, "make some."

So the imp showed him how. "Take a leaf from this oak tree," he said, "and rub it in your hands; gold will fall to the ground."

Ivan took some leaves and rubbed them; a shower of gold fell on the ground. "This is dandy," he said, "for playing games with children."

"Then let me go," the imp said.

"Well, why not?" He took his pole and pried the imp free, saying, "I don't care what you do, God knows."

No sooner had he mentioned God than the imp sank into the ground like a stone into water, and nothing remained but a hole.

VI

The brothers had built their houses and were living separately. Meanwhile, having finished with the harvest work and brewed some beer, Ivan invited his brothers to celebrate with him. But they wouldn't come. "We are not accustomed," they said, "to joining in the celebrations of peasants."

So Ivan invited some peasants and their wives. He himself drank heartily, grew tipsy, and went out into the street where people were singing and dancing. He went up to them and told the women to sing a song in his praise. "Then," he said, "I'll give you something you've never seen before in your life." The women laughed, and sang a song praising him. When they had finished they said, "Well, let's have it!"

"I'll bring it," he said, "right now." And he grabbed a seed bag and ran off to the woods.

"He really is a fool!" the women said, laughing. And they forgot about him. But behold! Ivan was running back, carrying the seed bag full of something.

"Should I give it out?"

"Yes, give it out!"

Ivan took a handful of gold and threw it at the women. Lord, how they rushed to pick it up! And up came the men, scrambling and fighting over it. One old woman was almost crushed to death.

Ivan laughed. "Oh, you fools!" he said. "Why crush the old granny? Take it easy—I'll give you more." And he began to scatter more of it. They scrambled for the gold and Ivan emptied the whole bag.

Then he said, "That's all. I'll give you more some other time. Now let's have some songs and dancing."

The women struck up a song.

"Your songs are no good," he said.

"What songs are better?" they asked.

"I'll show you," he said. "Right now."

He went to the barn and got a sheaf of grain. He beat out the grain, stood the sheaf on its bottom end, and tapped it. "Now," he said, *"My serf would as lief thou wert no more a sheaf, but every straw a soldier."*

The sheaf burst apart, and turned into soldiers playing

drums and bugles. Ivan ordered the soldiers to play a
march, and then he led them out into the street. The
people were amazed. The soldiers played some more
tunes, and then Ivan led them back to the barn, saying nobody should follow them. There he turned the soldiers
back into a sheaf, and threw it back on the pile. Then he
went home and lay down to sleep in the stable.

VII

The next morning the eldest brother, Semyon the
Soldier, heard about these things and went to see Ivan.
"Tell me," he said, "where did you get those soldiers?
And where did you take them?"

"Why do you want to know?" Ivan asked.

"What do you mean, *why?* With soldiers, a man can
do anything. He can win a kingdom for himself."

Ivan was astonished. "Is that so? Why didn't you tell
me a long time ago? I'll make you as many soldiers as
you want. Thank goodness we threshed a lot—I mean
the girl and me."

Ivan took his brother to the barn and said, "Look, I'll
make them for you, but then you'll have to take them
away from here. Because if we had to feed them they'd
gobble up the whole village in one day."

Semyon the Soldier promised to lead the troops away,
and Ivan began to make them. He tapped one sheaf on
the floor—and there was a company. He tapped another
sheaf—and there was another company. He made so
many that they covered an entire field.

"Well, that should be about enough, shouldn't it?"

Semyon was overjoyed. He said, "Yes, that's enough.
Thank you, Ivan."

"All right. If you need any more, just come back here
and I'll make more. I have a lot of straw right now."

Semyon the Soldier immediately gave orders to his
troops, mustered them in proper fashion, and went off
to make war.

No sooner had Semyon the Soldier left than Taras the
Big-Belly showed up. He, too, had heard about what
happened the day before, and he asked his brother: "Tell
me, where did you get those gold coins? If I had that

much cash on hand, I'd use it to bring in money from all over the world!"

Ivan was astonished. "Is that so? You should have told me a long time ago. I'll rub you as much money as you want."

His brother was delighted. "Give me about three sacks of it."

"Well, why not?" said Ivan. "Let's go to the woods. But you'd better harness up the horse first. You won't be able to carry it by yourself."

They went into the woods, and Ivan began to rub leaves from the oak tree. Soon there was a big pile of gold.

"That should be about enough, shouldn't it?"

Taras was overjoyed. "It will do for the time being," he said. "Thank you, Ivan."

"All right," said Ivan. "If you need any more, just come back here and I'll rub some more—there are plenty of leaves left."

Taras the Big-Belly gathered up the money—a whole cartload—and went off to trade.

So the two brothers went away: Semyon to wage war, and Taras to trade. Semyon the Soldier won a kingdom for himself, and Taras the Big-Belly made a heap of money buying and selling.

The two brothers got together and revealed their secrets to each other: where Semyon had got his soldiers, and where Taras had got his money.

And Semyon the Soldier said to his brother, "I have conquered a kingdom for myself, and I live well, but I don't have enough money to feed my soldiers."

Taras the Big-Belly said, "And I have made a great heap of money. But there's just one trouble: I don't have anybody to guard it."

Then Semyon the Soldier said, "Let's go see brother Ivan. I'll order him to make more soldiers, and then I'll give them to you to guard your money. And you can order him to rub me more money so I'll have the wherewithal to feed my soldiers."

And so they went to see Ivan. When they got there, Semyon said: "Brother mine, I still don't have enough soldiers. Make me some more—from as many sheaves as there are in a couple of shocks, say."

Ivan shook his head. "You're wasting your breath," he said: "I won't make any more soldiers for you."

"But why? After all, you promised."

"I know. But I won't make any more."

"But why won't you, you fool?"

"Because your soldiers killed a man dead. The other day when I was going near the road I saw a woman coming down the road hauling a coffin, and she was wailing. 'Who died?' I asked her. And she said, 'Semyon's soldiers killed my husband in the war.' I thought the soldiers would play tunes, but they've killed a man dead. So I won't give you any more."

And he stood firm, and made no more soldiers.

Then Taras the Big-Belly began pleading with Ivan the Fool to make him more gold coins.

Ivan shook his head. "You're wasting your breath," he said. "I won't make any more."

"But why won't you, you fool?"

"Because your gold pieces took away Mikhailovna's cow."

"What do you mean, *took it away?*"

"They just took it away, that's all. Mikhailovna had a cow, and her children used to drink the milk. The other day they came to me asking for milk. I asked them, 'Where is your cow?' And they said, 'Taras the Big-Belly's steward came and gave Mamma three pieces of gold, and she gave him the cow, so now we don't have any milk to drink.' I thought you only wanted to play games with the gold pieces, but you took away the children's cow. So I won't give you any more."

And the Fool stood firm, and wouldn't give any more.

So the two brothers went away, and began to consider how they might help each other in their troubles. And Semyon said, "I'll tell you what we'll do. You give me money to feed my soldiers, and I'll give you half of my kingdom and soldiers to guard your money."

Taras agreed. The brothers divided their possessions, and both became tsars, and both were rich.

VIII

Meantime, Ivan lived at home, feeding his father and mother and working in the fields with the mute girl.

Now it happened that Ivan's old watchdog got sick, became mangy, and was about to die. Ivan felt sorry for her. He got some bread from his sister, Malanya, put it in his cap, took it out to the dog, and threw it to her. But the cap was torn, and along with the bread, a root fell out. The aged dog gobbled it up together with the bread. No sooner had it swallowed the root, than it jumped up and started to play—wagging its tail and barking. It had recovered completely!

Ivan's father and mother saw this, and they were amazed. "How did you cure the dog?" they asked.

And Ivan said, "I had two little roots that cure any pain, and it gobbled up one of them."

At that same time it happened that the Tsar's daughter fell ill. The Tsar caused it to be announced in all cities and hamlets that whosoever cured her would receive an award and, if he were a bachelor, would be given her hand in marriage. The announcement was made in Ivan's village, too.

His father called Ivan in and said to him, "Did you hear what the Tsar has announced? You were saying that you had one of those little roots left. Go and cure the Tsar's daughter, and you'll be happy the rest of your life."

"Well, why not?" he said.

And Ivan got ready to go. His father and mother helped him dress up, and he had just stepped out of the door when he saw a beggar woman with a crippled arm. "They tell me," she said, "that you can cure people. Heal my arm—otherwise I can't even put on my boots myself."

And Ivan said, "Well, why not?"

He took the little root, gave it to the beggar woman, and told her to swallow it. She swallowed it, was cured, and began waving her arm.

Ivan's father and mother came out to accompany him on his trip to see the Tsar. When they heard he had given his last root away and had nothing left to cure the Tsar's daughter with, they began to upbraid him. "You took pity on the beggar woman," they said, "but for the Tsar's daughter you have no pity!"

Ivan began to feel sorry for the Tsar's daughter, too. He harnessed up the horse, threw some straw into the cart, and climbed in, ready to set off.

"Where are you going, Fool?"

"To heal the Tsar's daughter."

"When you have nothing to heal her with?"

"Well, why not?" he said, and gave the horse a flick of the reins.

He arrived at the Tsar's palace, and no sooner had he
set foot on the steps than the Tsar's daughter recovered.
The Tsar was overjoyed. He summoned Ivan, had him
dressed in fine clothing, and rewarded him. "Be my
son-in-law," he said.

"Well, why not?" said Ivan.

So he married the Tsar's daughter. Not long after-
wards the Tsar died, and Ivan became Tsar. So now all
three brothers were tsars.

IX

The three brothers lived and reigned.

The eldest brother, Semyon the Soldier, lived very well.
He drafted real soldiers to add to his straw soldiers. He
decreed that throughout his realm, one household out of
every ten must supply a soldier; and that every soldier must
be tall, physically fit, and clear-eyed. He recruited many
such soldiers, and trained them all. Whenever anybody
opposed his designs, he immediately dispatched these
soldiers, and did whatever he wanted. So everybody began
to fear him.

His life was most pleasant. Whatever he thought of,
or whatever he laid eyes on, was his. He would send out
his soldiers, and they would seize and bring back whatever
he wanted.

Taras the Big-Belly also lived very well. He had not
wasted the money he had got from Ivan, but had made
lots more with it. In his kingdom he had set up a fine
system. He kept his money in coffers, and collected a poll
tax, and a vodka tax, and a beer tax, and a wedding tax,
and a funeral tax, and a tax for traveling on foot, and a
tax for traveling on horseback, and a tax on bast shoes, and
a tax on leg wrappings, and a tax on dress trimmings. And
whatever he took a mind to, was his. For money, people
would procure anything for him and do anything for him,
because everybody needs money.

Ivan the Fool didn't live badly either. As soon as he
had buried his father-in-law he took off all his royal
attire, gave it to his wife to put away in a trunk, and got
back into his peasant's shirt, peasant-style pants, and
bast shoes, and got ready to work. "I'm bored," he said.

"I'm getting a paunch, don't have any appetite, and I can't sleep."

He sent for his mother and father and sister, the mute girl, and started working again.

"But you're the Tsar!" people told him.

"Well, what's the difference?" he said. "Tsars have to eat, too."

A cabinet minister came to him and said, "We don't have any money to pay salaries to our officials."

"Well, what's the difference?" he said. "Don't pay them."

"But then they won't perform their official duties."

"Well, what's the difference? Let them stop performing their governmental duties, and they'll be more free to work. Let them haul away the horse shit—they've piled up enough of it."

People came to Ivan to try lawsuits. One of them said: "That man stole my money."

And Ivan said, "Well, why not? That shows he needed it."

Everybody realized that he was a fool. Even his wife told him: "They say you're a fool."

"Well, why not?" he said.

His wife pondered and pondered, but she was a fool, too. "Why should I go against my husband?" she said. "Where the needle goes, the thread must follow."

So she took off her royal robes, put them away in a trunk, and went to the mute girl to learn how to work. She learned, and began helping her husband.

And all the clever people left Ivan's realm. Only the fools remained. Nobody had any money. They lived, worked, fed themselves, and fed all the good people.

X

Now the Old Devil waited and waited to hear from the imps how they had undone the three brothers, but there was no news. So he went to find out for himself. He looked and looked, but didn't find anything anywhere except three holes. Well, he thought, it is plain to see that they did not succeed.

He started investigating, but the three brothers were no longer in their old places. He located them in their various kingdoms, all living and reigning. The Old Devil was highly incensed. Very well, then, he thought, I'll take care of this matter myself!

First he went to see Tsar Semyon. But the Old Devil did not keep his own form: he changed himself into an army commander first.

"I've heard, Tsar Semyon," he said, "that you are a great soldier. I myself am well skilled in such matters, and would like to serve you."

Tsar Semyon began to question him, and saw that he was a clever man; so he took him into his service.

The new commander began to teach Semyon how to build up a strong army. "In the first place," he said, "you'll have to draft more soldiers—otherwise you'll have a lot of no-good idlers in your realm. You must draft all of the young men without exception. Then you'll have an army five times bigger than it is now. In the second place, you must get new small arms and artillery. I will provide you with small arms that will fire a hundred bullets at once, so that they scatter like peas. And I will provide you with artillery pieces whose fire will simply incinerate things. Men, horses, walls, or whatever—all will go up in flames."

Tsar Semyon paid heed to his new army commander. He gave orders that all young men without exception should be drafted into the army; and he had new munitions plants built. He had new firearms and cannons manufactured, and immediately went to war with the king of a neighboring country. As soon as the other troops came forth to meet his, Tsar Semyon commanded his soldiers to fire their bullets and unleash their artillery on them. In an instant, half of the troops were crippled or incinerated. The neighboring king took fright, surrendered, and handed over his realm. Tsar Semyon was delighted.

"Now," said he, "I will conquer the king of India."

But the king of India had heard about Tsar Semyon and adopted all his new ideas, adding a few of his own. In addition to the young men, he drafted unmarried women besides, and his army grew even larger than Tsar Semyon's. In addition to copying all of Tsar Semyon's small arms and artillery, he had thought up the idea of flying through the air and hurling bombs from above.

Tsar Semyon set out to wage war on the king of India, thinking he would do battle in the same way as before. But what works once doesn't always work twice. The king of India, even before Semyon's troops could come within firing range, sent his women soldiers through the air to hurl down bombs from above. The women sprayed bombs on Semyon's army like borax on cockroaches. The whole army took flight, and Semyon was left alone. The king of India took over Semyon's empire, and Semyon the Soldier escaped as best he could.

Having finished off this particular brother, the Old Devil went on to Tsar Taras. He turned himself into a merchant, and settled in Taras's realm. There he set up a business, and began spending money freely, paying the highest prices for everything. Everybody in the country rushed to get some of his money. They got so much money that they settled their debts and even began paying their taxes on time.

Tsar Taras was delighted. Thanks to this merchant, he told himself, I'll have even more money than before, and my life will be better than ever.

And Tsar Taras began to dream up new schemes. He decided to build himself a new palace. He notified the people that they should bring him lumber and stone and come to work on the project; and he offered high prices for everything, thinking they would come in flocks to work for his money, as before. But what do you think? They all took their lumber and stone to the merchant, and the workmen all flocked to him. Tsar Taras offered higher rates, but the merchant went still higher. Tsar Taras had a lot of money, but the merchant had even more; and he outbid the royal offer. The Tsar's palace was started, but never completed.

Tsar Taras had planned a park for himself. When autumn came, he sent for people to come and plant the trees and shrubs. But nobody came: everybody was busy digging a pond for the merchant.

Winter came. Tsar Taras decided to buy some sables for a new fur coat. He sent a man to buy them; but the man came back and said, "There aren't any sables. The merchant has all the furs. He paid a higher price, and he's made rugs out of the sables."

Tsar Taras needed to buy some stallions. He sent some men out to buy them; but they came back and said the merchant now had all the good stallions: he was using them to carry water for his pond.

So all of the Tsar's enterprises came to a standstill. All of the people were working for the merchant, not the

Tsar. Their only dealings with him was when they paid him their taxes—in money they had got from the merchant.

Tsar Taras had amassed so much money he didn't know where to put it, yet life was becoming miserable for him. He had long ago stopped dreaming up schemes and just wanted to survive somehow; but he couldn't manage even that. There was a shortage of everything. His cooks and coachmen and other servants all left him and went to the merchant's. He even began to run out of food. When he sent to the market for something or other, there never was any: the merchant had bought up everything. Only one thing kept coming the Tsar's way: money from taxes.

Tsar Taras waxed furious: he banished the merchant from his realm. But the merchant settled directly across the border. Just as before, the merchant's money attracted everything to him and away from the Tsar.

The Tsar was in a really bad way. He hadn't eaten for days; and rumor had it that the merchant was boasting he was going to buy the Tsar's wife. Tsar Taras got panicky and didn't know which way to turn.

Semyon the Soldier came to him and said, "I need your help. The king of India defeated me."

But Tsar Taras, too, was at the end of his rope. "I haven't eaten for two days myself," he said.

XI

Having polished off both brothers, the Old Devil turned to Ivan. He changed himself into an army commander, went to see Ivan, and began trying to persuade him to raise an army. "It is not fitting," said he, "that a tsar should have no army. You have only to order me, and I will gather soldiers from among your people and form an army."

Ivan heard him out. "Well, why not?" he said. "Go ahead. But teach them to play their tunes a little better. That's what I like."

The Old Devil went through Ivan's realm trying to recruit volunteers. He announced that all who came to get their heads shaved and join the army would be given a bottle of vodka and a red cap.

Ivan's fools just laughed. "We have all the liquor we want," they said. "We make it ourselves. And our women make us all the different kinds of caps we want. They even make caps of many colors, with tassels to boot."

So nobody would enlist. The Old Devil came to Ivan and said: "Your fools won't volunteer. We'll have to bring them in by force."

"Well, why not?" Ivan said. "Go ahead and use force."

So the Old Devil announced that all of the fools had to come and enlist as soldiers, and that whoever did not would be put to death by Ivan.

The fools came to the commander and said: "You tell us that if we don't enlist as soldiers our tsar will put us to death. But you don't tell us what will happen to us in the army. They say soldiers get killed to death."

"Yes, that does happen."

When the fools heard this, they grew stubborn. "We won't enlist," they said. "It's better to be killed at home if it's going to happen one way or the other."

"You're fools!" said the Old Devil. "Such fools! A soldier may or may not get killed. But if you don't enlist, Tsar Ivan will be sure to have you killed."

The fools thought it over and went to see Tsar Ivan the Fool and ask him about it. "An army commander came," they said, "and ordered all of us to join the army. 'If you go into the army,' he told us, 'you may not get killed. But if you don't join, Tsar Ivan will be sure to have you killed.' Is that true?"

Ivan laughed. "How could I, all by myself, put all of you to death? If I weren't a fool, I could explain it to you. But I don't understand it myself."

"All right, then," they said. "We won't go."

"Well," said Ivan, "what's the difference? Don't go."

So the fools went to the army commander and said they wouldn't enlist.

The Old Devil saw that his plan wasn't working. He went to the king of Cockroachia and talked himself into his favor. "Let's go to war," he said, "and conquer Tsar Ivan. He doesn't have any money; but he has lots of grain and livestock and other things."

The king of Cockroachia went to war. He raised a big army, put the rifles and cannon into good working order, and marched to the border of Ivan's country.

People came to Ivan and said, "The king of Cockroachia is coming to make war on us."

"Well," said Ivan, "what's the difference? Let him come."

The Cockroachian king crossed the border with his army and sent scouts ahead to reconnoiter.

They looked and looked, but they couldn't find any army. They waited and waited, thinking surely it would show up somewhere. But there wasn't a sign of an army—there was nobody they could fight.

The king of Cockroachia sent troops to capture the villages. They entered one village, and out ran the fools, men and women alike, gaping at the soldiers in astonishment. The soldiers began taking away the fools' grain and cattle. The fools just handed everything over, and not a one of them put up a fight.

The troops went into the next village, and the same thing happened. They marched on for another day, and another, and everywhere the same thing happened: they handed over everything; not a single one put up a fight; and they even invited the soldiers to stay. "Dear friends," they said, "if life is not good in your country, come and live here with us."

The soldiers marched on and on, but they never met up with an army: just people living and feeding themselves and others, never resisting—just inviting them to stay.

The soldiers became bored. They went to their Cockroachian king and said, "We can't fight here. Take us somewhere else. A war would be fine, but this is like slicing jelly. We can't go on with this campaign."

The king of Cockroachia flew into a rage. He commanded his soldiers to overrun the country, lay waste the villages and houses, burn the grain, and slaughter the livestock. "If you disobey my orders," he said, "all of you will be put to death."

The soldiers were frightened and began to carry out the king's orders. They burned houses and grain, and slaughtered the livestock. But still the fools did not defend themselves: all they did was weep. The old men wept, the old women wept, and the little children wept. "Why do you want to hurt us?" they asked. "Why are you foolishly destroying good things? If you need them, why don't you just take them?"

The soldiers couldn't bear it any longer. They refused to go on, and the army fell apart.

XII

The Old Devil also went away, having failed to undo
Ivan with the soldiers.

He turned himself into a fine gentleman and came back
to settle in Ivan's country. His plan now was to undo Ivan
the same way he had undone Taras the Big-Belly: with
money.

"I want to do you a favor," he told Ivan, "to teach
you some common sense. I'll build a house here, and set
up a business."

"Well, why not?" said Ivan. "Go ahead."

The fine gentleman spent the night there; and the next
morning he appeared in the public square. He produced
a big bag of gold and a sheet of paper. "All you people,"
he said, "live like pigs. I want to show you how to live
properly. You build me a house according to this plan, and
I'll supervise your work and pay you in gold coin."

He showed them the gold. The fools were amazed.
They had never used money; instead, they bartered or
paid one another by working. They marveled at the gold.
"Those are pretty little things," they said.

And they began to exchange their labor and other
things for the gentleman's gold pieces. The Old Devil started spending his gold freely, as he had done in Taras'
kingdom; and the people began trading all kinds of things,
and doing all kinds of work, for his gold.

The Old Devil was elated. Things are coming along
fine, he thought. Now I'll fix the Fool the way I did Taras.
I'll buy him out of the running—innards and all!

But no sooner had the fools garnered their gold pieces,
than they gave them away to the women for necklaces.
The girls plaited them into their braids, and the children
played with them in the streets. They all had plenty of
them, and they wouldn't take any more. Meantime, the
fine gentleman's mansion was not yet half built, and his
livestock and grain provisions for the coming year had not
yet been taken care of. So he sent word that he wanted
people to come and work for him, to haul in grain, and
bring in livestock; and that for every product or every job
done, he would pay lots of gold.

But nobody came to work for him, and nobody brought

IVAN THE FOOL 201

anything to him. A little boy or girl might occasionally stop by with an egg to trade in for gold; but otherwise nobody came, and he began to run out of food. The fine gentleman got very hungry and went through the village trying to buy something for his supper. He went to a peasant's house and offered gold for a hen, but the housewife wouldn't take it. "I have plenty of it already," she said.

He went to a poor old woman's and offered gold coins for a herring. "I don't need any of them, kind sir," said she. "I have no children I could give them to as toys, and besides I already have three coins I picked up as curiosities."

He went to an old peasant for bread. But the old peasant wouldn't take any money either.

"I don't need it," he said. "But if you're asking in the name of Christ, just wait a minute and I'll tell my old woman to cut you a slice."

The Old Devil spat and fled from the peasant. Let alone actually begging *in the name of Christ,* just hearing the words hurt him worse than a knife-stab.

And so he got no bread, either. All the people had all the money they needed. Wherever the Old Devil went, nobody would give anything for money. They all said, "Bring something else to trade, or come and do some work, or else take some food in the name of Christ." But the Old Devil had nothing but money, and he didn't want to work, and he couldn't possibly accept charity in the name of Christ.

He became furious. "I will give you money," he told the fools. "What more do you want? With money you can buy anything and hire any workman."

But they wouldn't listen. "No," they said, "we don't need it. We don't have any bills or taxes to pay, so what do we need money for?"

So the Old Devil went to bed without his supper.

Ivan the Fool heard about all this business. Some people came to him and asked: "What shall we do? There's this fine gentleman who appeared among us: he likes good things to eat and drink; he likes to wear fine clothes; but he doesn't like to work, and he won't beg in the name of Christ. All he does is offer gold pieces to everybody. People used to give him everything he needed; but now they have enough gold pieces and won't give him anything more. What should we do with him? He might starve to death."

Ivan listened to their story, and then said: "Well, after all," he said, "he has to be fed. Let him go from farm to farm, like a shepherd."

There was no other choice for him: the Old Devil had to start making the rounds of the farms.

Eventually he came to Ivan's house. He arrived at supper-time, and Malanya the Mute was preparing supper. Often before, she had been tricked by lazy people. Since they hadn't been working, they could get there for supper before the others; and then they'd eat up all the porridge. So she had learned to recognize loafers by the palms of their hands. If a man had calluses on his hands, she would seat him at the table; if not, he'd have to wait for the scraps.

The Old Devil sidled up to the table; but the mute girl seized him by the hands and took a look. There were no calluses: his hands were clean and smooth, with long fingernails. She grunted and dragged him away from the table.

But Ivan's wife said to him, "You must excuse us, fine sir. My sister-in-law doesn't let people sit at the table unless they have callused hands. Just wait a little, and when the others have eaten you can have what's left."

The Old Devil was insulted that at the Tsar's house they were making him eat along with the pigs. He said to Ivan, "That's a stupid law you have in your realm—that everybody has to work with his hands. Do you think it's only with their hands that people work? What do you suppose clever people work with?"

"How should we fools know?" Ivan answered. "We're all used to working mostly with our hands and our backs."

"That's because you're fools. But I'll teach you how to work with your heads. Then you'll realize it's more profitable to work with your head than your hands."

Ivan was astonished. "Well," said he, "it's no wonder we're called fools!"

"However," the Old Devil went on, "it's not so easy—working with your head. You refused to let me eat just now, because I didn't have calluses on my hands. But what you don't realize is that it's a hundred times harder to work with your head. Sometimes your head even splits."

Ivan thought about it a minute, "But then why, my dear friend," said he, "do you make it so hard on yourself? There's nothing easy about getting your head split, that's for sure. You'd be better off doing easy work—with your hands and your back."

Said the Old Devil, "Why do I make it hard on myself? Because I feel sorry for you fools. If I didn't make it hard on myself, you'd remain fools all your lives. But now that I've worked with my head, I can teach you how."

Ivan was very impressed. "You teach us," he said. "And then whenever our hands wear out, we can switch to our heads."

So the Old Devil promised to teach them.

Ivan announced throughout his realm that a fine gentleman had arrived who would teach them all how to work with their heads; and that a man could work more profitably with his head than with his hands, so everybody should come and learn how.

Now a high tower had been built in Ivan's realm, with a straight stairway on the outside, leading up to a lookout platform on the top. Ivan took the gentleman up there so that he would be in full view.

The gentleman stood atop the tower and began to speak. The fools gathered around and gaped. They thought the gentleman would actually demonstrate how to work with your head without using your hands. But all the Old Devil did was talk—explaining how to live without doing any work.

The fools didn't understand a word of it. They watched a bit longer, and then went off to attend to their own business.

The Old Devil stood on top of the tower for one whole day, and then another—talking constantly. He got hungry. But it never occurred to the fools to bring some bread to the tower for him. They figured that if he could work better with his head than with his hands, it would be no trick at all for his head to provide him with bread.

The Old Devil stood up there on the tower for another whole day, still talking. People would come and take a look, then go away. Ivan asked, "Well, how is the gentleman doing? Has he started working with his head yet?"

"Not yet," they told him. "He's still jabbering."

The Old Devil stood on top of the tower for one more day, and began to grow weak. He staggered, and struck his head on a pillar. One of the people saw him topple, and told Ivan's wife. She ran out to the field where her husband was plowing. "Come and look!" she told him.

"They say the gentleman has begun to work with his head."

Ivan marveled. "Oh?" said he.

He turned his horse around and went to the tower. By the time he got there the Old Devil was already very weak from hunger and was staggering around, knocking his head against the pillars. Just as Ivan got there he stumbled and fell, crashing down the stairway head over heels, counting each step with his head.

"Well," said Ivan, "the fine gentleman was telling the truth when he said that sometimes his head splits. In his kind of work it isn't calluses you get—it's lumps on the head."

The Old Devil came tumbling down the stairway and rammed his head into the ground at the bottom. Ivan had started toward him to see how much work he had done, when suddenly the earth opened up and the Old Devil fell into it. Only a hole remained.

Ivan scratched himself. "Just look at that! How disgusting! Him again! But he must be the father of all the others—he's a big one."

Ivan still lives to this day, and everybody flocks to his realm to live. His brothers have come there, too, and he feeds them.

Whenever anybody comes and says, "Feed us," he says, "Well, why not? Make yourself at home—we have plenty of everything."

But there is this one custom in his realm: if you have calluses on your hands, you're welcome at the table; if you don't, you eat the scraps.

1886